The Secrets of Roscarbury Hall

The Secrets of Roscarbury Hall

A NOVEL

ANN O'LOUGHLIN

Skyhorse Publishing

First North American Paperback Edition 2019

First published by Black & White Publishing Ltd in the United Kingdom under the title *The Ballroom Café*.

This is a work of fiction. Names, places, characters, and incidents are either the products of the author's imagination or are used fictitiously.

Skyhorse Publishing books may be purchased in bulk at special discounts for sales promotion, corporate gifts, fund-raising, or educational purposes. Special editions can also be created to specifications. For details, contact the Special Sales Department, Skyhorse Publishing, 307 West 36th Street, 11th Floor, New York, NY 10018 or info@skyhorsepublishing.com.

Skyhorse® and Skyhorse Publishing® are registered trademarks of Skyhorse Publishing, Inc.®, a Delaware corporation.

Visit our website at www.skyhorsepublishing.com.
Visit the author's website at http://annoloughlin.blogspot.com/.

10 9 8 7 6 5 4 3 2 1

Library of Congress Cataloging-in-Publication Data

Names: O'Loughlin, Ann, author.
Title: The secrets of Roscarbury Hall : a novel / Ann O'Loughlin.
Other titles: Ballroom cafe
Description: First North American edition. | New York, NY : Skyhorse Publishing, 2016.
Identifiers: LCCN 2016020183 (print) | LCCN 2016024399 (ebook) | ISBN 9781510713727 (hardback) | ISBN 9781510739062 (paperback) | ISBN 9781510713734 (ebook)
Subjects: LCSH: Sisters—Ireland—Fiction. | Older women—Ireland—Fiction. | Family secrets—Fiction. | Adoptees—Fiction. | Adoption—Corrupt practices—Fiction. | Domestic fiction. | BISAC: FICTION / Family Life. | FAMILY & RELATIONSHIPS / Adoption & Fostering.
Classification: LCC PR6115.L6795 B35 2016 (print) | LCC PR6115.L6795 (ebook)
 | DDC 823/.92—dc23
LC record available at https://lccn.loc.gov/2016020183

Cover design by Brian Peterson
Cover photo: iStockphoto

Printed in the United States of America

To John, Roshan and Zia . . . my universe

The Secrets of Roscarbury Hall

One

Rathsorney, Co. Wicklow, March 2008

'You have four more weeks, Miss O'Callaghan. It is the way things are now; the bosses in Dublin want to see some effort towards paying the loan. Otherwise we are going to have to take steps to get our money back.'

Bank manager Peter O'Doherty leaned back on his swivel chair. Raising her head sufficiently to look him straight in the eye, Ella O'Callaghan spoke in a slow, firm voice.

'What do you propose I do: prostitute myself, Mr O'Doherty?'

'Miss O'Callaghan, there is no need to be like that.'

'There is no need to threaten to push me out of my home. I won't let you. Roscarbury Hall is my life. I won't let you take it.'

'Maybe there is something you can sell off to get in some money?'

'Like my extensive jewel collection, I suppose.'

Peter O'Doherty jumped to his feet, impatiently fingering his bunch of keys.

'Go home, think about it. Come back next week with some sort of plan for repayment.'

He put out his hand to Ella, but she ignored it.

'In all my prayerful life, I have never felt so crucified. I will die before I move out of Roscarbury Hall.'

If O'Doherty intended to answer, she did not give him a chance, sweeping out of his office, banging the door. What did he care about Roscarbury, how the old house folded around them in bad times, how it was the only place where she felt safe? The rooms were so cold in winter you could see your breath, the stairs to the attic creaked like a banshee, and the chill winds rattled the window latches in a din of constant tapping. The parkland dipped and rolled away to the lake, so it was impossible for Sheehy the farmer to get his hay cutter properly across it; the rills silted up every year, long after the cherry blossom flowers had gone dark brown and sodden and the oak and old horse chestnut trees had shed their leaves.

Roscarbury existed for the worn days of summer sun, when warm air lingered in the house and the hens had to be hunted from the open back door. It was the starlings gathering and chattering on the wonky television aerial strapped to the first chimney that woke Ella every morning. The crows and pigeons in the fir trees destroyed the stone slabs around the fountain and she had to scrub it down once a month. The overgrown kitchen garden gave fruit for enough tarts through the summer months and luscious pears in a hot spell. Ella could never leave Roscarbury: the mists of the past shrouding the old house webbed around her, keeping her calm.

Peter O'Doherty, if she told him, would not care for any of that. Ella O'Callaghan and her tumbledown house were a small, silly aggravation in his busy day.

★

Roberta O'Callaghan was sipping a dry sherry from a crystal glass when she saw her sister skirt around the house. There was a jizz on Ella; she knew by the way she was pounding along. Her stride was just a tiny bit longer than usual and her step heavier and more determined. Neither did Ella bother to linger at the fountain, as she usually did, to remember better times, when water had tumbled, gurgling and gushing on through the garden rills.

The urgent pushing on the back door, the sharp ping of a cup on a saucer and the powerful surge of tap water into the kettle indicated a heightened anxiety in Ella. Roberta pushed her hip flask of sherry deep in her dark-brown leather hand-bag and snapped the clasp shut. With a deep sigh she got up from the velvet armchair to hide her glass behind the old atlas on the third shelf of the mahogany bookcase. Ella thrashed about the kitchen, cupboard doors slammed, saucepans placed too heavy on the hob. She burrowed into the kitchen whenever she was troubled, baking her worries away, often lifting cakes out of the oven and scraping them straight in to the bin.

She had first turned to the solace of the kitchen the night their mother and father died. On the way home from a choral recital, John O'Callaghan had no opportunity to react when Sean McCarthy drove his tractor the short trip home from the pub, without even a small light showing. All three were killed in what Rathsorney later referred to as the tragic accident. For days, Ella and Roberta were surrounded by so many people, but within three weeks, the girls were on their own in the big, empty house. With their father gone, so too was his solicitor's salary. Neither had John O'Callaghan found time to provide for his daughters, so busy was he running Roscarbury Hall and throwing money after horses on a Saturday afternoon. Ella did not waste time on resenting her father's irresponsible attitude but took their new state of low financial means in her stride. She set to getting in as much money as possible to keep Roscarbury Hall standing. She baked cakes for the Rathsorney shops and took in ironing to keep up with the bills. Roberta continued doing the outside jobs, as best she could. They got in to a routine every day of doing their chores and delivering the bread and cakes in two big bags, while at the same time catching up on their necessity shopping. They did not move far from Rathsorney, but were sometimes called upon by the department store in Arklow to do relief holiday work and also helped out at the local hardware shop on busy weekends.

When the fountain pump broke down, there was no money to repair it. When the garden needed tending and the plants needed pruning, they did not bother until they had to. When rain leaked into the attic rooms, through gaps left when the slates slipped, they called in Hegarty, the local farmer, who brought his extension ladder and gingerly went out on the roof to tack the slates back in place. When the job was too big for the handyman, Ella managed to organise a loan from a sympathetic bank manager.

Tired of the noise from the kitchen, Roberta made for her bedroom, stopping in the hall to read the note Ella had placed there.

Gerry says he will collect a bit early for 10 Mass. Be ready. Don't make us late. E.

Ella waited until she heard the knocking of Roberta's walking stick on the landing overhead before she rang her cousin Iris.

'I need your help. I think I have a good plan; it is about keeping Roscarbury and making money. I think you are going to approve.'

'Shoot it out for God's sake, girl.'

'No, I don't have time now. Ten o'clock Mass in the morning.'

She rang off before Iris had time to protest.

★

Ella chose the blue swing coat for Mass, a fitting backdrop to her favourite Weiss brooch, nine balls of Montana blue crystals in a simple circle setting. Her mother had only worn it on special occasions. There wasn't another one like it, she told her daughter, and Ella believed it. Carefully, she fastened the brooch to her left lapel and stood in front of the mirror, tugging her coat lightly to straighten it. Not that anybody took much notice of her these days.

Gerry O'Hare's Mercedes lumbered up the avenue. She watched as he eased his immense frame from the driver's seat, a cigarette hanging from the corner of his mouth. Leaning against the fountain, he puffed quietly as he waited for the O'Callaghan sisters.

Roberta was already in the back hall, wearing her black coat ringed with fur at the sleeves and collar. Her large grey handbag and gloves reflected the patina of her shoes. The sisters took each other in, without saying a word.

'Good morning, girls. How are we this morning?'

Gerry O'Hare collected the sisters every Sunday, to bring them to and from Mass. He did it out of kindness, though his

Christmas box from the O'Callaghans was exceedingly generous. They put up with his silly ways and sometimes even looked forward to his fake, flirtatious line of talk.

Iris pushed in to the seat beside them, towards the middle of the church.

'You got me to Mass, Ella. What is it you want?'

Ella stayed looking ahead.

'Come home with us and we will discuss it.'

'Couldn't you spit it out now?'

Ella stiffened on her seat.

'Mass first, discussion later.'

Iris groaned, refusing to stand when the priest came out onto the altar, and fidgeted so much during the service that Ella elbowed her in the ribs.

'You will come in the taxi with us?'

'I won't set foot in anything owned by Gerry O'Hare. He is no friend, advising that husband of mine with his nuggets of wisdom over a pint. Isn't it Gerry O'Hare who told my wonderful husband he should fight me tooth and nail for everything I have? He is not a cab driver but a DIY divorce expert.'

'You will have to walk then.'

'Not a bother. I will only be a bit behind that slowcoach O'Hare. Is that a tractor he drives?'

When the Mercedes pulled up at the back door of Roscarbury Hall, Roberta marched straight to the hall table and loudly slapped down a note.

I know you are up to something. I do not give permission for any of your stupid plans. R.

A fast walker, Iris was only ten minutes behind. Slightly out of breath, she pushed open the back door.

'Come and join me here,' Ella called out.

She had changed into her walking shoes and pulled on her old hat to cross the farmyard to the walled garden. Her hair tumbled in loose curls from under her velvet hat, giving her face a youthful look. The paths were still clear in places, but where there used to be drills of carrots and onions was now a mess of overgrown weeds, briars and nettles, all competing and taking the best from the soil, which had once yielded prize-winning vegetables.

'I am going to set up a café. This is a good place for all-day sun, but do you think we could tidy it up, put a few tables out here?'

Iris shook her head.

'Too much work. Better to fix up the fountain and have the tables at the front. We will only have to cut the grass and trim the hedges. The rhododendron and azaleas will be in flower there soon. Brightens up the old house lovely.'

They walked side by side, past the buildings that were falling down and the hay barn that was cavernous, cold and empty. Roberta nodded to Iris as they walked into the kitchen, taking her time making her tea, so she could eavesdrop. As she passed through the hall, she flung another note on the table.

Not that I think they will ever come to anything, these feverish plans of yours, but you most certainly do not have my permission to let people tramp all over Roscarbury Hall. Iris spends too much time here. R

'Why don't you start small? A few tables. They have those collapsible ones in the catalogues. With a fancy tablecloth, nobody will know,' Iris said, her arms folded, leaning against the sink.

'But where would I put them? It is a bit cold at the front in the mornings.'

Iris jumped across the kitchen and trotted up the hall. Ella followed, snatching the note from the hall table, glancing at it as she went. Iris turned the knob of the drawing room and swept in.

'Isn't it perfect for starters? A few tables in the middle.'

'What will we do for a drawing room?'

'Ella O'Callaghan, you have one week; we don't have any better ideas. It is not as if you even use the room. All we have to do is rearrange the furniture. Let's give it a whirl.'

'But who will come? It is a daft idea.'

Ella crumpled the note into a tight ball and pushed it deep into her pocket.

Iris gripped her cousin tight around the shoulders.

'Believe you me, all the ninnies that go to morning Mass will be falling over themselves to have a look at your best china.'

Ella moved to the window.

'I don't think I can do it, Iris. Roberta will have a fit.'

'What does it matter what Roberta thinks? You are the one who has to go and see the bank manager every other week.'

Ella did not answer. The frost was tight on the briars; a robin flew low, looking for grubs; and in the distance, a child called out to his friend to hurry up on the lane across the field. A rat flitted past the fountain. She did not need to be outside to know the late morning sunlight was sheeting across the top windows, so that they glowed gold.

'Nobody will want to come,' she said, taking in the formal, stuffy room with high-backed chairs and a chandelier that looked out of place, too big for the setting. The desk at the window was cluttered and dusty. Somebody had shoved a stack of letters on to the windowsill, where, over time, they yellowed and crisped. 'The house looks a mess from the out-side and is no better inside.'

'Which is why we will call it the Old Café?'

Ella guffawed out loud.

'You mean the Old and Dusty Café.'

'That's the spirit,' Iris said, pushing the big green velvet chair closer to the fireplace.

'There are a lot of cobwebs and the chandelier will need a thorough rinsing. What will we do about the front door?'

Iris put her hands on her hips.

'You are looking for excuses, Ella; we will use the French doors to the side.'

'I just could not bear to be a laughing stock again; it has happened too often in the past.'

A tear splattered down Ella's cheek.

'Ella, there has been a lot of sympathy, but the O'Callaghans were never a laughing stock.'

'I just don't like being put under the microscope.'

'Then find something to sell, Ella.'

Ella slumped onto the couch, making the leather crack.

'This is only a home, Iris; nobody is interested in any of it. It is the home of two biddies who don't have anything to say to each other in a house with maybe too much history. I am tired of pushing at doors that never open. Roberta is drinking more; I am finding bottles stuffed everywhere. If she even gave up the money she spends on her sherry, we might be able to ride this mess.'

Iris sat down beside her.

'When did Roberta ever think of anybody else but herself? We can do it together.'

Ella grabbed her hand and clenched it tight.

'I hope you are right, Iris, because as it stands, there is not much of a market for these old antiques and if anything has to be sold it will be the house.'

'Let's not go there. We will do as much as we can today. I will ask Muriel to spread the word about the café, grand opening 9:15 a.m. Wednesday. Though we will need more than four tables, if Muriel is involved.'

'Four tables are enough to test the waters,' Ella said, moving to the sideboard where she kept the best china.

Two

It was a cold, damp morning. Kiely's bus slipped down Main Street, revving high around the corners, the growl of the engine left hanging in the air. The milkman tinkled bottles on the doorsteps; the stray dog holed up in Maurer's doorway stretched its front paws elaborately, before settling in for a scratching session.

Pat McCarthy, lifting up a bundle from the newspapers stacked at his front door, nodded politely at the stranger as she walked past, her head down, her hands deep in her pockets. Slicing the plastic seal from the *Irish Times*, he watched her as she flitted across the street, darting fast glances from side to side, before stopping to linger outside Rahilly's hardware. A tightening of her coat belt signalled a decision made. With a whip of her shoulders, she set off at a faster pace, taking the Arklow Road out of Rathsorney. McCarthy, muttering under his breath, threw two empty chip bags and a beer can out onto the street, before fiddling with the ground-level lock and pushing up the window shutters, the tearing steel screeching the start of the town day.

Debbie, hunching up her shoulders against the cold wind blowing in from the sea, walked past a cluster of red-roofed houses and a cemetery set across a hill of two fields. At the bridge she lingered, leaning over to watch the hurrying water. It whooshed out Rob's name, a rhythm she could not get out of her head: the quiet murmur of the funeral crowd as they remembered her father.

After everybody had drunk enough, talked enough about Rob, buried him twice over, after everybody had run out of words, she was in the attic looking for nothing or something, filling in time, nudging boxes around corners, when she saw the small one greased with dirt, stuffed under the water pipes. It was sealed with brown tape and a pink label splotted dirty grey was curled up on one side, probably from where the heat of the hot-water pipe had dried it out. She could just about make out the neat handwriting: 'Baby Bits.'

She picked up the box, shaking off loose mouse droppings, and made her way carefully to the spare room. Battered old suitcases lay opened and discarded on the red sofa bed. A stack of yellowed newspapers was spilled on the floor.

'Debs, are you finished up there yet?'

Aunt Nancy thumped up the stairs, swiping the sweat from her forehead with her hand, her breath wheezing.

'Don't be bothering yourself with all that junk, dear. We can get somebody to clear it out.'

'I want to pick a few things.'

Nancy caught Debbie tight by the shoulders.

'You do what you have to do, sweetheart, but memories don't hold dust.'

Nancy kicked at the newspaper stack and stood back, taking the room in.

'Your mother would have a fit if she knew how the place had turned out. Look at the dirt on the curtains: the finest embossed cream silk, she ordered specially from the store in Cleveland. Bert said he would come at five to fill up the U-Haul. Is that everything in the sitting room? It's very little.'

'Yes, but the rocking chair on the porch as well.'

'Not worth taking, but suit yourself. Let's have tea. What about the box of baby bits?'

'It'll fit on the front seat.'

'Your mother was so good with storage. Look at that neat labelling. She really was something.'

'I know.'

'It was a long time ago. This house will have new owners and the unhappiness will fade away.'

'Except in our hearts.'

The freight train pelted through to Chicago, the clatter of the railroad crossing penetrating the lonely air. Nancy shuffled about the kitchen; Debbie sat tracing shapes on the red Formica tabletop.

Several days passed in New York before she got around to opening the box. A whoosh of dust punched the air as she pushed the flaps of dirty cardboard to the side, ripping open the top.

Layers of thin tissue paper sprinkled with lavender were stacked on top of each other. Removing five neatly creased squares of soft paper pressed like a cushion into the centre of the box, Debbie ran her hand along the silk and lace of a christening gown she did not know. As her fingers slipped across the cream silk, whispers fluttered in her ear, words like butterflies blotting away the tears but creating a new, persistent angst.

Two crocheted bootees tied with narrow pink ribbons were tucked to one side. Gently, she shook the robe so that the musty aroma of stale lavender wafted through the room, wispy ghosts of Agnes coasting about her for a few moments, cushioning her from the ingrained memory of her loss. A battered pink rabbit and an envelope, small and white, half concealed, were at the bottom of the box. Scanning at first, she was not sure what it said and some of the words were joined together so tightly they were hard to make out. Agnes's sweet perfume surrounded her, now strangling at her throat.

The letter had haunted her every minute until she came to this place. Would that she had left it, marked it down as a part of forgotten family history.

A rubbish truck reversing drew her back. She ran her hand along the smooth cold of the stone bridge, her palms fizzing red as she dawdled over to the heavy iron gates, set back to one side of the riverbank. An old house lay half hidden beyond the trees. The driveway was pocked with weeds and tough grass, the padlock on the gate rusted. A jeep bumped across the bridge and pulled in beside her.

'You are out early. Are you looking for somewhere?'

The man yanked at the lock and pulled a key out of his back pocket. He clicked the gate open and watched it shudder back.

'I was wondering about the house and the café.'

'It is some old place all right. The old dears who live here won't mind if you walk up the path. I am only the gardener,' he said, before jumping back in behind the wheel. A dog scooted up the avenue after the jeep, only inches from the back wheels.

Three

Ella O'Callaghan watched the small dog in the garden running, sniffing, pissing as if it were in a public park. She stayed behind the curtain, easing the big leather armchair out of her way, leaning to the left to get a better view. It was a cold, sharp morning. The frost lingered in the dark, heavy corners of the rhododendron. A wagtail foraging for crumbs flew in to peck the ground closer to the house. The woman, who had followed the dog in behind the high wall and iron gates, was standing on the gravel avenue, smoking a cigarette. 'It is a dirty habit,' Ella snorted to herself as she looked at the stranger propping up the broken fountain, blowing smoke rings towards the house.

Roscarbury Hall was a sight to behold: a sorry pile, three storeys high. Long neglected, it looked empty. The dirty windows were covered in a thick layer of grime. The wisteria was out of control, its gnarled stems woody and bare. The front door, with the dull, brass knocker, was covered in decades of blown dust built up and mixed with layer upon layer of dried-out, peeling paint. Leaves, trapped in the corners at the threshold, were stuck with cobwebs. It did not matter; the front door at Roscarbury was never opened any more.

Ella shrank back from the window as Roberta came in to the room and switched on the second bar of the heater. It let out a low hum and the dry heat choked her throat. Bristling with indignation, because the heater would now pong out the place, she sighed loudly. She could not move to the back room, which was so cold there was a layer of thin ice on the far wall.

She saw the woman, her hair falling into her eyes and her walk ungainly, trudge across the grass towards the lake. Ella moved from the window, stopping to switch off a bar of the heater on the way. She paused in the hall to pick up a red note.

Order a roast beef from the butchers. We also need onions, and cream for the apple tart. Tell Iris to stop polluting the house with her filthy smoke. R

Ella's kettle was already boiling when Roberta shuffled from the drawing room, halting her walking stick long enough to check the note had been removed and to scrunch Ella's note into the hall bin.

Taking down her rosebud teapot with matching cup and saucer, Ella set them on a tray. Swirling the boiling water fiercely to scald the pot, she reached with one hand for the box marked 'Ella's Tea.'

Roberta stood beside her and slowly placed her kettle on the gas ring. She patted the tight bun at the back of her head, humming a tune to herself.

Her china teapot on the tray, along with a small jug of milk and a spoon holding three cubes of sugar, Ella walked past her sister and out of the room.

No word was spoken between the two, but this was not surprising: no word had been exchanged between the two sisters in decades. Those who knew the sisters well were aware of the hard frost, thick and deep, between them. It had, at one time, been the source of extreme speculation, but as the years went by, the interest of others in the travails of the O'Callaghan sisters receded.

Ella, on the way back through the hall, slapped down a reply on the table.

You give up the booze, I will tell Iris to give up the cigarettes. Pigs might fly as well. E.

She settled back in the drawing room and sipped her tea. The hot drink warmed her and she turned off the last bar of the electric fire. She listened to her sister fuss around the kitchen, tidying up her things: each mug and plate in its place and her provisions labelled 'R' tidy and in a separate cupboard. She stayed on in the drawing room because it was, this morning, the warmest room in the house. On a walnut table, framed photographs of the sisters were smeared with greasy dirt. Happy days when they played tennis on the grass in front of the house and had day-long picnics by the sea. There were only two frames that were polished regularly: the wedding photograph of their mother and father and the wedding-day picture of Ella O'Callaghan and Michael Hannigan.

She touched the picture glass, remembering the warm summer's day they had exchanged vows. Swinging around to the congregation, the light flashing on the aurora borealis stones of her Weiss brooch, those in the front rows had predicted a happy and long union. Small but exquisite, the brooch was a cluster of flowers with big petals made out in brilliant white cabochon stones. Smaller, delicately coloured, sparkling aurora borealis stones peeped through the gaps. She had picked this brooch because it was the first her father gave her mother.

'Young and foolish,' Ella muttered, impatiently wiping the glass with the end of her skirt before carefully setting down the heavy silver frame in its place. She noticed the stranger lingering by the front door. Sighing impatiently, she stuck her head out the drawing-room French doors.

'Have you come about the job?'

'What job?'

'Come in; keeping the door open is making a draught run through the house. I need help in the café. God knows, I could do with a good pair of hands. Are you interested?'

Ella O'Callaghan stepped back so she could sweep the length of her visitor. Nice-looking. Her silly years were definitely behind her and she might have half a sensible head on her. Her jeans were faded, washed too many times, and her hair was too long for a woman her age; she would have to tie it back.

'Ma'am, I'm not looking for a job. I'm on vacation. Is the café open? The lady in the post office said it's very good.'

'I don't need big signs when I have Muriel Hearty. You are too early. I have only just got the buns and cakes out of the oven and the tables have to be set yet. A girl from the town promised to help this week, but she has skedaddled: more money cleaning out rooms in the fancy hotel off the N11.'

'I can help.'

Nervousness made Debbie's voice sound too high-pitched.

Ella flustered with her apron strings, her cheeks pinching red with embarrassment.

'Not at all. It is easily done, only a few tables. Give me an hour, maybe less.'

'If you're sure. I waited tables during summer vacation at my local diner. A while back, sure, but it's like riding a bike, isn't it?'

Ella grimaced, as if she had heartburn.

'It is a very kind offer. Just for this morning, mind. My name is Ella. Ella O'Callaghan.'

She held out her hand and grasped the other woman's firmly.

'From America?'

'Yes, Deborah Kading; call me Debbie.'

'Roscarbury Café has only been open a few weeks. Just a few tables in the drawing room, but we are doing nicely. If I could only find proper help, it could be magic.'

She walked over and pushed open the heavy cream door. The walls were a dull gold and a chandelier hung low over four small tables with lace tablecloths. A leather couch veined with age was pushed up against the bay window; bulky armchairs blocked the front of the fireplace.

'It is simple, but the food is good and we give an extra cup of coffee on the house, which goes down well with the ladies after Mass.'

Deborah walked over to a side window draped in heavy gold brocade curtains and overlooking the rhododendron grove.

'This is a very lovely place.'

'Thank you,' Ella said quietly and moved quickly towards the sideboard. 'You will find all you need here. We only serve tea and coffee in the best china cups. They were my mother's. I am not sure she would be happy with the women of Rathsorney turning them over every day, but needs must. Three settings per table. I will be in the kitchen. Shout if you need any help,' Ella said, walking smartly from the room, tightening her apron at the waist.

The sideboard door was stiff, so Deborah tugged it, making a sweet-smelling mahogany cloud puff around her. Stacks of china cups and saucers were neatly tucked together, plates to the side. Each was decorated with lilac and blue thistles, the stems rough, contrasting with the delicate bite of the china rims. She walked between the tables, carefully placing each setting, her hand hovering over every cup as it rattled into position. She was pulling out a drawer looking for cutlery when Ella came back in with two silver platters of cake, crumbly warm, arranged in neat rows, and scones, buttered and laid out flat. Two big flasks of coffee and tea she placed on the sideboard beside the platters.

'They will be along in the next ten minutes. The old priest races through in a rush back to his bed. We have time for a cup before they descend on us.'

Ella did not ask but took two china cups and poured strong coffee, the aroma curling past them, fading into the mustiness of the room.

'Can you just do this: set up a coffee shop?'

'I don't know, I just did it; if we don't get extra money in, the house will fall down around our ears.'

'It is very brave letting people into your home like this.'

Ella snorted loudly. 'Stupid, more like, but it is not as if I have much of a choice.'

'I would never have the nerve. I've been a teacher all my life and getting up in front of classes full of teenagers doesn't bother me, but I could never do this.'

'Necessity brings out all sorts of hidden traits.'

Ella jumped up when she heard the sound of gravel scrunching under the heavy but swift steps of the twelve ladies who bothered each morning to rise to hear Father Hurley stumble too fast over his words, his eyes heavy with sleep still and his hair tousled at the top of his head.

'You pick the seat near the window; that is the best,' Ella told Debbie, ushering her along gently as the mumble of women chattering got louder.

Ella pulled open the side French doors, greeting each woman by name. The cold of the early morning air freshed out the room, settling on the pleated drapes at the window.

Each took a cup and saucer and lined up at the sideboard to help themselves, nodding politely as they passed Debbie and squeezing in too many to a table, so they did not have to share with a stranger. Aware of her intrusion, Debbie slipped out the French doors when the hum of chat in the room lowered to a contented level. Strolling down a side path, she stopped at the stone fountain to light a cigarette.

There was a faded quiet about the place, which she liked. It reminded her of home in Bowling Green, a house lost on the outside but brimming with memories. What a fraud she was. Rob Kading would never have let her work in the diner. The skirts the waitresses wore were too short, the shifts too late. Mr Peabody from out of town grabbed the waitresses' butts.

The ladies of Rathsorney were a loud lot; she could hear them still, the lilt of their conversation fluctuating with the importance afforded to each subject. Muriel Hearty's shrill could be heard above all others.

'There you are. I thought you had left.' Ella seemed out of breath.

'I was daydreaming.'

Debbie stubbed out her cigarette quickly with her fingers, flitting her hands through the air to break up the smoke.

'Won't you come back to the house? The girls are heading and we can have tea and cake in peace.'

'That's kind, but I should be getting along.'

'Maybe another morning? I hope you will come to the café again, though at the moment we are only open until eleven. Until I get my permanent help sorted.'

'I hope you find someone soon.'

'Yes. Enjoy your holiday.'

Ella watched her for a few moments, sauntering down the avenue, before she turned back for the house. If she got a nice woman like that to help out, she just might be able to hold off the bank. Spying Roberta lurking at her bedroom window, Ella hurried to the back stairs so that she would not have to hear her sister slap down another note. Already this morning she had made the hall table shake as she banged down two red notes in quick succession.

Taking in strays now, are we? Our mother and father would be ashamed of you. R.

Muriel Hearty says you are the laughing stock as far as Gorey, with your highfalutin ideas for a coffee house. R.

Her head thumping with the silent fuming of her sister, Ella moved swiftly to her room and her dressing table. The crows were bickering in the high trees. Closing her eyes, she imagined it like she had done so many times, every detail just right: the buzz of conversation, the ping of china cups, the crunch of the gravel as people came and went to her café, the old house humming with life.

Reaching into the silver jewellery box, she took out the green brooch. Shaped like a pansy flower but coloured inky black-green, her mother grumbled loudly it should have been purple, yellow or even all black. Bernie O'Callaghan wore it once with her dark coat, but it was never accorded another outing.

'I like a flower to look like a flower,' she said, clicking her teeth in annoyance that her husband should have wasted his money on something she could not like.

Ella loved the Weiss pansy, the green stones glistening and the darker crystals shimmering, outlining perfectly the curved petals of the flower. The centre was black, except for one green crystal shaped like a teardrop.

John O'Callaghan, when he entered into correspondence with the Weiss jewellers of New York City, also thought the idea of a pansy in varying green hues was both beautiful and different. Mr O'Callaghan ordered two brooches a year, from Weiss, New York. The family-run jewellers were happy to post the small parcel care of Rathsorney post office, so that Bernie O'Callaghan never fully realised the lengths to which her husband would go to show her he loved her.

In all the years, Ella only wore the brooch once. Intent on keeping it for a special occasion, she lost her moment. The time came when the only significant event left in her life was the funeral of her husband. Just before his coffin was taken from the house, she pinned the brooch to the wide collar of her black swing coat. Those who saw Ella that day said she never looked so pale, stylish, heartbroken or so alone.

Even after her parents died, there was a delivery from New

York, as if the love of John O'Callaghan for his wife was inde-structible. Ella still kept those brooches in the same small cardboard box they arrived in.

Muriel Hearty had run up the avenue, her forehead furrowed; she was stuttering her words. 'I got it in yesterday and I saw Mr O'Callaghan going down the street. Next thing I was distracted; I should have called out to him. I will never forgive myself.'

Opening up the brown paper and separating the two folds of the lid to reveal the two brooches carefully wrapped in white tissue paper, Ella took out the topaz and orange rhine-stone brooch. It would have perfectly matched her mother's new burnt-orange coat, the one she had bought in Gorey and was saving for her birthday. The brooch, with a circle of smoky topaz and dull yellow stones, was highlighted with deep orange rhinestones, which radiated, like shafts of sunlight, from a central topaz. Held to the light, the orange stones sparkled.

It was the other brooch that Ella adored: a simple square of clear stones that, when trapped in the light, threw out the colours of the rainbow. It would have sat so perfectly on the floaty dress her mother had fashioned for the night of the choral recital.

She had felt an anger rise in her, that Muriel Hearty had not stopped her infernal gossiping and run after her father.

Ella had dispatched a postal order for the amount of the brooches and also wrote to Mr Weiss as to the tragic accident, which meant no further pins would be ordered by the O'Callaghans of Roscarbury Hall.

A month later, Muriel Hearty had rushed up the driveway of Roscarbury, again in an agitated state of excitement. 'It is another box,' she shouted.

Even Muriel Hearty had been silenced when Ella ripped it open to reveal not one but two exquisite black brooches. The letter of sympathy attached was graceful and dignified. Ella took out the second brown box and looked at the two brooches. At the time, Roberta declined to accept her brooch, and though Ella never wore hers these days, in the first year after the death of her parents, she found comfort in the pin, which was a simple black flower.

Pushing the box to the back of the drawer, she pulled on her heavy coat. Stopping in the front hall to take out a small compact from her handbag, she strained to see in the tiny mirror. Carefully she powdered her face, shoving her powder puff in the creases under her eyes, for a moment squashing her wrinkles so she looked like the young Ella with the big, some would say sad, eyes.

Banging the back door behind her, she waved to Iris, not slowing her pace, moving quickly through the back yard to the well-worn path across two fields and through a small wood, to the cemetery.

Quickly, she walked to the small plots to the right. Shaking her head so the tears had no time to lodge and swell her face, she turned to the small grave under a single cypress tree. Once Carrie's grave had been alone at the far end of the graveyard, but now there were well-worn paths to nearly an acre more of the dead.

BELOVED DAUGHTER

Carrie Hannigan, who Died Tragically on June 23, 1959.
Deeply Missed by Her Mother, Ella, and Father, Michael.
Gone, but Never Forgotten.
Another Angel in Heaven.

A wave of impatience rolled over her, like it always did.

Walking quickly away, she unfurled her shopping bag. Slowing her pace, she dithered at the narrow, overgrown track around the outside of the cemetery wall. Two years they had been married. Slowly, she walked up the path and stood at his grave, leaning down to scrub the dust off the plain wooden plaque.

Private Michael Hannigan.
A Soldier with the Irish Army
Died September 4, 1959.
Sadly Missed by His Loving Wife, Ella.

Straightening, she spotted the dog, a leg up against a pot of plastic flowers on McDonald the grocer's grave. Iris was forever letting that dog roam free; she would have to tell her to keep it tied up in future.

Four

Bowling Green, March 1968

Rob Kading, pulling in to the driveway, saw the porch door swinging open. Stepping out of the driver's seat, he stooped to straighten a supporting rod on the raspberry canes and waved to old man Haussman across the way. Placing his briefcase in its usual spot inside the door, he called out to Agnes softly before making his way to the kitchen. Surprised the table was not set for dinner, he called to his wife again as he moved across to the dining room.

He unfastened the leather strap of his watch and checked the time against the dining-room clock before placing the timepiece carefully on the mantelpiece. Hearing a light step on the outside porch, he was so sure he called out 'Aggie.'

'Mr Kading, it's Moira Rochdale. Silly of me, but I wondered is Agnes all right? She didn't turn up to teach her flower-arranging class.'

'Moira, I think she's gone out. I'm just home from work. Maybe she was called away.'

Moira Rochdale angled closer on the porch.

'The ladies were so disappointed. Agnes isn't usually like this. So dependable. Usually,' she twittered.

Rob Kading was not listening. He noticed her raincoat and her handbag were missing from the coat rack.

'Mr Kading, is everything all right?'

'My wife must have an urgent appointment. I will convey your concerns to her,' he said, as he manoeuvred Moira Rochdale's ample frame back out onto the porch. He didn't know why exactly, but Rob Kading felt very strange. A nausea of worry crept through him and settled. 'Can I drop you home, Moira?'

Moira Rochdale fluttered like a girl asked out on a first date.

'Not at all, the stroll will do me good; you must have so much to do.'

She skipped off across the road as Rob jumped into his car, coasting down the incline to Nancy's house.

Nancy Slowcum was drinking tea and on page two of her *Ladies' Home Journal* when Rob burst in.

'Is she here?'

'Who?'

'Agnes—her bag and coat are gone, do you know where she is?'

'Maybe she took a bus somewhere; no need to panic.'

Rob slumped onto the chair beside the kitchen table.

'She's been acting so strange lately. Nancy, what's wrong with her?'

'She's tired, Rob, did that ever occur to you?'

'She's unhappy, has it in for Debbie all the time.'

'It will pass.'

'She never said she was going anywhere today.'

'Give her a bit of time. Can't a woman move from her routine without the police being called?'

Rob jumped up. 'Where's Debbie? Wasn't she with you today?'

'No, never on a Tuesday. Maybe she and Agnes decided on the spur of the moment to do something.'

Rob guffawed out loud. 'You know, Nance, Agnes isn't capable of doing anything on the spur of the moment. I must find Debbie first.' Without waiting for an answer, he made for the door.

'She's probably playing in her room; Debbie does that a lot lately.'

'Will you come with me, Nance?'

She reached out and touched his arm. 'It'll be all right Rob, maybe she just wants a bit of space.'

'She's been talking to you. Hasn't she?'

Nancy bustled about, closing the kitchen door behind them. She did not answer Rob, and when she sat in the passenger seat beside him she put up her hand to stop any further questions. 'Let's find Debs,' she said.

Debbie was swinging on the gate waiting for either her mother or father to come back. When she saw her father arrive home from work, she presumed her mother was already back. When she saw Rob rush off as quickly, she worried and she waited.

'Mommy isn't here.' He wrapped his arms around her, so she could smell the tobacco on his lapel. 'Darling, let's not worry about it. I am sure Mommy will be home soon.'

'Why don't we tidy up the kitchen and get some food going, for when Mommy comes home,' Nancy said, her voice high-pitched with worry.

Taking in her father's harried look, Debbie moved in beside her aunt. Rob pulled Nancy aside. 'I'm gonna cruise around and call on a few of her friends. I'll check back in an hour. The bus from Cleveland gets in around that time; if she's not on it I'm going to the police.'

'Wait until ten; that's when the last bus pulls in from anywhere.'

'Will Mommy bring me a present when she gets off the bus?'

Nancy gently hushed her niece. 'Well, if she does, we better have this place looking nice.'

She ushered Debbie into the kitchen.

★

Order of Divine Sisters, Rathnew, Co. Wicklow, March 2008

'We had a lot of wealthy Americans in those days who wanted to help out. There is really nothing unusual about this letter. I am afraid I cannot help you.'

Mother Assumpta handed the page across her desk. A smile crawled across her mouth, as if she had been examining a child's drawing. She concentrated on straightening the box of pencils in front of her. Flicking her eyes to the wall clock, she pulled her diary forward. Flinching as if cold, anger shuddered inside her: not at this woman, but that she had to cover up once more. How many times had she seen such a letter? Double digits she supposed, and all before her time.

Consuelo she had always admired for her natural savvy, a quality that was obviously lacking in her early years, when she had put pen to paper. Assumpta flared inside at the pompous gratitude expressed in the letter.

Order of Divine Sisters,
Ballygally,
Rathnew,
Co Wicklow.
May 15, 1959

Dear Mr and Mrs Kading,
Please find enclosed a receipt for the £300 paid to us in April for services offered. Without the help of good Catholic families in the United States, we would not be able to help so many women and children. I thank God for people like you, willing to give a good home to these unfortunate children.

We will continue to pray for you and your family. We wish you happiness with your little girl. I am sure under your guidance she will become a good and loyal daughter.

Yours sincerely,

Sister Consuelo

'I must have been adopted from here: why else would my parents have this letter?' Debbie said firmly.

Mother Assumpta, turning the pages of her desk diary, impatiently looked over her black-rimmed glasses.

'I have checked the records book myself. I am sorry to say you are putting two and two together and getting five. There is no mention of an adoption by Agnes and Robert Kading from the US. It was a very kind donation, but that is all.'

'Why give a donation to a convent in a country they didn't know? Sister Consuelo, is she still here?'

'Sister Consuelo is an old woman now and won't have the memory for this sort of thing. It is the records that count.'

'You did give out children for adoption in the States?'

'Of course. We got fine Catholic homes for a lot of orphans.'

'But not a baby to my mother and father?'

Mother Assumpta clicked her tongue loudly. 'I realise you have come a long way, Miss Kading, but really it is a wasted journey. There is nothing—'

'But there must be something. Can I see the records?'

'And violate the sacred privacy of so many unfortunate women . . .'

'I didn't mean it like that.'

A heavy woman, Mother Assumpta pushed herself out from behind the desk. 'I am sorry, Miss Kading. I am afraid we are quite familiar with this situation. Sometime in all the years that have passed, the information has somehow been changed, interfered with. It is nobody's fault.'

'Surely you can search again, in case you made a mistake.'

A shadow flickered across Mother Assumpta's eyes. 'I have checked the records, Miss Kading, and even two days either side. There is nothing further I can do to help you, only to wish you luck in your quest.'

She stood up and walked to the door. 'Maybe this business is best left. Don't get bogged down in the small details of the past; it will only bring bitterness. You have had a good life: look forward, not back.'

Debbie remained seated. She turned to Mother Assumpta, who was tugging a loose thread from her skirt. 'Is there anything I can do to get access to the records?'

'Like what, Miss Kading?'

Debbie swallowed. 'A donation.'

Mother Assumpta opened the door with an agitated flourish. 'These are different times, Miss Kading. Thankfully this order no longer relies on the handouts of rich Americans. Accept the answers to the questions you have asked. We will include you in our prayers.'

When Debbie stood up, Mother Assumpta ushered her out of the room quickly.

'Are you doing any sightseeing while you are here?'

'I have no plans . . .'

'What a pity . . .'

Debbie's lip quivered; tears threatened to burst out. 'Is there any way?'

'I am afraid it would be like trying to find a needle in a haystack. Our sisters all over the country, and other orders too, took in poor girls and found good homes for their illegitimate children.' She put her hand on Debbie's shoulder. 'Be thankful for the life you have and leave all this in the past,' she said gently.

Debbie shrank from the heaviness of her touch. 'I can see myself out,' she said, slipping down the first steps of the staircase sweep.

Mother Assumpta waited until she reached the front door before disappearing back into her office to take two tablets for her thumping headache.

Outside, the sturdy door clicking shut behind her, Debbie breathed in the fresh air, angry tears spouting from her. The gardener, who was tending to flower pots on the stone steps, stopped to look at her.

'Are you all right?'

Debbie swiped her hand across her eyes. 'I'm good. Thank you.'

He shrugged his shoulders, dropping back to the pots on the bottom stone step.

She wanted to throw up. She was stupid; she had taken all those tablets this morning on an empty stomach. Last time she did that, she threw up in Dr Lohan's office in Manhattan. He remained smiling as splats of vomit landed on his desk, his calendar, his light-blue carpet stained dark by a woman who was not sure who she was.

Her throat felt dry and tight. She rushed down the steps, and when the puke came she directed it into a bed of daffodils that had yet to bloom, before wiping her mouth with her coat sleeve. A grey fog curled around her.

She pushed her hands in her pockets and, feeling the late afternoon damp creep up under her coat, she pushed forward to her car. Pain coursed through her; tears tumbled down her face.

Driving through Rathsorney a few minutes later, she pulled in to have a coffee in Molloy's; Ella's café was too intimate a place when she was in a state like this. Curse the Baby Bits box: her life had been so tidy, structured and predictable before.

Five

The sun shining through the glass seeped across her. She sat in the warm glow, but inside she felt cold. The harsh spring rays pierced at her eyes; the hum of Molloy's coffee shop faded away.

Funny how accustomed she got to the idea that Agnes had gone away. It did not mean she did not want her to return, just that she was used to her being away. They waited the first night and most of the next day. Agnes did not phone and she did not come back. Rob paced the porch. After twenty-four hours, Agnes was declared missing; police were asking questions, putting up posters, checking bus and train lists.

Somebody thought they'd seen her get on a bus to Cleveland. Rob drove there, cruising along the streets, like a criminal looking for trouble. When he came home he was tired; he said his eyes were out on stalks.

The neighbours were sympathetic, then fearful to mention Agnes when more than a week had passed. Debbie and Rob were lost. He spent his days looking for his wife and his nights pacing up and down, a bottle of whiskey for company. After four days and four nights, Nancy insisted they move in with her.

'Rob Kading, if she is going to come back, don't you think she'll know where to find you?'

'It's like we're giving up.'

'It's like you're accepting an offer of some normality in the midst of this awful mess.'

Debbie's normality was that Agnes was gone. Sometimes she dreamed that Mommy would come back. She would slowly pace from Nancy's porch to the fence, willing Mommy to be coming down the little hill. Some days, she imagined Agnes came running from the other side, her hair bouncing about her shoulders, all apologies, all stories about why she had been delayed by weeks.

She wanted that warm feeling of relief to course through her, like a waterfall rushing, to feel Agnes's excitement, be enveloped by her Blue Grass perfume, to finally show her the gold star she got that day for spelling.

'I can see you are lining up with the opposition.'

'Excuse me?'

'There are only two coffee places in town.'

'Yes, of course.' Debbie was stammering, not sure of the intent behind the observation.

Ella saw the red veins in her eyes, the blotchy swollen skin underneath. It had only been a few days, but Ella thought the woman had aged at least a decade. She should have walked by, but she felt sorry for this stranger so far away from home. 'Tell me to go away if you like, but are you all right?'

Taken aback, Debbie pressed her fingers under her eyes. 'I got bad news today. I don't know what to do.'

Ella sat down. 'I know we don't know each other very well, though you have handled some of my best china.'

Debbie smiled. 'I don't know anybody else who would trust me like that. My mother always called me butterfingers.' She stopped suddenly, as if she should not be raking up unnecessary memories.

Ella made to stand up. 'I am intruding.'

'Please sit down; we can talk about other things.'

Ella motioned to the waitress to bring her a cappuccino. Out of the corner of her eye, she saw Roberta take a window seat and order a pot of tea. 'We all have strange stories in our families. That woman over there with the drawn-out look is the O'Callaghan one: my younger sister.'

'She lives in the old house with you.'

'Yes, but we don't talk.'

'And you don't mind?'

'Of course I mind, but don't tell her that or she will keep it up forever.'

'How long has it been going on?'

'The silent treatment? Decades: too many years to count. I think we are rather used to it by now. Probably would not know what to say to each other, if we started to talk.'

Debbie spluttered, the last of her tea falling back in the cup. 'You can't be serious.'

'Unfortunately, yes.'

'Why exactly?'

Ella smiled. 'We will have to get to know each other better before we start sharing those secrets.' Her coffee arrived and she used her spoon to scrape off the frothy foam. They sat silent as she stirred in two sugars.

'It would be so much nicer in your china cups, don't you think?' Debbie said.

'With a chocolate stick on the side to scoop up the foam,' Ella said, and they both started to giggle.

'Take the café job?'

'I'm only here for a short time.'

'Take it?'

Debbie hesitated. 'I'm only on vacation.'

'It will be something different, an adventure to talk about back home. A distraction, even. I have Iris, but she has to pull around the gardens. To be frank, I don't want her anywhere near my china. Just until I can get somebody to help out full-time. It might be fun.'

'You have a way of persuading a person.'

'I wish the bank manager felt the same way. I am thinking of expanding, converting the old ballroom.'

'There's a ballroom?'

'Once the talk of the town between here and Dublin. We will look at it tomorrow, when all the ladies have drained their cups.'

'Won't your sister object?'

'To you or the ballroom?'

'Both.'

'Yes, she will, but what can she say?'

Listening to their loud giggling, Roberta prickled at the back of her neck. She rose quickly from her seat, threw a five-euro note on the table and rushed out of the café, banging the door.

'Don't mind her; she does not like anybody to enjoy them-selves. Will I see you tomorrow?'

'I guess.'

'Eight-thirty on the button,' Ella said, before she whipped away to cut across the fields and beat her sister home.

★

The next morning Ella was in her bedroom powdering her face when she saw Debbie approach from the lakeside. Walking across the grassland, she was stooped against the cold morning breeze pushing past the house, gathering momentum on the parkland on the way to ruffle the lake. She saw her check her watch and nip in behind a tree to light a cigarette, puffing out large clouds of smoke, which were whisked away by the wind. Tramping towards the house, cupping the cigarette in her hand, at the fountain she stopped to stub it out and throw the butt under an old butterfly bush. Ella clicked her tongue, annoyed that the butt should be discarded so casually. She went downstairs to open the front door for Debbie.

'There is a biting wind out there; come in and have a cuppa before you start,' Ella said.

'Let me get the tables set and then I can relax.' She slipped off her coat before making her way to the sideboard.

'Have it your way. Come to the kitchen when you are ready. The lemon cakes are rising nicely, cracking on top.'

Ella stopped in the hall to pick up a note left there since late the night before.

Do you want us to be a complete laughing stock? There is talk that your cake is too sweet and the coffee too weak. Give up now for all our sakes. R.

She scrunched the paper and pushed it in her apron pocket. Ten minutes later, she heard Debbie make a lot of noise as she walked with heavy steps down the hallway before she cautiously pushed at the door.

'All done,' she said, nervously sitting at the kitchen table.

Ella pulled three cake tins quickly out of the oven. She used a darning needle to pierce each cake five or six times, drizzling lemon and melted sugar across the surface of the cakes and pushing it towards the holes until it slipped down out of sight.

'It makes them lovely: a mouthful of sour and sweet at the same time. You can't beat it. It is the only cake that can stop Muriel Hearty talking for a few minutes,' Ella said, knocking out two other cakes onto a wire baking tray.

'Looks like a secret ingredient. There was a bakery near me in New York that injected cream and jam into its muffins.'

'My secret is to get it all into the cake while it is still hot.'

Debbie pressed a few crumbs on the table into her mouth with her finger. 'Mmmm.'

'You might stay here after all.'

'No. That's not going to happen.'

Ella would have answered, but she heard Muriel Hearty's screech as she scurried up the driveway, desperate to get in from the cold. 'The hordes of Genghis Khan are upon us.'

Debbie helped pour the teas and coffees, handing out slices of lemon cake and buttering plain scones. Muriel Hearty tried to put talk on her, but she demurred and escaped to the stone fountain.

The pain up her side was persistent and her stomach was queasy. She heard the ladies push back their chairs and leave soon afterwards, and Ella locking up the French doors and making her way to the fountain.

'You are not fed up of us already, are you?'

Ella was standing behind her, idly fanning her hand along the cold stone of the fountain.

'That's not it. I have a lot on my mind.'

'Can I divert you?'

Debbie nodded.

'I promised to show you the ballroom. Come on. I will warn you nobody has been in here in a long time,' Ella said, as she led the way inside. They climbed the dark staircase, past the sombre portraits of a family, long since faded. 'Good-looking relatives: they have the O'Callaghan nose—long, we won't say beautiful,' she giggled.

Opening a door halfway down the hall, Ella stepped back to take it all in. She did not see the mouse droppings, or the cobwebs so thick they resembled a stage prop, nor the window-panes dulled with dirt. They stepped into the long hall; Debbie whistled under her breath. The oak floor was soft with dirt. A thick layer of dust ground and scraped the wooden boards as they stepped across. Shafts of sunlight were thrown about, as if discarded in the rush to leave decades earlier. Damask curtains, now torn and no longer regal, were half hanging on poles, some with dirty tears and rips from where bigger than a mouse had lost its footing in a panic. In the fireplace grate were the stiff remains of a crow that had crashed into the chimney top, its wings still half splayed wide.

'It must have been grand at one time. Of course, we only ever used it as a skating rink. When I was a young woman, I imagined nice wooden tables with tablecloths and chairs with cushions, where people would come and sample my cakes and drink my tea. There would be window seats overlooking the garden, where customers could enjoy the sunshine and pay good money for refreshments.'

Ella walked over to a window and spat on a pane of glass; tucking her sleeve over her fingers, she rubbed fiercely.

'Old glass. It shines up lovely, even after all these years of neglect.'

Debbie copied her, scraping away the dirt from another pane so she could look out. Underneath, the fountain was empty; the rhododendron spread without direction; the fields tumbled away to the sea.

'It would be so nice to sit at this window. Why didn't you ever do it before?'

Ella had been asked such a simple question. Would she tell her that she had been frozen in pain for so long? Would she tell her the emptiness inside her meant that fulfilling dreams was nothing but a silly notion that, from time to time, brought a certain comfort? How could she, even now, articulate the pain of a husband and child dead, within months of each other, the grief and loss that left a permanent longing? What would this woman from a grand city know how it was to be alone, to have lost time and time again, to be forever grieving?

'I just never got around to it.'

'You should do it now.'

'We will have tea. The damp goes into your bones, if you stay on this floor for too long. The radiators were never enough to heat the place. We will have to get a few plug-in heaters.'

Ella walked back across the ballroom, leaving neat tracks in the dust.

Roberta, sitting at the kitchen table heard the murmur of voices. Pulling her notepad from her pocket, she scribbled another note.

What was that woman doing upstairs? I won't have it. What's next, guided tours? R.

Pushing the kitchen door so hard it crashed into the free-standing fridge, making it shake and shudder, Roberta made a beeline for the back yard. Grabbing her emergency coat from the shed hook, she set off for the front gate. When she'd phoned Gerry O'Hare earlier, he said he could be there in fifteen minutes and it was nearly that now.

'Feeling like a trip out, Miss O'Callaghan?' he said, as he helped her into the car.

'Just drop me in the town, Gerry. I need to get out of the house.'

She barely said goodbye when he pulled in at Hearty's post office. Standing rearranging her coat, she did not see Muriel come up behind her.

'Are you going for a cuppa, Roberta? Matthew has taken over and I am gasping.'

Roberta did not indicate either way, but the two women fell in to step beside each other.

After they ordered, they sat on two hard chairs, so they could be within easy hearing distance of each other.

'I see the Yank has almost taken up residence with you,' Muriel said, jigging on the seat, to get comfortable.

Roberta did not answer but fiddled with the Peter Pan collar of her blouse.

'You know she is going to be around for a while, has taken my flat for four weeks in all.'

'Hmmph.'

The two women leaned back so that the waitress could put down the large cappuccinos.

'Would you like a bun with that?'

Muriel looked at Roberta.

'Wouldn't the taste of something sweet be nice?'

'I suppose,' Roberta answered.

'Two currant scones with butter and jam, please,' Muriel said to the waitress.

Roberta sat stiffly on her chair. 'So, what has all this got to do with me, Muriel?'

'I hear she was the only one who wanted the job in the new café,' Muriel said, rearranging the pleats of her skirt.

'I don't know anything about a job. That might be putting too much of a spin on it. She is helping out, that is all. Any talk of anything else is pie in the sky.'

'Well, I think they might be keeping you in the dark there. Iris herself told me Molloy's will be closing down soon. She talks big, that one, says the American will mean a bigger café and more time for her to whip the gardens in to shape. What would your poor mother have said?'

Roberta felt hot. The waistband of her skirt was pinching her skin. Spikes of sweat pushed through her hair.

'I really don't have time to sit around all day gossiping. You enjoy the rest of your coffee,' she said, rising abruptly from the table.

Gathering up her coat, she slapped a few euro coins on the counter before making for the door.

Never a woman to waste anything, Muriel reached across and threw Roberta's cappuccino into her half-empty cup and began to butter her scone.

Gerry O'Hare, who was passing after picking up paint at the hardware shop, saw Roberta rushing out of Molloy's, her coat flowing around her.

'Is everything all right, Miss O'Callaghan?'

'Take me home, Gerry, please.'

Nothing further was said until the Mercedes pulled around the back of Roscarbury Hall.

'Are you sure you are all right, Miss O'Callaghan? Will I talk to Ella for you?'

'That will not be necessary. Thank you.'

Roberta pushed cash into Gerry's hand before rushing off, stopping in the kitchen to take a note wedged between her sugar bowl and milk jug on her tray.

Butt out. You are not the one who has to deal with the bastards in the bank. E.

Six

Mother Assumpta was reading the paper in the top-floor sitting room when Sister Marguerite, out of breath and excited, called her to come quickly.

'Two minutes in the day I take, to read and pray for the poor souls of those suffering all over the world. It had better be a matter of supreme importance.' Assumpta did not move, but shuffled her newspaper loudly to convey her annoyance.

'It is the American on the phone, looking for Consuelo. Will I say you are at prayers, Mother?'

Assumpta carefully folded the newspaper, her hands trembling and jerking as if she were trying to parcel an awkward item. 'No need for that.'

Spinning Marguerite out of the way, she swept along the narrow corridors to the main house. Stomping down the stairs, she stopped on the widest step of the sweep to compose herself before marching into her office to pick up the phone.

'Miss Kading, dear, is there anything wrong?'

'I want to talk to Sister Consuelo.'

'What good would that do? There are no records of your birth here.'

'She would be able to clear it up. I will have to go further if you don't let me talk to Consuelo.'

'Miss Kading, if that is a threat, you are very silly indeed. I am not going to subject an old woman to your senseless, emotional ravings.'

'Mother Assumpta, I just want some answers.'

'You have got your answer, Miss Kading: there is no record of your birth here.'

'Please, can I talk to her?'

'Sister Consuelo is no longer at this convent.'

'Tell me where she is and I'll visit her.'

'I have no intention of doing that.'

'Maybe you would, if you could understand why this is so important to me.'

Assumpta sighed loudly. 'Miss Kading, there is no one more sympathetic than I, but there is simply nothing I can do to help you; you must understand that.'

Debbie was about to answer when Mother Assumpta cut across her.

'We will leave it at that, Miss Kading. You will not harass members of this community. Go home, Miss Kading, to the family we gave you, and thank God for them.'

Mother Assumpta replaced the receiver gently, shaking her head: a sharp pain was needling the back of her neck and soon she would have a full-blown migraine. The last time she had had such a troublesome enquiry she had managed to frighten the woman off with the prospect of a court order and the ensuing publicity. She dialled Consuelo's mobile, becoming mildly irked when Consuelo answered with a soft, singsong voice as if she were being interrupted mid recreation.

'Mother, what can I do for you?'

'Sister, I have had another bothersome enquiry. Please do not engage in conversation with the latest person, an American. I am sure she will run you down and we certainly do not want such an embarrassment on our hands.'

'I never did anything but find homes for those unwanted children.'

'We both know we are in different times now and the less said is the best approach.'

'Who is she anyway?'

'A Deborah Kading from New York.'

'I don't remember a Kading offhand, but there were so many applications in those days.'

'Quite.'

Consuelo sighed when she heard the frosty edge to Assumpta's voice. 'I found good homes for lost souls; that is what I did. I don't see them traipsing back to thank me. "Ungrateful" springs to mind.'

'That debate is for another time, Consuelo. Please do not engage with this woman, if she makes contact, which I am sure she will. Do not engage in any way. Do you understand?'

'I understand.'

'Make sure you do. God bless.'

'God bless, Mother.'

Assumpta took two painkillers from a drawer and called Marguerite to bring some sweet tea. When she had been elevated to this position two years ago, she imagined presiding over a productive and happy convent and spent hours on plans to improve the accounts and the kitchen garden. When one of the older nuns remarked that her promotion might be a poisoned chalice, Assumpta put it down to bad feeling. Now, as the dark clouds of uncertainty loomed over her patch, Assumpta wondered why indeed she had been picked for this job; maybe it had something to do with her age and the fact that she had so few links to the murky history of the community. She needed to ask Consuelo for the details of all the adoptions she had facilitated, but today she did not have the stomach for it.

*

Debbie stuffed her hands in her pockets and walked against the wind on Main Street. She had been mad to come here; she felt that now. She did not notice when Muriel Hearty waved as she closed up the post office for the day or when Pat McCarthy, chatting at his doorway, saluted her. She was grateful for the family this place had given her, even with all that had happened, but why now, especially now, were there no answers to her questions? She felt like a child again who was not being told, protected from the truth for whatever reason. The sense of helplessness was the same as when sad Rob had tried to build a type of normality back into their lives.

She and Rob, they had stayed with Nancy for two weeks. It was a Saturday morning, early, when Rob announced they were going to move back home. Nancy was dismayed and ushered him to the side, whispering fiercely that it was too early and pleading that the child was not ready. When he could not be moved from his decision, she pleaded to be allowed to keep Debbie.

'I need her help back home. She knows what to do. God knows, she spent long enough at her mother's elbows.'

They walked the two blocks side by side. Neighbours pretended not to notice. He quickened his pace as they got closer and she had to scurry to keep up with him.

When they reached the front gate he moved even faster, covering the stone driveway in three strides and lightly skipping up the front steps, as if he were a ballet dancer on stage. He beckoned Debbie to follow.

'I don't want to have to push you in, but I will. It's best to get it over and done with.'

She tried to shrink back among the raspberry canes and flower beds. A red cardinal sat on a window ledge, pecking at the sill. In one stride, Rob came to her and, grabbing her roughly by the arm, pulled her towards the house. Her feet slid across the porch as she half-heartedly resisted her father's urgent grip.

'I don't know any other way. Mommy has left us like this. Now we must get on with it, until she decides to come back.'

He was slightly out of breath, but he did not hesitate for a second. He turned the key and pushed the door. It gave way freely, the door fanning back so they could see the height of the stairs. Sunshine flooded into the hall. The kitchen clock ticked loudly. The floor tiles were polished and the coat stand was empty.

'I thought you might like to have something of Mommy's in your room. The necklaces; I thought you would like to mind them for Mommy, and her dressing table. We can move it into your room, if you like.'

Shrinking back, Debbie shook her head fiercely.

'Sweetheart, I'm only trying to help.'

Debbie knew she would never want the sparkly necklaces. They still belonged to her mother; she had declared her rights to perpetual ownership. Hadn't she told her so, screamed at the top of her voice two days before she left that she was never to look at or touch the jewellery again? She could still feel the softness of her spit spraying over her, when Agnes had stuck her face in hers. Tiny holes in her skin were clogged with fine brown powder; her nostrils flared red.

Mommy had been in such a good mood when Debbie came home from school, singing as she pushed the power pedal on the sewing machine. Debbie, who was sent to tidy her room, saw a new pearl necklace had been laid out on Agnes's dressing table. The whirr of the machine on a long, straight seam gave her the confidence to step inside the room. Three lines of pearls and a diamante clasp were draped side by side. It hypnotised her with its perfect simplicity. She should have left it at that, but, mesmerised, she could not leave. The only thing she could do was reach out and touch one of the strands, picking it up and letting the beads run through her fingers. So transfixed was she by the feel of the pearls, like light rain on her cheeks, she never realised the machine had come to the end of the long evening-skirt seam.

'What's going on?' Agnes asked.

'I was just looking.'

'Really? Who gave you permission to put your grubby little hands on my pearls?' Her mother's arms were folded across her chest, her eyes cold and hard.

'I was just looking and then I picked it up. It's beautiful.'

She held the pearls closer. She did not expect her mother to hit her, so when the slap came stinging across her cheek, it knocked her sideways, making her stumble into the dressing table. The pearls shot out of her hand, skittering across the floor; bottles rattled and two tubes of make-up slipped to the floor.

'You are a thief in the making. Don't think you can even look at my jewellery. Do you understand? It's mine. I don't want your dirty paws near my necklaces again.'

Pushing Debbie roughly out of the room, Agnes banged the door shut. Debbie ran to her own room, where she curled up tight on the bed, sobbing, her tears dampening the pillow.

Seven

Mother Assumpta paced up and down, keeping an ear open for O'Hare's car. When Consuelo had asked for permission to visit she'd wanted to refuse, but knew it mattered little because Consuelo would do as she pleased anyway. Considerably older than Assumpta, Consuelo had expected to be appointed to the chief's chair when Mother Bridget died two years ago. She not only showed her surprise but also her disgust when the much younger Assumpta was named as Bridget's successor.

'After all I have done for this community and those on the outside. There are children across the world who have me to thank for their very good fortune and lives. Not that I ever would go seeking their thanks or gratitude, but I would have expected some recognition within my own community,' she muttered to anybody who cared to listen.

When the first flush of indignation had passed and Assumpta settled into her role, Consuelo appeared to begrudgingly accept the inevitability of the situation. In the past six months, however, as more and more came to make enquiries about their birth mother and named Consuelo as the adoption facilitator, tensions between the two nuns had grown.

Assumpta sat in the armchair by the window. She felt weary. She should have been more forceful with Consuelo when the woman from Donegal had come asking questions four months ago. It was a familiar story: there was no record of the birth, but of course she had Consuelo's name and a goddamned letter the nun had penned in a fit of simpering gratitude, decades earlier, to the adoptive parents.

Consuelo refused to budge, sticking to the mantra that she had done no wrong and the God Almighty could be her judge. When the young woman threatened to go to the newspapers, Assumpta retaliated with the threat of an injunction and the public humiliation of having her name in the newspapers for harassing the convent.

The strategy worked, but Assumpta, upset by the aggressive stand she had had to take, moved Consuelo to the Moyasta convent in the hope her unavailability would turn away even the most determined.

She watched the daffodils swaying in the breeze, the blur of gentle yellow across the park a sad reminder of the indignity of pregnant women put to weeding and planting bulbs for the whole of the month of October, rain, hail or shine. Little did those who admired the swathes of daffodils, snowdrops and crocuses know of the back-breaking toil and knee-grinding pain involved for the women, many of whom were in their final weeks of pregnancy.

Closing her eyes, the sounds of the convent were her calming backdrop: the faraway shimmer of Sister Christina's giggle as she indulged in gossip Martha's sewing machine, which fell silent at eleven each morning when she went to the kitchens for a coffee; and the hens clucking loudly, waiting still to be fed, because Sister Bernadette had dallied too long at the pig sty. That this normality would be upset by Consuelo was a major aggravation for Mother Assumpta, who decided to take a painkiller.

Gerry O'Hare's car swung to the steps; he got out to open the car door for Consuelo.

She pulled her big frame from the back seat and rummaged in her handbag until she found her purse. She pushed a generous tip into the palm of O'Hare's hand on top of the fare after he neatly placed all her luggage in a line beside the front door.

Assumpta waited for Marguerite to greet the visitor, before sitting at her desk, pretending to be writing a letter. Consuelo's voice bounced through the hall as she bustled into Assumpta's office without knocking.

'It is so lovely to be home. This is where I started out and this is where I always want to be. You understand that, Mother Assumpta, surely.'

Mother Assumpta rose up and smiled gently, motioning with her hand for Consuelo to sit down. Consuelo ignored her, walking over to the fireplace.

'You really should have an open fire; there's a fierce nip in the air today.'

Mother Assumpta waited patiently for the chatter to stop.

'The cases, Consuelo?'

Consuelo whipped around and flopped into a comfortable chair at Assumpta's desk, her face suddenly serious. 'I have to take the bull by the horns, so to speak. I am moving back. You can't deny me that as I approach my twilight years, Mother.'

'You never said, when you requested a meeting.'

'I need to be among my own; I have done my time in Moyasta. I want to come home.'

'It is hardly proper to be moving in before even applying to move.'

Consuelo stood. 'I was never one for formality, Mother. Is it this nonsense with the American that has upset you?'

Consuelo was very good at turning the conversation around, Assumpta thought, and she felt anger stab through her. She stiffened in her chair and straightened the writing sheets on her desk.

Consuelo walked over to the window. 'I miss this place and the daffodils; I so wanted to see them in bloom. I remember when we planted every single one.'

Assumpta cleared her throat. 'That may be, Consuelo, but I do not think we have room.'

Consuelo swung around and clapped her hands. 'The young girl, Sister Marion, is desperately homesick. Why not let her go back to Moyasta? She is from those parts and I can take over her quarters; I am not fussy.'

Assumpta felt her hands clench to fists, and she placed them on her lap. 'Quite impossible. Sister Marion is an important and integral part of our community here and must learn to swallow her homesickness.'

'Are you refusing me?' Consuelo marched across to the desk and stood leaning over Assumpta.

'Until this thing about the American blows over, the safest and best place for you is Moyasta.'

'You are afraid I will shoot off my mouth, aren't you?'

'I don't know what you are talking about and I do not want to know. What I am saying is, having a high profile in the community here would not be helpful at the moment.'

Consuelo looked deflated, like a child told she could not go swimming after all. 'You are not seriously going to send me back, are you?'

'I am asking you to go back, Consuelo. We can manage to put you up for tonight, but that is all.'

Assumpta could hear the tick of the hall clock as Consuelo sat down massaging her fingers.

'I did the best I could for every child; nobody can say different. Just because some people won't accept the answers in black and white, the official records of this convent, does not mean I should be penalised.'

'You are not being penalised. We simply do not want the whole thing blowing up in our faces.'

'What is new in these parts?'

Assumpta smiled to herself. Consuelo would never admit she was beaten, but merely changed the subject.

'Jimmy Doohan, the farmer who owns the fields across the way, has died,' Assumpta said, trying to make her voice sound conversational and friendly.

'We will need to show our faces at the funeral. If the family sell off the land around the convent, our privacy will be gone.'

'We will cross that bridge when we come to it.'

Mother Assumpta stood up as the lunch bell sounded, catching Consuelo gently but firmly by the elbow.

'Ella O'Callaghan has set up a café in the house.'

'At Roscarbury Hall?'

'Upstairs. Father Devine says it is wonderful. He has coffee there every morning after late Mass.'

Sister Consuelo turned sharply to Assumpta. 'What sort of madness has come over her, letting people into the house?'

'The front door has been opened up. The place is looking good.'

Consuelo pulled in a whistling breath. 'There must have been a sea change in Ella O'Callaghan. Sure, she would not let you past the kitchen. A gardener once told me he had to piss outside, because there was no point asking about going upstairs to the loo. Rusted up a right good plant in the process, he did.'

'Sister Consuelo, please watch your language.'

There was a loud whoop of welcome for Consuelo when she walked into the basement kitchen and took up her usual position to the right of Mother Assumpta at the long, rectangular table.

One woman stood by the Aga, ladling food from different saucepans onto plates, which were then passed from sister to sister along the table. The same was done at the end of the table, where another nun, wearing a charcoal-grey jumper and jeans, handed out glasses of juice. Consuelo chatted loudly to the woman on her right.

'The way this country is being run, there will be no young people left. McInerney in the High Street, his three sons have left; he does not think any one of them will want to come back and make a life here.'

'Consuelo, you always were the heartthrob of the town. A few minutes back and you have us all up to date; I don't know how you do it,' Sister Marion said, in an attempt to join the conversation.

Consuelo, buoyed up by the praise, straightened in her seat, throwing her shoulders back. 'Years of practice, Marion, mean I am very much in tune with the common man or woman,' she replied, her voice at a high pitch. Her habit of looking over her glasses made her look pompous, as well as sounding it.

Assumpta quietly picked at her stew, wondering if Consuelo would leave tomorrow morning or if she would hatch up another plan to stay.

Eight

There was such a flurry of activity around Roscarbury Hall over one weekend that those who lived in the town could not but notice something big was afoot. But it was Muriel Hearty who decided to make the trip down the road to find out. After the post office closed for a half day, she had her husband drop her at the big gates.

Ella and Debbie had gone on a special shopping expedition to Gorey, ordering fifteen round wooden tables for inside and wrought-iron round for outside, red and white check table-cloths, and plenty of strong chairs. Little red candles in glass holders were purchased for the centre of each table along with boxes of cutlery. Red napkins were bought in bulk, and new cake tins and bun trays by the dozen. Debbie's advice was taken on a sophisticated coffee machine and a hot-water geyser.

Back at Roscarbury, they set to work with a renewed vigour, dragging the cobwebs from the high ceiling and hoovering up runaway spiders. Ella and Debbie donned thick rubber gloves and washed and swabbed until they ached. The dust was beaten out of thick old carpets, and window nets were dipped in bleach before being rinsed and put back on the tracks immediately, to avoid creasing. Rolled-up balls of newspaper were used to make the old window glass sparkle, and the silver and brass were polished until the cloth went black. Leather chairs were massaged with sweet-scented furniture polish, and years of grime scraped away. Velvet drapes were sent for dry-cleaning, and the upholstered couches sponged and left near the window to dry. Pots of cut flowers were placed about. The hall table was sprayed and polished, the walls washed and the floors scrubbed until they gleamed.

One morning, Debbie took down the big key from its nail beside the front door and left it to soak in oil, pouring an ocean more into the old lock.

'This grand house needs the front door,' she said.

Ella did not tell her that the door had remained shut since the day of Michael's funeral; she did not let on she had wanted it that way. They sat and had tea with thick slabs of chocolate cake as the oil softened years of rigid dirt.

An hour later, giggling like a nervous schoolgirl, Ella walked up to the heavy wooden door, last opened when the coffin of Michael Hannigan was carried out after he had been waked for a day and a night. Ella attempted to turn the key. Stiff at first, reluctant to let go of its rusty lethargy, the lock slowly clanked to life, coaxed by the big key, and the bolt slid back with a dull thud. It took Debbie, heaving and pushing from the other side, lending her weight to the door, to make it give way with a rasping creak, and it groaned after decades of sitting tight with neglect and let the light spill into the hallway.

Debbie worked like a woman possessed, brushing down the

door and the lintel, the dust falling into her hair, the indignant spiders and beetles racing around her feet in frantic chaos. The water went brown several times over as the door was washed down and layer upon layer of dust picked out of the corners. John Sheehy was tidying the rhododendron when he saw Debbie wiping down the door. She scrubbed with a heavy brush before spraying the wood with disinfectant. So intent was she on the work she did not seem to notice a run of water was drenching her shoes and the ends of her jeans.

She was exhilarated, but an awful fatigue was taking her over and she hoped she could last the day until she could go back to her place and lie down.

'I see Ella has roped you in as well.'

Debbie did not turn from her work. 'I am glad to help her.'

The gardener plucked a half-decent bloom from the rhododendron and held it out to Debbie. 'Tell Ella I will start digging out the rills tomorrow morning. I am knocking off early today.'

She did not know what he meant by either the flower or the message. Before she could formulate anything in her head, he was heading to the jeep. He waved as he drove past, and she smiled.

Concentrating on the doorknob and handle, she scrubbed and polished; the lock she tried several times, until it was free running. Weeds were picked out of the cracks on the front steps, which were brushed and sluiced with warm water. The postman stopped to admire the work and left the letters on the hall table.

Ella stuck her head out the drawing-room French doors and called her. 'Don't overdo it, Debbie. Have you an admirer?'

Debbie felt a blush rising in her.

Ella got some fresh cloths and scouring pads from the press and they set off to the ballroom. Debbie got down on her knees and scrubbed the ballroom floor with a soapy steel pad, her trousers sodden with dirty water, her fingers red from the combination of the hot water and the frenetic scrubbing. When she finished polishing the oak floorboards, they looked as they had done when Ella's great-grandaunt had had fine gatherings in the big room with a view. An invitation to such an evening was like gold dust; revellers were prepared to travel from as far away as Dublin to spend time at Roscarbury Hall.

'We will have to ask Mulligan to put putty in the windows and give them a lick of paint,' Ella said. As she finished polishing the ballroom's bevelled glass, she spotted Muriel Hearty beetling up the avenue. 'Well, I knew it would not take her long.'

Roberta also saw Muriel come up the driveway and up the steps to the front door. She pushed her hip flask deep in her handbag and stayed out of sight in the side library. But Muriel Hearty knew her way around Roscarbury Hall and rapped on the window. She waved, forcing Roberta to fix a smile on her face and go to the front door.

'Roberta, how are you?' Muriel Hearty shot into the hall before she was even invited. 'Well now, what has been happening here? I even thought the garden looked all spruced up. Are ye expecting important visitors or what?'

'Haven't you arrived, Muriel?' Roberta said, making her visitor beam with pleasure. 'How are things at the post office?' she added.

'Oh, you know, up and down. Gerry O'Hare keeps getting letters from the Revenue. Don't know what all that is about.'

'Aren't we lucky we don't get much post or you would be able to tell us what is happening in our lives as well.'

Muriel giggled uncomfortably. 'Ah sure, I mean no harm. Actually, I am here because there is a huge parcel delivery, several boxes, coming out of Gorey for Ella.'

'Of course, I would know nothing about that.'

The two women listened as they heard Ella clumping down the stairs.

'I will leave you to it,' Roberta said as her sister arrived in the hallway.

'Ella, there is a delivery coming in from Gorey for you. You are going to have to get Gerry O'Hare to collect it,' Muriel said, already peering up the staircase.

'Muriel, you could have phoned. There was no need to come out of your way like this.'

'Ah sure, the fresh air is good for me. Now tell me, some in town say you are setting up a bed and breakfast and others say an even bigger restaurant. Which is it?'

'A café, Muriel, in the old ballroom on the first floor, and in the garden in the summer. Come on up and I will show you.'

Muriel made a straight line for the stairs, eager to see at first hand the goings-on at Roscarbury Hall.

'Have you heard that Tom Mason's wife has left him?' She did not wait for an answer. 'Just packed her bags last night and said she had found a new man, who could love her, and off she went. I believe he opened the butcher shop as normal, though when I went to get a bit of steak I saw he was putting a lot of oomph into the cleaver chopping.'

Ella did not say anything, but led the way down the long corridor to the ballroom door. 'It is still a bit of a mess, but we are getting there.'

She opened the door. The floor dazzled and the windows

sparkled, throwing light onto the two tables, set up in red and white.

'Now let's sit and have some tea,' Ella said, directing Muriel to a seat by the window.

'Well, haven't ye done a fine job? I can see myself having a lot of cuppas here. What a great place for a chat.'

'And a gossip,' Ella added, though she tried to dilute the barbed tone of her voice.

Debbie appeared with a pot of tea for two and ginger cake cut into neat squares, a dab of cream on the side.

'I could get used to this,' Muriel laughed.

'Tell me more about Tom Mason. I always thought he and Tricia were happy.'

'So did all of us, and I think so did the fool Tom Mason. She won't get better than a butcher. Sure, people eat meat in good times and bad.'

'She hardly married him for the meat,' Ella said.

'Well, the lad she has gone off with is younger than her. They say he is a mature student, whatever that is. I wonder what he saw in her. For God's sake, Ella, she is in her sixties if she is a day. She must be mad, throwing up a good man like Tom Mason. So good he never asked her once to help out in the shop. He said a lady of her gentility should not have to look at dead animals. What I wouldn't give for a man like that.'

Ella did not answer, but Muriel continued regardless.

'You know what will happen. That young man will throw her over next month or maybe next year and that saint of a butcher, the fool, will take her back. Well, I for one will never talk to her again. She can buy her stamps somewhere else.'

'They might be in love,' Ella said.

They sat quietly for a moment, each in their own way envious of the butcher's wife.

'It will come to no good end. I know that for sure,' Muriel snorted.

'Maybe,' Ella said.

A van trundled up the driveway.

'You are getting another delivery, Ella.'

'A few pots of flowers to brighten up the front.'

Behind the screen, Debbie slumped against the sink, her head down, pain gripping her insides, a sick feeling rising inside her. She pulled over a small stool and sat, her head resting on the cool stainless-steel rim of the sink, her body stiff with pain. Pulling deep breaths, she waited, hoping this episode would pass. She had only a few weeks left in this place; why she was wasting it helping set up the Ballroom Café, she simply did not know.

Nine

Bowling Green, October 1968

Agnes had been missing exactly a month when Debbie's birthday came along. They had a small cake with eight candles and she blew them out quickly, the pain in her heart too much that Mommy was not there. That morning she had got up and sat by the window until Rob called her, taking her into such a tight bear hug she could feel the well of grief inside him. When he produced the cake, she loved him because he remembered and because he was so strong for her.

It was the first year there was not the usual trouble around her birthday.

Every other year an agitation infused Agnes, who became crotchety and cross with her daughter. Debbie only picked up on the tension as she approached her fifth birthday.

For weeks she pestered Agnes about a party. She thought of cake and balloons and her mother happy and beautiful. Mary Power's mother had baked and iced a cake to look exactly like their house, with Mary waving from the top window.

'If we try to do that it will look a mess, because your father never bothers about the upkeep of the house.'

Agnes surely griped a lot more, her mouth contorted, her eyes narrow, but Debbie did not listen. She tuned in for the last bit, which came loud and clear.

'You can forget about a party this year. I am just not up to it.'

She went upstairs to lie down and was still there when her husband came home from work. The house was quiet; his daughter was sitting, her arms folded, at the kitchen table.

'What's wrong, baby face?'

Debbie threw herself at him and began to sob.

'Hey, hey, what could be so bad?' He took out his handkerchief and dabbed her eyes gently.

'Mommy says I can't have a birthday party and I've told everybody at school I'm going to have the best party ever.'

'I'm sure Mommy didn't mean that exactly. Let me go and talk to her.' He tucked her up in a blanket with a plate of cookies in front of the TV.

She waited until she heard him go into the bedroom before tiptoeing up the stairs.

'Aggie, you can't do this to her. She is only four, for Christ's sake.'

'"I want, I want, I want." I'm not running myself ragged over this.'

'Aggie, she's excited. Remember when she was born? We were so happy.'

There was a loud crash. When she looked through the keyhole, Debbie saw her father ducking down by the dressing table; the mirror was smashed and a lamp was lying on the floor broken.

'Aggie, have you taken leave of your senses?'

'Don't talk to me about when she was born. Where were you?'

'You know I couldn't be there. We've been happy, haven't we, all these years?'

'Happy. Is this what you call happiness?'

'Aggie, don't say things you'll regret later.'

'It's what I feel.'

'Aggie.'

Rob made to go to his wife, but she shouted at him. 'You always take her side. I will not change my mind. That is the end of the party talk.'

'All right, all right. I'll talk to Nancy.'

'Aren't we so lucky to have Nancy?'

'I'll leave you to it.'

'You're good at that, Rob Kading,' she shouted at his back.

Debbie raced down the stairs, but her father saw her slip across the hall to the sitting room. He stopped to give her time to settle herself in front of the TV before entering the room.

'Baby face, why don't we do something totally different? Five is a big birthday, big enough for a party away from the house.'

'Where will we go?'

'Let me talk to the folks at Ed's Diner.'

She smiled at him. His face was a grey colour and the frown on his forehead made him look old. He cooked fried eggs for their tea and made a big thing of explaining that Mommy was tired and needed to rest.

'Don't worry about your birthday. We'll have a great party,' he said with a jolly smile she wanted to believe.

'Will Mommy come to my birthday?'

'Of course, darling, Mommy would love to go to your birthday.'

Agnes stayed in her room all evening; even when Debbie was going to bed and lingered at the doorway she did not turn from her position, curled up in a tight ball and facing the wall.

'She might be asleep. Let's leave her,' Rob said, gently guiding his daughter to her bedroom. He stayed with her until she fell asleep.

When he checked on his wife, she threw a hairbrush at him. Out on the porch, he sat on his rocking chair and unscrewed the bottle of Jack Daniel's he had been saving for an occasion. He did not bother with a glass, but swigged from the neck.

When Debbie woke in the early hours, she did not know at first why her legs and sheet were wet. She called her mother; she did not come. Afraid to disturb Agnes, she went looking for her father and found him asleep on the rocking chair on the veranda; a half-empty bottle of Jack Daniel's still in his hands. He did not wake when she softly called his name. Yanking the bottle from his grip, she grabbed his shoulder and shook him hard. He rose up from the chair with such ferocity that it rocked violently. The bottle fell from her hands; Debbie shrank back into the shadows, afraid.

As he wiped the sleep slobber from around his mouth, Rob Kading saw his daughter cowering by the sitting-room windowsill.

'Little darling, I'm sorry if I frightened you. Daddy didn't mean to.' He held out his hands to her and she ran to him. 'It's not the whole party thing, is it?'

She could only whisper in his ear.

'Oh, don't worry. That's easily sorted.'

He led her by the hand and she helped him take off the wet sheet and turn over the mattress. After they had tucked in a new sheet, he sat Debbie on the bed and helped her change into a fresh nightgown.

'We don't need to tell Mommy about this.'

She nodded with relief and closed her eyes, the smell of whiskey from her father in her nostrils.

When Agnes got up the next morning, it was as if her outburst of the evening before had not taken place. She cooked pancakes for breakfast, stacking them high, humming a jaunty tune. Rob winked at Debbie, and it made her happy.

*

At the gates of Roscarbury Hall, Debbie stopped to check her make-up and dot concealer under her eyes. The dark patches were only a little muted, but she figured Ella would be too jittery to notice. Ella was standing nervously at the front door when she rounded the bend in the driveway.

'I did not sleep a wink. My stupid ideas. I should never have gone this big. I am sure I have baked too much. It will be a terrible waste.' She stopped to look at Debbie. 'Are you all right? You look a bit peaky.'

'Hard time sleeping, too.'

Ella gave her an odd look, but Iris, screaming from upstairs, made them take the stairs two at a time. The café looked like a sauna, white steam puffing across the room.

'I am nearly scalded with this coffee machine,' Iris shouted.

Ella shouted to open some windows as she ran to switch off the machine. 'Iris, stick to the garden or the washing-up. All you had to do was turn the dial.'

'I only wanted to sneak a cappuccino.' Iris stopped Ella's hand moving for a china cup. 'I need a mug; I am so nervous.'

The steam dissipated, clearing to the corners. Debbie, checking out the windows, saw as many as twenty coming in the gate. When they had got past the bank of rhododendron, she took Ella by the hand and pointed to the group flowing towards the house.

'My good lord in heaven, I am not going to have enough to feed them. I don't even know some of them.' Her voice was shaking, a tear rolling down her face. 'Do I look all right?'

Debbie nodded. Reaching over, she opened two buttons at the top of Ella's cream blouse and loosened her golden hair from behind her ears. 'Now you look great,' she said.

Ella, pink on the cheeks, was embarrassed but felt ridiculously happy.

'I don't want to meet any of that crowd. Time for me to exit,' Iris said, rushing down the stairs and outside to the kitchen garden.

Muriel Hearty led the charge. She had not just spread the word about the café; she had promised more.

'They have opened up the old house. Sure, we have to have a look. No stranger was ever allowed past the downstairs before,' she babbled on to anyone who would listen.

Many went to gawp. Those who thought they might find some clues as to the tragic history were disappointed but seduced, instead, by the flowing fountain and garden rills, the view from the café windows, and both Ella and a quiet American behind the counter.

Ella patrolled the garden tables and the aisles of the Ballroom Café, personally checking with each customer if they were happy. At one stage, Roberta swept by to hand her sister a red note.

Are you happy now the whole of Rathsorney has come to gawk? Don't take this as a measure of your success but as a level of the notoriety of the O'Callaghan sisters still. You have had your fun. For pity's sake, stop now. R.

Ella took the pencil from its place balanced at her ear and wrote a reply, holding it out at eye level so her sister could scan it.

The Ballroom Café stays open. Like I said, put up or ship out. E.

By lunchtime, all the scones were gone and people sat inside and outside with tea and coffee and slices of cake. To make everything go further, Ella had to halve the slices of cake, but nobody seemed to notice, so enchanted were they by the delicate china and the faded elegance of the old house. When the last person left, at four o'clock, Ella shut the hall door and asked Iris to put a closed sign on the main gate. Debbie had already started the washing-up.

'Leave that, dear; your feet must be killing you.'

'I want to get along.'

'Sounds like you have plans.'

She saw her shoulders hunch up, a shiver of tears making Debbie stoop further over the sink.

'Debbie, what is wrong? Has someone said something to you? Those women can be awful cruel: they don't mean it, but they are vicious gossips.'

Debbie turned, her face patched red from crying. 'It's not the women. Everybody was perfectly nice to me.'

'Darling, what is it?' Ella put her arm around her shoulders, steering her to a small table for two.

'It's my birthday today. I lost my dad recently. Silly, really, at my age to be so caught up on a birthday.'

'You poor thing! I would not have had you working if I had known.'

Debbie snorted her tears loudly, so Ella patted her gently on the shoulder as she reached into the cupboard under the sink for a bottle of Baileys.

'I was going to put some in the whipped cream, but I thought why bother wasting it on the gossips of Rathsorney.'

She took down two small china cups, delicate blue flowers mossed in and topped with gold rims, pouring a generous measure into each. Whipping a chocolate muffin from the cake stand, she stuck a lighted match in it.

'Blow it out, quick, before we blow up the place. Happy birthday.'

Debbie blew hard and the match toppled onto the table. 'Thank you for being so kind.'

'Drink up; it will warm you up and leave a sweet taste. Tell me about your dad.'

Debbie took a gulp from her teacup. 'He was always there for me. My mom . . . she hasn't been in my life for a long time. Dad passed away a short while ago; there's nothing much to tell.'

'Not easy. In time, the memories themselves will bring you comfort.'

'Maybe.'

Ella got the bottle and topped up the teacups.

'Do you have children, Ella?'

'Yes . . . my girl died a long time ago.'

'I'm sorry.'

'She drowned at the harbour; she was only a baby. We have to take what life throws at us.'

Debbie did not know what to say. She could hear herself breathing. They sat as the light began to dull, sipping from the china cups; there was no need to talk.

'Do you mind if I ask a personal question?' Ella asked after a short while.

'I suppose not.'

'Why have you come here to Rathsorney? It was hardly for employment in the Ballroom Café.'

Debbie gulped some more from her teacup, before sitting back. 'No reason for Rathsorney in particular. I'm trying to trace my roots, so I needed a base.'

'Right.'

Debbie got up and walked to the window. The trees were beginning to blend into the late-afternoon sky. She spotted a fox creep up the parkland to Neary's farm, and in the distance a boat was heading out to sea for a night's fishing. She kept her eyes on the rills, following them to the pond, looking at the lake in the distance as she spoke.

'It's not as simple as that. I was adopted from the convent orphanage in Ballygally.'

Ella followed her to the window. 'That's why you are here?'

Debbie swallowed back the tears. 'They have no record of me. I've tried everything.'

'Oh, you poor darling.' Ella stroked her hair lightly.

Neither of them heard Iris come up the stairs.

'Drinking in the early evening, ladies? This café has not got a licence,' she cackled.

Ella whipped around. 'You won't want a Baileys then?'

'Ella O'Callaghan, you are bold. Remember, make it a mug,' Iris said, plonking into a chair and patting the one beside her to call Debbie over. 'You are the talk of the town, madam: you and the café. I will put my money on an even bigger crowd tomorrow.' If Iris noticed the tear stains across Debbie's face, she did not let on.

'Ella here should run a great American day: hot dogs and mustard, blueberry muffins, donuts. Pecan pie maybe?' Iris laughed.

Ella plonked the mug in front of her. 'You are losing the run of yourself, Iris O'Callaghan. No offence, Debbie, but we are not running a diner.'

'None taken. I really must get along.'

Ella jumped up. 'Please, can you wait a few minutes? I have something for you.'

Before Debbie could answer, Ella scurried off to the next landing and her room. She knew exactly what she wanted to give her: the Weiss butterfly brooch, delicate, to match the look in her eyes. She had no daughter who would ever wear it now. Taking it out of the box, she held it up to her shoulder. Delicate pinks, blues and lilacs; the stones glittered and glowed in the light. She had had such grand plans when Carrie was born of ordering a Weiss brooch for her birthday each year. She wrote to Weiss of her daughter and how even the butter-flies fluttered down to kiss her face.

Holding the brooch close, Ella skipped down the stairs to the café.

'I want you to have this,' she said to Debbie. She reached out and pinned it to her shirt. 'It is time for it to fly to the outside world.'

Debbie took Ella's hand. 'Please, I cannot take this. You hardly know me.'

'I know you enough to know you will cherish it, and it's the only type of jewellery you will wear.'

'How do you know all this?'

Ella turned over Debbie's hands. 'There are no marks from rings and I have never seen you wear a necklace.'

'Can you tell me what I'm thinking as well?'

'I will need a few more days for that,' Ella answered solemnly, and they both giggled.

'Time for me to hit the high road,' Iris said, elaborately downing the rest of her liqueur.

Debbie hugged Ella. 'Thank you for making this birthday so special.'

Debbie squeezed her elbows and Ella felt suddenly lonely.

'On time in the morning, mind you.'

'Without a doubt.'

When Ella heard the front door bang gently, she stood back from the windows, watching Iris and Debbie walk down the old avenue, too busy chatting to even look back. The bile of loss rose up inside her, so she moved away to put the chairs up on the tables and mop the floor.

Ten

Debbie turned up at Roscarbury the next day with the brooch pinned to the multicoloured thin scarf she liked to wear loosely around her neck. Ella did not show her surprise and she did not say she had expected it to be for good wear only. Iris readied the outside tables and Debbie the upstairs café. Ella cut thick slices of coffee cake, making sure to press a candied orange slice into the icing.

Roberta, for the most part, hovered out of the way, leaving notes for her sister beside the kitchen ovens.

The health inspectors will be calling on you soon. Do your customers know when they eat your cake that your kitchen is so filthy? R.

Ella scribbled a caustic reply.

My side of the kitchen is perfectly clean. It is the drunk on the second floor who does not clean up after herself. E.

She has stolen your jewellery. R.

Butt out. Mind your own beeswax. E.

May Dorkin was always the first to arrive. Because she was visiting somebody's house, May never arrived empty-handed but always had a small plate of homemade scones or a small, sweet cake. Ella accepted the gift each morning with a fixed smile and a polite thank you.

'May, you know you shouldn't. You will have some?'

'I will not. I will have the chocolate cake. One of these days, I am going to get your recipe; it is delicious.'

Ella laughed before going behind the screen to the kitchen, where she threw May's offering in the bin.

'The hens are going to develop a real sweet tooth,' she fussed.

Ella saw James McDonagh park his tractor and jump from the seat as she served a customer at the centre window seat. She hurried behind the counter to Debbie.

'I don't want to have to talk to McDonagh. Will you serve him?'

'What if he asks for you?'

Ella looked agitated. 'I will stay behind the service screen. Just say I am too busy.'

When he came in the door, James McDonagh was on his mobile. 'A latte,' he said, gesturing to Debbie.

As she prepared the coffee, he asked after Ella. 'Will you tell her my mother sends her regards?'

Behind the screen, Ella sat on the bin, biting her nails. 'I am sure she does. He is only here to see me fail. Walking in here as if he owned the place,' Ella muttered, jumping up and marching onto the ballroom floor. Her teeth grinding with determination, she walked over to James McDonagh. 'Excuse me for disturbing you, Mr McDonagh, but could I have a word in private, downstairs?'

'James. Call me James, Miss O'Callaghan.'

Ella led the way to the front drawing room.

'Mr McDonagh. Thank you for frequenting the Ballroom Café, but it will not be requiring your custom.'

'That is a bit harsh, Miss O'Callaghan. We are, after all, still family.'

'I am not related to you. The day my husband died is the day I stopped having any connection with your family. Tell your mother she might be Michael Hannigan's sister, but she is no friend of mine.' Her voice was prim and her mouth so pinched she was spitting out the words like bullets.

'My mother is ill and wondered would you visit. She wants to make things right.'

Ella staggered back before shaking herself, rising up and covering the space between them in one long stride. 'You tell your mother she was not there for me when I needed support. What she was good for was spreading the gossip and wrongly accusing me. I loved my husband, not that anybody in Rathsorney thought that by the time she was finished. Tell your mother she was responsible for my husband, her only brother, taking his own life: she has to live and die with that.'

James McDonagh retreated, his hands in the air. 'Don't shoot the messenger. Couldn't you find something in your heart for my dying mother?'

Ella O'Callaghan, a woman who abhorred bad manners, spat on the ground, the glob of saliva landing on the rug to the left of James McDonagh. 'Get out! Get out and don't even come back to tell me that interfering bitch is dead!' she choked.

James McDonagh would have answered but for the strong voice that interrupted from the doorway.

'Please leave, Mr McDonagh, and realise that some pain of the past can never be assuaged.'

Roberta was standing straight, her walking stick propped behind her back. She stepped back to allow James McDonagh to walk past.

'And please remove your tractor from Roscarbury Hall. It is quite unsightly,' she added, as he quickly marched out the front door. Roberta looked at her sister, who had slumped into the armchair. She saw Debbie come down the stairs and she called her, closing the drawing room door as she did. 'My sister is in a bit of a state. Will you bring her a coffee when you next come down?'

Debbie made to push past into the drawing room, but Roberta put a hand out to stop her.

'She could do with a few minutes. Put a few sugars in the coffee, please.'

Roberta wrote a note, propping it against a jug on the kitchen table. The hall table was unthinkable during café hours; neither of the sisters wanted the nosey parkers of Rathsorney knowing their business.

You drew him down on us. How dare you? You have opened up our house to the public. What do you expect? Undesirables will come too. R.

Debbie presented Ella with a hot mug of sugary coffee. Ella said she might take a bit of time in her room. Mary

McDonagh, Michael Hannigan's sister, she had not heard from since her husband's death. That she should try now to make amends for causing the pain that had festered and swelled over the last decades was no surprise.

Mary McDonagh was a pious, church-going woman who would leave nothing to chance in her quest to make it directly to the pearly gates. That she had done a wrong to Ella O'Callaghan all those years ago was clearly on her mind as a reason she might trip on the path. Ella remembered it was the Weiss yellow-framed flower brooch with the aurora borealis stones that set Mary off. A practical and dour woman, Mary McDonagh saw the alluring brooch at Ella's neck. A small piece, a cluster of yellow crystals circling the iridescent stones of a little flower, it relied on the sparkling stones to give it a delicate brilliance that was both captivating and beautiful. For Ella it was exquisite in its simplicity. Mary McDonagh thought it was a very expensive piece of jewellery for the wife of a soldier to be wearing, especially when he was away. She took to visiting Ella at all times of the day or night when Michael Hannigan was on manoeuvres, and though she never collated any physical evidence of a woman cheating on her husband, she was convinced because of the different and extravagant pieces of jewellery she thought were flaunted. Mary McDonagh never raised her suspicions with Ella. If she had, she would have been told the truth: that Ella O'Callaghan, alone and under pressure, had found solace not in the arms of another man but in an old love affair—that of her father and mother.

Instead, Mary McDonagh discussed her suspicions with all and sundry; and in the telling, convincing herself so absolutely as to the veracity of her claims that they came to be fact. She took it upon herself to write to her brother as to the sorry state of events: that his wife was unfaithful. Michael Hannigan, grieving the death of his baby daughter, buckled, and within two days was found, his head half blown off, as he slumped beside his metal bed in the Army barracks.

It was not until his personal effects were dispatched to Roscarbury Hall that Ella saw the letter. When confronted, Mary McDonagh stood firm in the absolute certainty her brother was the aggrieved party in a sordid affair, which Ella O'Callaghan had concealed. If, in later years, she reconsidered her position, she never broached the subject with Ella, who had cut off all communications and banned the Hannigans from entering O'Callaghan property. Ella also reverted back to the O'Callaghan name.

Scrabbling under the bed, Ella used her long umbrella to sweep in to the wall and push out the old Army tin box, rusted brown with age. Levering the side handles up, she wrenched hard to open it. A musty, dark smell of a long-dead man pushed past her. She moved his cigarettes and thick woollen Army-issue socks out of the way, along with the spare laces and the boot polish.

A copy of the *Evening Press* newspaper, which had been folded neatly, was at the bottom along with a small stack of letters. Michael Hannigan always had been an obsessively tidy man. He would have read his newspaper and folded it along the creases before taking out his rifle and wedging it tight between the back of the wardrobe and the wall, so when he pressed the trigger it blew half his head off.

A small group of letters contained all the notes Ella had sent him during his previous trips from home. On the top was Mary McDonagh's letter, written in a careful and slow hand.

Castle Street,
Rathsorney,
September 2, 1959.

Dear Michael,
It is with a heavy heart that I write to you to inform you
of the goings-on in Rathsorney. I am sorry to tell you your
wife Ella is having an affair, by all accounts with a rich
man who can buy her expensive jewellery to adorn
herself. I don't write on a whim but after careful
consideration, and I know how devastated you will be by
this news.

I know too that a woman who has lost her child in
such tragic circumstances must not be right in the head
and I have tried to take that into account. But, frankly,
she is flaunting new jewellery every day, even at Mass.

I can't have word reaching the McDonaghs. This could
badly affect my prospects. What would they think of us
all? People are beginning to talk. It is time you came
home and controlled your wife.

I remain Your Loving Sister,

Mary.

That Mary, who had married soon after her treachery, should
now want absolution for her sins, after living a happy and ful-
filled life, made Ella O'Callaghan shake with anger. Afterwards came the wrenching tears, big wet drops of bitterness
she had cried many times before. It lasted several minutes.
With a familiar resignation, she went to the bathroom and

sluiced her face with water before patting it dry. She redid her make-up, paying extra attention to her eyes. Before she returned to the café, she closed up the old Army box and pushed it hard into the far corner under the bed.

She smiled at Chuck Winters as she entered the café, and his heart skipped; she looked so vulnerable, so gentle. Placing his crossword on the table, he hoped Ella would stop to chat.

'Wonderful cake, Miss O'Callaghan, as always.'

She nodded politely and he wondered why her eyes looked so troubled.

'Won't you take a break and we can discuss the recipe?'

Ella shook her head, but she smiled kindly at Chuck, whose complexion had deepened pink. She ducked in behind the screen.

'Are all the orders out?' she asked Debbie.

'Yes. Don't worry. And you?'

Ella faltered a little. 'Fine. We should clear off some of the tables. Get a head start on closing.'

Eleven

When Sister Marguerite burst in without knocking, her voice high-pitched, her body spinning across the room, Mother Assumpta knew something dreadful had befallen the community. She carefully replaced her pen on her desk and waited for the younger nun to get her breath. Marguerite reached behind Mother to the window ledge and switched on the radio, all the time whimpering like a dog that knows that trouble has visited.

'Do you want to share with us why you want in particular to trace your mother, Debbie?'

There was a lull, and Mother Assumpta put her head in her hands, listening intently.

'I dearly wish to meet her, before I die.' Debbie's voice was calm and steady. 'I don't want to go from this world not having met her or knowing about her.'

'Are you going to die, Debbie?'

'In a few weeks: things are going to start getting bad pretty soon. Gall bladder cancer.'

'What can we do to help you, Debbie Kading?'

'I want my mother, if she's out there, to get in touch. I was born on April 15, 1959, and adopted by the Kadings of New York. Sister Consuelo of the Divine Sisters handled the adoption.'

'Couldn't the sisters help you?'

Debbie sighed deeply. 'I've tried, but there's no give there, not even in my case.'

'Shouldn't you be at home in the arms of your family at this moment?'

'My mom isn't around any more, and my father passed away two months ago. He didn't even know about my cancer; I didn't even know about it then.'

There was another silence, which the interviewer did not try to fill.

'I want to look in her eyes, to talk to her, to know her touch, to find out if she likes what I like. If she has passed on, I want to hear stories of her, stories that will keep me strong in the difficult weeks ahead.'

★

It came out of the blue. Ella, washing up, stopped: her hands treading the sink water, sludge circling around her elbows, the water going cold. Debbie's voice was low to start with. She had never said she was going on national radio, did not even hint at it. Ella wiped her hands dry, sitting down to take it all in.

Roberta, downstairs, the open bottle of sherry in her hand, forgot to pour a glass, the air around her crowding with the words. Debbie spoke slowly and clearly, as if she had all the time in the world. Everybody listening knew this was something that would go wider and deeper, like the circles to the far shore when a small stone sinks. She had started with a hesitant voice, but ended it with tears, full of thanks to the good people of Rathsorney and, above all, to Ella, who ran the Ballroom Café.

'A romantic name, for sure; what sort of establishment is it?' the presenter asked.

Debbie giggled, the lightness of her voice conveying more than the description that followed of the best little café this side of the Atlantic. Ella felt her cheeks glow red with embarrassment and pride, despite the tears streaming down her face, plopping into the dish water. She dried her hands carefully, as if she were about to collect a prize, and decided to get up an hour earlier the next morning, to throw a few extra cakes in the oven. It might be time to try out a lemon meringue pie, though she worried she would not have the time or patience to stand at the stove and stir to get the required thickness of the lemon curd. Maybe a duck-egg sponge cake with a dusting of icing sugar. She needed extra anyway, because even the lackadaisical would make an effort after hearing that interview.

★

Mother Assumpta sat down, stress pains flashing across her stomach. Consuelo could protest all she liked, but this business had all the hallmarks of ballooning into a scandal and it was she, Assumpta, who would have to deal with the fallout.

That Consuelo should refuse to go back to Moyasta, even now, made Assumpta very angry. The knife still in her hand from peeling the spuds for dinner, Consuelo, in Assumpta's office, looked like a raving maniac as she invoked God to justify her past decisions.

'I am named to the country as a criminal when all I did was the Lord's work and help those young girls who had done wrong and shamed their families.'

'I doubt it is going to stop there. The Donegal woman has also come on the radio. It is most unpleasant.'

Consuelo placed her knife on the table. 'Where the hell would those people be if I had not got good homes for them? Sure, their mothers were only delighted to be getting rid of them. I have nothing to hide.'

'Don't you, Consuelo? We both know that times back then were harsh on unmarried women, and while we got homes for their children, we treated the women like dirt.'

Consuelo banged the table so hard with the palm of her hand the bowl of oranges trembled. 'How dare you, Mother. I gave my life to finding good homes for the bastard children nobody wanted.'

Assumpta shook herself, to get Consuelo out of her head, and sat down to draft a statement for the press. In it, she offered to help anybody who came forward but declared that Consuelo herself, who was now in her 70s, was too ill to be of benefit to any inquiry.

If she kept Consuelo contained within the convent walls, her strategy might even work.

★

Ella watched her dawdle up the avenue, dragging her feet and pulling on a cigarette. At the fountain she paused, puffing quickly before stubbing out the cigarette butt on the lichen-stained stone. A teacher waiting on tables in the Ballroom Café: that was something Muriel could put in her pipe and smoke. Curse the life she had been dealt, though. Ella snorted. Frustration rising inside her, she set to rearranging the tables at the window. Debbie lingered at the front door, idly scraping her shoes slowly along the steel of the foot scraper. Roberta, hovering at her bedroom window, watched as she stamped her feet on the top step.

Roberta had already slapped down two notes.

Never in all my life have I been so ashamed. How dare she talk about Roscarbury on the radio. Is this what you want: to be talked about on the national airwaves? R.

An hour later, another note in bigger writing was pushed on top.

She has showed us right up, telling the whole world her business and ours. If you don't tell her to get on her bike, I will. R.

Ella did not bother to respond, but baked five extra cakes, because the whole of Rathsorney would surely come to the café that day. Lemon, chocolate, carrot, a light ginger cake, and a marble cake because it was easy and looked so complicated.

'Just in time to grate the carrots. How are you, Debbie?'

'You're not cross, are you?'

'Furious, more like, that you did not tell me these past weeks, and I working you to the bone. You poor thing, I even had you lifting heavy furniture and scrubbing floors. What must you think of me?'

'I wanted to, but . . .'

Ella reached over and squeezed Debbie across the shoulders. 'The whole world knows now. You don't have to work. I remember I forced you in to it.'

Debbie pulled away, her face swelling with anxiety. 'Ella, this place is like home to me.'

'It will be harder on you now that the gossiping ninnies are on your case.'

'I think I can handle Muriel and her bunch.'

'If you are sure.'

'I am.'

'How did you swing it, getting on the radio?'

'It was you, Ella: remember you introduced me to that local reporter? Next thing I got a call; he had contacts at the station.'

'You could have told me. I would have come along, given a bit of support.'

Debbie reached over and gently rubbed Ella on the shoulder. 'I was too afraid I would chicken out. I had to go on my own. If you'd been there, I'd have just ended up crying on your shoulder.'

'There is nothing wrong with a bit of support. You are one for keeping things in, all right, but no matter: what's done is done. It is all out there now.'

'Ella, I'm sorry; I should have told you.'

Ella shook out a tea towel. 'I just don't like that you thought you were better on your own. Anyway, enough of that. After the carrots you can measure out a load of caster sugar, and the tables have to be laid.' Ella clapped her hands in mock impatience.

Debbie did her best to smile as she tied her apron behind her back.

'Have you heard the latest? It was on the news: there were so many people coming forward with the same story as you, there is going to be a full investigation; other convents might be involved.'

'It's not going to do me any good. I have to get back.'

'Working here is not good enough for you.' Ella pretended to throw her nose in the air.

'You know it's not like that,' Debbie laughed.

The two of them set to laying the café tables.

'I suppose I could stay a bit longer,' Debbie said, folding napkins neatly on each table.

'What have you to go back to?' Once she said it, Ella regretted it. She saw Debbie's shoulders shake. 'I am so sorry. Curse the O'Callaghans; we were never known for our diplomacy.' She stroked Debbie's hair, like she would a child's. 'Stay longer, but leave that awful dive Muriel Hearty maintains is a studio apartment. You could move in here.'

'But what will your sister say?'

Ella turned around. 'Thankfully she won't say anything, but she will of course be furious.'

They both giggled.

'Oh my God.' Ella had her hand to her mouth, staring out the window. 'I think the whole town is coming in on top of us. Quick, put an extra setting on each table. Tell Iris to bring up some extra chairs.'

They rushed about with china cups and saucers, so that they were out of breath when Muriel Hearty led a very big posse up the stairs.

'Darling Debbie, what can we do to help?' she said, her voice loud so that everybody could hear her.

Embarrassed, Debbie did not answer.

'For God's sake, Muriel, will you stop your fussing and leave the woman alone to do her day's work,' Ella said.

'She should not even be working today, Ella.'

'Mind your own business, Muriel. By the way, Debbie is moving in here.'

Muriel Hearty put her elbows on the table. 'A bit of a comedown, I would have thought, Ella. You do know it is breach of contract, it is. I turned away very good offers on my apartment to let her have it.'

'Muriel, you know that is not true. Is it the marble cake today? I put a light dusting of cinnamon on top, mixed with a little icing sugar.'

Muriel, afraid of the adverse attention of the room, let it go and ordered the marble cake.

By the time Debbie slipped the plate of cake onto the table at her elbow, Muriel had turned the whole episode to her advantage. She took Debbie by the hand and in a booming voice, pushing through everybody else's conversation, she announced loudly, 'Darling, you do what makes you happiest. You won't get any trouble from me. We all want the best for you and to see you reunited with your mother. How are you, dear?' Muriel sat back in her chair, waiting for a detailed account.

'Just fine, thanks.'

'You are not on your own.'

The other women pushed closer together, clucking in agreement. Debbie nodded, moving from one foot to another before bolting downstairs to clear the garden tables. She was carrying a tray stacked with crockery when Roberta approached.

'On the radio, that was a sad story you told.'

Debbie balanced the tray on the corner of the table nearest the door.

Roberta motioned Debbie to sit down and arranged herself carefully into a garden chair opposite before she continued. 'I want you to go away, leave my sister alone. She does not need you here; she can run this place on her own, for as long as it lasts, anyway.'

'You should have more confidence in Ella.'

Roberta shifted in the chair and fixed her coat over her knees. 'The gossips will keep the place busy, until the next alluring venue turns up. A few weeks and it will shut down.'

'I think you're wrong.'

'Does it matter what you think?'

'Ella is determined to make a success of it.'

'You talk as if you know my sister very well.' Roberta leaned across the table. 'You don't know her at all.'

Deep circles of red formed on Roberta's cheeks as she spat out the words. 'You have no business being here, stirring up trouble, dragging our good name into the mud, so that people propping up the counters in public houses are gossiping about us.'

Roberta pushed her face closer.

'Don't you ever think you are part of Roscarbury Hall.'

Iris came striding across the parkland. Roberta turned and walked inside the house, slapping a note on the kitchen table as she passed through, on the way to the back garden.

I have told that Yank to leave. She has three days, no more. She is not wanted here and neither is the riff raff this café of yours is attracting. Don't I have a say in who tramps through our home? R.

'See you met Roberta. Was she nasty?'

'I'm afraid so.'

'Don't take it personally; she is nasty and bitter to everyone, especially herself. There was a time Roberta was the same as the rest of us, but life has dealt her some blows and this is how it has left her.' Iris shook herself. 'I had better not say anything. It is up to Ella to tell you the family secrets.'

Debbie walked further on and leaned against the side wall of the house as she lit up. Her head was thumping and she had a queasy feeling that would not go away.

Dr Lohan told her she would be fine until she was not. Then she would have to fix up her financial affairs.

She must talk to Nancy. She had always told her smoking would kill her; well, it wasn't going to now, that was for sure. She puffed out three rings of smoke and watched them glide past the rhododendron, losing shape and disappearing among the shiny, broad leaves.

★

Bowling Green, October 1968

Saturdays changed so much after Agnes left. Before, it was all about Mommy and her preparations; now it was about Rob and Debs making do.

Saturday, early afternoon, Agnes, with Debbie by her side, would begin her elaborate preparations for her night out with her husband. Emerging from a hot shower, she smelled of steam and lavender soap, making Debbie's nose twitch until she had to itch. In a big, blue towelling bathrobe, she sat at the dressing-table mirror and arranged all her bottles on one side, brushes and make-up the other. Not a word was spoken. If the young girl, unable to resist, wandered closer, Agnes put up her hand to keep her at a distance.

First Agnes plucked her eyebrows into a high arch and lathered her face and neck with moisturiser, massaging with elaborate, slow, deliberate movements. A special white square of cotton was used to wipe down the excess, before she patted

her face hard. Finally, she moved to the thick brown founda-
tion and the powder from a big glass jar with a red ribbon.
The blusher was pink and discreet, the eye shadow blue and
garish. Thick false lashes were glued to her eyes and painted
deeper with a mascara stick. Only then did she let her hair fall
around her shoulders and brush it until sparks flew, as it
crackled and shone.

Sometimes, Debbie sidestepped closer, her hand twitching
to touch the glossy golden locks. Her mother always spied her,
snapping to get back. Deep-pink lipstick was the last to be
applied, Agnes smacking her lips like a fish to make sure it
would hold. Twirling off the dressing-table stool, she dropped
her bathrobe like a film star before stepping into a new satin
dress, ruched at the neckline and tight around the hips.

It was then that the palaver with the jewellery began. There
was a drawer full of the stuff, sparkling necklaces mostly, which
Rob Kading could ill afford but which his wife said she could
not live without. When she pulled back the drawer and opened
the velvet casings, the stones twinkled, enticing the little girl to
come closer. Sometimes, if she was in a good mood, Agnes let
her daughter choose for her, but more often than not, she tired
of the child staring and told her to leave the room. Through the
keyhole, Deborah kept watch as her mother tried out several
necklaces, craning her neck, twisting from side to side in front
of the mirror before deciding on one.

Flicking pieces of fluff from the satin, she stepped into her
slingbacks before making her way downstairs, where her husband was waiting at the bottom of the stairs, ready to let out a
low whistle of appreciation.

Now, Debs liked hanging out with Rob. As the leaves fell

from the trees, they had a leaf-raking and diner routine every Saturday.

'Gather them in to a heap, little one, and help Daddy.'

She knew she made the job slower. When the pile of leaves was high enough, Rob always gave the first kick, spreading the crinkly colours across the driveway. She threw bunches at him and he shouted and pleaded to her to stop, until she had him on the ground, covered and squealing for mercy. Later, he would send her inside to pour his coffee and heat a hot chocolate for herself. When she came back out on the porch, the leaves had been cleared up and he reached for his newspaper, which she knew signalled quiet time.

She sat on a small chair with a hard cushion and watched the neighbours go about their Saturday duties: washing cars, going to the mall, tending to gardens and repairs, and even sweeping up the autumn leaves. She watched her father methodically reading every page and she waited for the moment he would scan the front and back pages and say, 'I'll get to them later.'

It was the start of their time, when she would sit on his lap and they would chat before wandering to Ed's Diner for dinner: a burger and fries for her and a large coffee and a cigarette for him. It was the only time of the week he seemed happy.

They sat in their usual spot beside the window, which overlooked the stacked flowerbeds. They shared a donut, he dunking his piece in the last of his coffee.

They fitted in well together.

'We are doing all right, baby face?' he said.

She grinned and tucked into her half of a vanilla-iced donut.

'Your mom wouldn't like us eating so many donuts. She always said no additives, no preservatives: just good fresh food.'

Debbie did not answer, but watched a boy across the road wash his father's estate car, spraying the neighbour's cat when he thought nobody was looking.

'Do you miss Mommy?'

Rob Kading seemed surprised at the enquiry.

'She is a gorgeous woman. I love every funny bit of her.' Rob stopped, afraid of burdening his young daughter further. He put on a bright smile and dunked his donut.

'Did you always love her?'

'Yes, I did, even when she was throwing half the room at me. I loved her from that first day I saw her. She was walking along Broadway. She was so beautiful; women looked on with envy and men walking out with their wives sneaked backward glances. When she asked me a question, I was so shocked I nearly forgot to answer.'

'What did she ask?'

'I don't know exactly, but I remember the sparkle in her eyes, her golden hair in a neat bun. She was lovely, and when we started to talk, it turned out she was from Ohio.'

Debbie began to fiddle with her napkin.

'She loves you, sweetheart. She prayed for a daughter and then you came along. She loved dressing you up and taking you for walks when you were a baby. From when you were three, you went to the hairdresser with her every Saturday morning.'

'I remember it; Edna gave me candy.'

'Remember the good times, darling; that's what I do. It's what Mommy would want as well.'

She nodded and asked if they could go, running ahead to the machine for a jawbreaker.

Twelve

That woman is bad news, but she will have to leave if the health inspector closes down the café. R.

Ella ignored the note, pretending she had not seen it, but slipped a note of her own beside it.

You say one thing and I will make sure everybody knows what a lying, cheating bitch you really are. E.

Enraged, Roberta marched into the kitchen and propped a further note by Ella's teapot.

You are no saint either, Ella O'Callaghan. If you had looked after your husband, he would have been happy at Roscarbury. R.

Ella bided her time, until her sister was sitting at the kitchen table the next morning, fiddling with the spoon beside her mug. She placed a long, handwritten note in front of her.

Dear Roberta,

It may not have come to your notice, but we don't have any money. The bank is insisting we repay the loan granted for the costly necessary repair of the back roof. If we cannot meet our obligations, then we will have to sell Roscarbury Hall.

I trust you realise the seriousness of the situation: even through your sherry-soaked ether, you must know this is a crisis. The only way out I can see is to attempt to bring some money into the house, something you stopped doing a long time ago. Even if you could forego one of your numerous bottles of sherry a week, it would help.

The Ballroom Café stays open and long may it remain that way, because without it, we would both be out on the streets. Debbie Kading is a very important part of the popularity of the café and I will not have you insult her.

You might as well know, she is moving in today. I am warning you, I will not have rudeness or bad manners towards our guest and my friend.

As for the other matter mentioned in your communication, can I remind you of your own role in all of this? I hope the flush of shame and guilt is coursing through you, as it should be.

Your sister,

Ella.

Roberta folded the note in four and slowly pinched it to

shreds, until there was a heap of paper beside her mug of tea. Ignoring the paper mound, she moved to her cupboard and took down a small crystal glass.

She poured a sherry from the hip flask in her handbag, before taking a long and extravagant sip. Smiling at the loud sighing of her sister, Roberta topped up her glass. Exasperated, Ella bustled out of the kitchen to answer a knock on the front door.

Debbie had only one pull-along case.

'Debbie, welcome. Do you mind if I show you the room later? Muriel Hearty rang and said there was going to be a huge crowd this morning. The Women's Guild has decided to meet at the café.'

'Did you bake extra?'

'I did, and I also found time to tell my sister to behave herself, so you need not worry on that score. When we close up shop tonight, we must have a Baileys to celebrate your moving in. Come on upstairs; there is work to be done.'

'I'd like that, but I think we'd better set some extra tables; otherwise Muriel will create a fuss.'

'She will create a fuss anyway, but let's hope it is not about that,' Ella said, as she spooned the coffee into the machine. 'Any developments on the other thing?' Ella said, her voice slow and vague, as if she had more important things to think about.

Debbie knew what she was doing: tiptoeing for fear of causing upset. 'A guy from a government department rang me and said the Minister has asked the nuns to account for themselves. A judge is to look into it.'

Ella stopped, the coffee scoop in mid-air. 'And it took you until now to tell me.'

Debbie began to stutter. 'I suppose it's a step forward.'

Ella grabbed her hand and squeezed it. 'Have patience.'

'I'm afraid I've wasted this precious time.'

Ella squeezed Debbie's hand tighter, loosening her grip when she saw her wince with pain. 'That is mad talk. How do you think they put damask curtains and swags on the wide windows of the convent? Only with the blood money they took from desperate women and couples.'

'Whoa, what a load of fighting talk,' Iris said, striding in to the café, her face expectant. 'Tell me what I have missed, every detail.'

Ella snorted loudly. 'Aren't you supposed to be digging out the old rills?'

'Now you're beginning to sound like your sister.'

Debbie smiled as Ella pulled a sour face, her eyes narrowing and her chin disappearing into her long, once graceful neck.

'Come on, less talk and more work,' she said, as she carried a tray full of sugar bowls to the far end of the room.

Iris began to fiddle with the cappuccino maker.

'Iris, let Debbie do it; we don't want the Women's Guild to be swimming in steam,' Ella snapped.

'All right, hang on to your hair,' she said and sneaked a chocolate-chip cookie into her pocket when she thought nobody was looking.

Iris was making her way down the stairs when Ella called after her, 'You should try the shortbread as well: very tasty and all butter.'

The ladies of the Women's Guild pulled up in two mini buses. Ella went downstairs to greet them, as Muriel and her band hurried up the avenue. They alighted in a gaggle of chat, but one woman pushed herself forward.

'Ella, Ella O'Callaghan; you have not changed a bit.'

The woman, with a large bosom, hair dyed mahogany brown, dangling earrings to her shoulders and lipstick that leaked from her lips, grabbed Ella in a tight bear hug.

'You have no idea who I am, have you?'

'I am awfully sorry, I am afraid I don't.'

'Wendy, Wendy Marsham.'

'Wendy?'

'Remember when you and Michael were on your honeymoon, you met Barry and me at the seafront in Bray. We got married the same day.'

Indifferent to the confusion in Ella, Wendy turned to the crowd.

'She pledged to keep up contact, but of course we only did if for a year; then it drifted. You never did write to me in Australia, Ella O'Callaghan. No matter, we have so much to catch up on. I had to move back when my Barry died. You want to be near family, don't you? I had nobody over there,' she said, grabbing Ella by the arm.

Ella allowed herself to be walked across the small lawn.

'It is so nice to see you, Wendy, and you look so well.'

'You always were kind, Ella; I look like a cow with too-bright hair and loud make-up, but I don't care. Who is going to be interested in me now anyway? Barry died last year.'

'I am sorry to hear it.'

'We had a good life and a happy one, which is more than can be said for a lot of couples still hanging in there together. How about you? Where is your handsome soldier?'

Ella stopped in the hall and looked at Wendy. The woman, wrinkly fat curling under her chin, was sweeping her eyes up to the stairs. 'This is a great place, Ella.'

'Michael died a long time ago, Wendy.'

'Oh my dear, I did not know. I am so sorry.'

Ella gripped her elbow and steered her to the stairs. 'We are two widows: who would have thought?'

'I don't like the sound of widow: too lonely. Can't we be two old birds who have seen a bit of life instead?'

'Too much of life, you mean,' Ella snorted.

Debbie swung around as the group began to fill the room, the chatter loud and friendly. Muriel, out of breath by the time she got to the top of the stairs, had to bash a china cup with a spoon to be heard.

'Ladies, you are now in the famous Ballroom Café, mentioned on radio this very week. Take a seat and I will get around to each table in the course of the next hour. Proprietor Ella O'Callaghan will answer any questions you may have about the café.'

Wendy leaned over to Ella. 'Some day, somebody will oust Muriel and there will be a lot less earache.'

'And probably less fun too. What would we have to complain about then? She keeps us on our toes, if nothing else,' Ella said, as she moved away between the tables, taking the orders down in an old notebook.

'If you are into spiteful gossip and faux concern,' Wendy called after her, before settling in with a group from Gorey.

Ella had not a moment to think; she stood at the coffee machine, dispatching cup after cup and sending out pots of tea. Debbie, her face red with the rush, walked among the tables with large platters of cake, doling out slices with big tongs. When they ran out, Ella raced downstairs and cut some more, slicing thin so there was more to go around. Iris shouted up the stairs that some more guests had taken over the outside tables and could somebody come down to take their orders. Ella heard her, but in the rush promptly forgot until a well-dressed gentleman stuck his head in the café door.

'I can see you are swamped. We were hoping for coffee and any cake you have.'

Ella recognised him, but did not let on. 'I am sorry. Give me two minutes,' she said, instructing Debbie to take the order.

When Debbie came back up the stairs, she was smiling. 'The man down there said to pass on his regards.'

'Fergus Brown?'

'He didn't give his name; I guess he figured you would know,' Debbie said, her smile growing broader. She detected a certain flustering in Ella and thought it made her look vulnerable and pretty.

'The tables near the windows need to be cleared,' Ella said, her voice stiff.

They worked solidly for two hours, Ella staying behind the partition, washing up, Debbie waiting on the tables. At one stage Wendy Marsham swept behind, but Ella ushered her back to the counter.

'I don't want you getting your nice outfit dirty,' she said.

'This thing? Picked it up in a charity store. My Barry invested all our money and this is the way it has left me: skulking around charity shops, looking for something decent to wear.'

'We are all finding it hard, Wendy; that is why I am running the café, to keep a roof over our heads.'

'Ah, but you have family around you; we were never blessed with children.'

Ella looked alarmed. 'You mean my sister, Roberta.'

'Your daughter. You are so lucky.'

'Debbie is just working here for a few months. My daughter died when she was very young.'

Wendy stretched over and took Ella's hand. 'I am raising ghosts, like kicking a bunch of dead leaves. I am so awfully sorry.'

'You weren't to know, Wendy, you weren't to know,' Ella said, pulling her hand away too quickly. 'Will you have another coffee?' She knew it was a pathetic effort to cover her discomfort.

'No, I think Muriel has arranged a tour. We must follow the boss.'

Ella stepped out from behind the counter to say her goodbyes to the Guild women, who had begun to push back their chairs and ready themselves for the off.

'We made in a few hours what we normally make in two days. Muriel Hearty wrecks my head, but she is good for the pocket,' Ella told Debbie, as she tidied up the last tables. 'We might as well close up for the day, because there is nobody left in Rathsorney to have a cuppa after this morning. C'mon, I will show you your room.'

Ella led the way to the next landing. 'Sandwiched between the warring sides you are going to be, but at least we will be quiet. Don't mind my sister; just stay out of her way, and if you are using anything in the kitchen, make sure it is from one of my cupboards.' She stopped, her hand halfway to the brass doorknob. 'It makes us sound really odd, doesn't it?'

'What family isn't a little bit odd?'

'I suppose.'

She waved Debbie into a small, light-filled room with rich mahogany furniture and a bed covered with a bright-pink duvet. There was a chair at the small dressing table by the window and a television on the chest of drawers.

'It's like Mom and Dad's room back home: furnished with such taste.'

'I can't take any of the credit. My mother picked out all the furniture in the house, spent my father's wages on furnishings. She said they would last, that was her excuse; I suppose she has been proved right. I usually have dinner at six; I will put your name in the pot, unless otherwise told.'

Ella was already halfway down the stairs when Debbie stepped out onto the landing to collect her case. The other doors had large 'private' signs, old and crooked, secured with nails. On the wall, a framed black and white photograph showed a happy group on the front steps of Roscarbury Hall.

When Debbie placed her hand on the brass knob of one of the doors marked 'private,' it clicked loudly, so that she sprung back. Gingerly pushing the door, she formed an excuse in her head. The dark landing left behind, she stepped into a big room with floor-length windows. Heavy net curtains blotted out the landscape and formed a barrier, the light filtering through in spots.

Shivering from the chill lingering in the room, Debbie ran her hand across the purple eiderdown covering a heavy brass bed. A block mahogany wardrobe took up one corner. Her heart thumping, she tiptoed across the room, taking in the faded blue wallpaper, the clothes neatly folded on a chair, the big silver boxes on the dressing table. She wanted to sit, take time to sift through. She might have chanced it, but a shriek of laughter from outside made her panic and rush back to the landing, like a mouse scuttling away at the glimpse of a cat.

Nipping into the bathroom to take her breath, she splashed cold water on her face.

Tantalised by the other door, she hesitated again on the landing. Stretching to turn the knob, she peeped in. A similar room with long windows, it was furnished in muted, warm tones of orange and peach and was full of bric-a-brac, piles of old newspapers and one shelf of very large handbags. The bed was covered in differently coloured cushions and a glass decanter on the bedside table was full. When her phone rang, Debbie jumped, twirling around and sprinting to her own room.

'Deborah, it is Dr Lohan.'

She closed her eyes and listened.

'Debbie, you're running out of time. You need to come home. Soon you won't feel as well as you do now; you need to come back,' he said.

'I want to stay here a few more weeks.'

'Two weeks, Debbie, no more than two. The hospice bed is ready. I can't hold it any longer than that. You need to be with people who can look after you.'

'OK.'

She sensed the exasperation in his voice. 'Are you taking your medication?'

'There's so much of it.'

'Debbie, you need to. It may keep you stable while you're over there.'

'OK, but I feel sick all the time.'

'That's to be expected at this stage. It's time to come home.'

'All right.'

Slumping down, she rolled into the soft hollow of her bed and, tired, she fell into a sort of half doze.

★

When she woke up, Debbie set off walking across the parkland, not sure where she was going. Where Iris had dug out the rills near the house, the water was flowing, but already the cherry blossom was surfing, waiting to dive and clog up the channels once again. McInerney's brown cat slipped quickly past, darting fast glances as it made for the far wood. Two weeks: enough for the grass to grow and need cutting, for the fuchsia to start its buds, for the tulips to go bald. Two weeks: that was when her insurance on the apartment was up for renewal, when the attorney said the probate would be through on her father's estate. Two weeks: the right amount of time for a small holiday.

Iris called out and waved from where she was digging out the rill that flitted across the land to the far lake. 'Where are you off to?'

'I just needed some fresh air.'

She saw a group of children scurry past the gates, late and deep in chat. Old man MacCreevy was leaning on his walking stick by the bridge, like he did most fine days, before limping up the avenue for a cup of tea: two sugars, no milk.

'Ye are not closed, I hope,' he asked anxiously.

'Ella has just opened up. The kettle is boiled.'

'Enjoy the fresh air. It will do you good. Ninety years and I put it all down to the clean air. Nothing like it.' The old man paused, his face pinking with embarrassment. 'I'm a bit of a straight talker. I was sorry to hear about yourself.'

'Thank you. You're lucky.'

He stopped shuffling. 'I would say lonely. There is nobody around these days I would want to knock around with. All gone. Anyway, I will have my tea and the Madeira cake, like my mother used to bake it.'

Tremors fluttered through him as he set off shuffling, only slowing his sliding pace to round a pothole, every step deliberate and careful, lest he trip.

Debbie crossed to the bridge. The water, swelled by the rains and the mountain, flowed noisily between the rocks on the way to Rathsorney and beyond. Two weeks was no time, she knew, to find her mother.

★

Bowling Green, October 1968

Debbie imagined Mommy had taken her beautiful ball gown with her when she left. She had only seen it on her once, the week before she disappeared. It was the night Debbie stole to the porch to sit on the rocking chair.

Wrapped up in a dark-grey blanket, quietly rocking, she saw Mommy in the garden. Dressed in a stunning gown, Agnes drifted around the small front patch, like a woman greeting her guests at a ball. Transfixed at her loveliness and the strangeness of her behaviour, there was an awful worry in Debbie that Mommy would spy her. She hunkered under the blanket, keeping a slit open, so she could see what was going on.

Agnes, her three-strand pearl and silver necklace and matching earrings glinting in the half moonlight, was humming to herself, moving between the raspberry canes and the pavement, as if she were waiting for somebody.

Fear flushed through Debbie. She should call her father, but she was more afraid of his reaction, if she exposed her hiding place.

Debbie had never seen the dress before: navy blue with silver beads on the bodice and around the hem, twinkling as she swished across the flowerbeds. Agnes paced the perimeter of the front garden, once stepping onto the sidewalk and scuttling back onto the grass. She seemed to fixate on the space where the sunflowers were planted, kicking the ground.

Her frustration rising, she fell to her knees to draw her hands across the packed earth, before taking her silver sandals and digging the heels into the ground in an attempt to pierce it. Debbie could hear her sobbing and muttering, but even when she stiffened her whole body and strained her ears, she could not make out what her mother was saying.

She imagined she could run to her and hug her, and Mommy would be so relieved to see her daughter, she would ignore the fact she should be in bed and forget to get cross.

But Debbie could not move. She saw the despairing strength as her mother hit against the ground, intent on digging up the garden in the middle of the night. A dog began to bark in the distance. Agnes stopped briefly and pretended to be fixing her hair when a car swept by. Debbie saw her face was streaked where her tears had made rivers through her thick make-up; mud was caked on her forehead. She looked straight at Debbie, or so the little girl thought. Agnes's eyes were blank; there was no flicker of recognition. Debbie, trying to massage away pins and needles, was making the chair shake, but Agnes, though staring straight at the porch, did not seem to notice.

'Aggie, Aggie; what are you doing?' Rob Kading rushed out on to the veranda in his underpants.

Agnes spiked her heel into the earth, pulling at the grass.

'Agnes.'

Rob stood for a moment, suspended between the normality of watching the garden from his veranda and the knowledge that Agnes would more than likely react badly when he tried to persuade her inside. Tentatively, he stepped off the veranda.

'What is it, Agnes? Have you lost something?'

She did not answer, but her attempt at digging became more frenzied.

'Can I help at all?'

He got down on his haunches, but she did not register his presence, until he placed his hand on her arm.

'I want to dig it up; I have to.'

'Dig what up? There's nothing there.'

She did not answer, stabbing her sandal into the earth beside his hand.

'Don't do that, Agnes. Why don't we go inside?'

'I have to dig it up.'

Placing his two arms around her, he made to haul her to her feet, but she pushed him away.

'Agnes, you're spoiling your lovely dress.'

She looked down at the dress, touching the sequins. 'I sewed it nicely.'

'You did. Let me see it in the proper light of the sitting room.'

She dithered, before a smile came over her face, lighting up her eyes. She stood up, offering her hand to Rob, as if he had asked her out on the dance floor. Sweeping up her sandals, now worn and dirty, he slowly led Agnes to the veranda.

When they walked inside to the sitting room, Debbie uncurled herself from the rocking chair and peeped through the window, as Rob held his wife in his arms and slowly rocked her to sleep, until he was able to put a blanket over her and a cushion under her head.

It was then that he came back out on the porch.

'You shouldn't be spying on your mother. Go to bed at once.'

Debbie stepped out of the shadows.

'Bed now,' he said, turning to the kitchen.

She followed him, slipping quickly past the sitting-room door, lest her mother wake up.

Thirteen

Ella was sipping her tea from a china cup when she saw Fergus Brown walk up the avenue. His step was slow and deliberate, his walking stick more of an accessory than essential equipment. She could tell his distinctive lumber anywhere, leaning too much to the right. She felt a flutter of excitement that he should have returned to Roscarbury Hall.

She watched him as he doffed his cap to two young girls, causing them to giggle. Draining her cup quickly, she fixed her hair with two hands and applied a slick of lipstick.

Slightly out of breath, Fergus Brown stepped into the hall. Sitting in the old oak captain's chair, he took off his hat. It had taken him fifteen minutes to walk from his house; he had to allow for the same back, which would give him a leisurely half-hour break here.

For one hour a day, Fergus Brown could be himself. The rest of the time, he had to look after Margaret, when he was a babysitter, cleaner, servant and a major annoyance to his wife of thirty-five years. He knew that, because she never stopped telling him so. For one hour a day, and a Saturday afternoon, he left his home, seeking out conversation and company, sometimes just peace and quiet, among a happy gathering where he could feel part of a world less demanding of his attention.

When he heard that Roscarbury Hall had opened up its doors, something stirred inside him, an interest reignited. Ten years previously, he had met Ella O'Callaghan at a choral society recital in the hall in Gorey. Margaret was busy behind the counter, helping with the teas, and he was at a loose end.

At first, he noticed the way she dressed: folds of fabric flowing around her thin hips as she walked on moderately high heels, so that from behind she would pass as younger. He made sure to sit beside her.

'Fergus, how are you?'

'Very well.'

'You don't know me?'

'I am not sure.'

'Ella O'Callaghan.'

'How silly of me. So nice to see you again.'

He remembered he was taken aback when she said her name and tried not to show it. The last he had heard of her was when he was working abroad and his mother said she had gone slightly mad. Both the sisters had, after tragedy on tragedy had been heaped on them. Too much of a gentleman to allude to the past, he enjoyed her company and the whiff of her perfume every time she leaned towards him, her big eyes wide, her warm smile giving her face a much younger aura. In dark moments in the decade that followed, as his wife slipped deeper into a greyness of the mind, he often fell back on the badly lit room and the serene woman beside him, wearing royal blue and green and smelling of exotic perfume.

Ella met him at the door.

'Fergus, I am sorry for ignoring you yesterday; I am afraid we were run off our feet.'

'Ella, it is so good to be here. The café is wonderful.'

'I am just closing; it is a half-day on Wednesdays.'

He threw his hands in the air. 'Silly of me not to check.'

'I suppose I could rustle up a cuppa and a piece of sweet cake.'

She liked the way he beamed at her and the way he let her up the stairs in front of him. 'Are you back in these parts on holiday?'

'I live not far from here now, moved here in the last few weeks to a small place by the sea.'

'Sounds nice.'

There was a short moment when neither of them knew what to say.

'Where in Rathsorney are you?'

'At the harbour. Do you remember the night of the choral society?'

She arranged some china cups on saucers and made a fuss of cutting two slices of fruit cake. 'Everybody thinks I put too many cherries in, but I think a fruit cake mean on cherries is not worth serving.'

When she placed the plate in front of him, her hand lightly brushed against his and he thought it was as light as the touch of a bird's wing.

'The cherries are pouches of velvet,' he said.

She smiled because he was trying to please her.

'It is a fine place you have here. Do you have family who can look after it?'

'There is just my sister.'

'Well then, it makes it all the more remarkable.'

She liked, particularly, that he pretended not to know of the O'Callaghan history.

'You are doing a wonderful job turning the place around. The café has quite a name for itself already.'

'We are new, so people are coming to check us out. Let's see, after the first few months.'

'If you don't mind, I will be one of your regulars.'

'That is kind of you. What made you move here?'

'My wife and I moved here last month. I thought it might help her, being back. You remember her: Margaret O'Brien?'

There was a sharp intake of breath from Ella as she reached out to a small window box of tulips and pretended to check them. 'Yes, I know Margaret. She does not come out with you?'

'My wife is very ill.'

Fergus Brown faltered and Ella put her arm on his shoulder. He reached into his pocket, for his handkerchief. 'I don't mean to keep you.'

'I am sorry, Fergus.'

'She won't know you. Some days she looks at me and I know I am a stranger to her.'

Distracted, Ella plucked a stray hair from his jacket.

'I am a misguided old fool who thought if I brought her back to her birthplace it would be easier, but that is not the case.'

'We can only do our best,' Ella said gently.

Fergus checked his watch. 'I have only a certain time. I must get back. Would you come up and see Margaret? It might stir something in her.'

Ella's head was hurting. The thought of Margaret O'Brien

back in Rathsorney made her feel sick. If she did not go to see her, she knew she would worry, and worry brought worse headaches. 'I could walk with you now. Let me get my coat.'

Surprised, Fergus Brown agreed and made to get up.

Ella gently put her hands on his shoulders. 'I will be back in a few minutes.'

Quickly, she touched up her make-up in front of the hall mirror, before pulling her best cashmere coat from the cupboard under the stairs. If she had to meet Margaret O'Brien, she was going to look her best. She called lightly to Iris in the back yard that she would only be an hour. Fergus Brown was standing, watching the water flow in the fountain, when she went out the front.

'I am afraid I won't be able to walk you back to Roscarbury Hall. I can't leave Margaret on her own. If you like, I can arrange a neighbour to run you home afterwards?'

'That would be lovely. Anyway, it is a good day for a walk.'

'I will warn you, she is not the woman she was.'

'None of us are.'

Fergus Brown stopped and leaned on his stick. 'I was very sorry to hear of your great loss.'

Ella fiddled with the buttons on her coat.

Fergus Brown stretched his hand to her. 'I know Margaret did you a wrong. If she could say sorry, she would. I know in later years she cursed she was such a busybody.'

Ella felt a stab of pain through her head. 'We were both young and foolish. It hardly matters now anyway.'

'She learned a lesson. She said you had a mean right hook.'

They had been such pals. Margaret stayed weekends at Roscarbury Hall. They got dolled up and went to dances together. But after Ella met Michael Hannigan, she forgot

Margaret and all the fun they had, chatting and putting on the glam. They drifted apart so much that by the time of the wedding Ella did not think to invite her former friend. When they met a month later, a bitter and rejected Margaret O'Brien ignored Ella.

Peeved, Ella ran after her and asked why Margaret had not answered her salute. She could feel the sting of the words still.

'High and mighty Ella married to a soldier. Ask him how he spends those long evenings. He is not always confined to barracks, you know.'

Ella hit Margaret O'Brien square in the face. As she doubled over, roaring in pain, Muriel Hearty ran out saying she had seen it all and somebody should call the Gardaí. Tom Mason helped Margaret into his shop, where he put a side of cold round steak on her face. Ella walked home, her hands stuffed in her pockets because she could not stop them shaking. It was a whole week before she could face going in to Rathsorney again for the messages.

'The house is second on the right,' Fergus Brown said as they turned down to the harbour. 'She has forgotten most things. Don't worry if she does not recognise you.'

When he walked in the door, his voice changed, became louder. A woman in a nurse's trouser suit put on her coat and said goodbye.

Fergus took Ella to the garden, where his wife was sitting, smiling at the birds as they pecked at the feeder.

'Margaret, this is an old friend. Ella. Ella O'Callaghan.'

The woman beside him had aged well, with only laughter lines visible around her eyes. She wore navy trousers and a soft blue cardigan. When she extended her hand to Ella with a smile, it was strong and confident.

'It has been a long time,' Ella said.

'It has?'

'Since we met last.'

Margaret let go of Ella's hand. 'Do you live here?'

Ella looked confused. 'At Roscarbury Hall.'

'Roscarbury?'

'The big house.'

'I like a big house. Miles does not come and visit. Do you think he will come today?'

Ella looked to Fergus for help.

'Darling, you know Miles can't come. He is dead.'

Margaret swung around, anxiety across her face. 'Poor Miles is dead?'

'Yes, a year ago.'

'Oh.'

She sat down and picked up the cat and began to stroke it. Ella mumbled she must go.

'Stay for tea,' Fergus said.

'Maybe another time.'

Rattled, Ella insisted on walking home. She barely noticed the cars as they hurtled by. All the times she had wished ill on Margaret O'Brien; now she could not even register a well-turned-out cashmere coat. Nothing mattered any more. The cashmere coat did not matter, and neither did it really matter that Margaret O'Brien had been correct in her assessment of Ella's young husband.

The house was quiet when she returned, so she brought a bowl of cereal to her room as supper.

She sat at the dressing table to catch the last of the natural light and reached for the velvet pouch. The brooch was a small but perfect heart, with twelve tiny rectangular, almost smoky stones and bigger circular stones offering a simple raised gold rose. It was a pure and clear statement of love. She remembered the day Bernie had unwrapped it, fondly chiding her husband that he was a mad fool with his money.

'You will have to bring me somewhere fine to wear such a brooch. It needs a dress of silk, taffeta or maybe chiffon. Something beautiful that floats,' she said.

John O'Callaghan answered he would find a place, much grander than anywhere she could imagine, where they could dance cheek to cheek.

Ella ran her fingers along the heart outline. She could see her mother wearing the brooch, pinned on the wide white satin collar of her ivory chiffon dress with the satin cuffs and small-button detail. It had taken her two weeks to stitch the dress and four long nights under the fluorescent light of the kitchen to secure the buttons and sew neat buttonholes by hand. Sometimes she called on Ella to try on the dress, so she may best judge the alignment of the darts, but was prone to get cross very quickly if her daughter dared to attempt a twirl.

On the night the O'Callaghans went to the Gresham Hotel, Dublin, they left Rathsorney on an early train, a simple tweed coat cloaking the dress and brooch until they reached their destination. Mrs O'Callaghan wore her black hair up and on her feet were high strappy sandals that had cost a small fortune in the expensive shoe shop in Wexford.

When they returned the next day, Bernie O'Callaghan said it had been the best time of her life. She carefully placed her brooch in its velvet pouch and declared that the only place she would wear it, or the dress, again was the Gresham Hotel.

'There is nowhere like it, girls. Someday we will go back,'

she said, carefully wrapping a sheet around the chiffon dress in the wardrobe.

There was not another outing to the Gresham and a moth ate a large hole in the front panel of the chiffon dress.

Fourteen

May Dorkin walked in to the café and slapped her small rectangular cake heavily on the counter. She was dressed up, wearing a cloche hat with a feather on her head and the coloured summer raincoat. But it was the determined look in her eye that made Debbie enquire whether she should get Ella.

'Please; I have a business proposition to discuss,' May said, reaching out to tidy a stack of plates on the counter.

Ella threw her eyes to heaven. 'No doubt there is some harebrained idea for the café. I might as well listen to her; it will move her along faster,' she grumbled to herself as she moved to the counter. 'You are looking well today, May. Is it an occasion?'

'Taste my cake and then we can do business,' she said, her voice a little shaky.

When Ella did not immediately respond, May pulled the cling film from the cake and reached for a knife. 'Best carrot cake there is,' she said gruffly.

'May, I don't know what you are at, but I am very busy.'

May Dorkin took a step back, her nose tipped. Her voice

was slightly hoarse. 'Ella O'Callaghan, I am trying to help you out here. I will bring three cakes each morning, eight good slices in each: that is twenty-four euros, but twenty-two to you, and you can sell them on at whatever you like.'

'I am not buying your cake, May.'

'But you will happily take in a whole cake without any qualms every day. You must think I am a right old fool. Sure, don't I know you are selling it the minute I am out the door?'

'I only sell my own cake, May Dorkin, and very popular it is too. I have no need for yours. I told you, May, I can make my own cake.'

'Nonsense, Ella, just taste it.'

Ella could not hold it in any longer. 'I am not in need of these cakes.'

'People are getting tired of the same old thing. Molloy's will be happy to take them, but I will give you first refusal.'

Exasperated, Ella slapped down a teacloth heavily. 'Tell Molloy's they are welcome to them.'

May Dorkin was furious: two red spots ringed on her cheeks and her little hat slipped an inch to the side of her head, making her look like a crazy exotic bird, as she began to shout at Ella.

'There is no fear you have changed a bit, Ella O'Callaghan, thinking you are better than everyone else. Everyone says when the milk of human kindness was flowing down the road the O'Callaghans were behind the wall. You were willing to take my cakes every morning when they were free.'

Chuck Winters, who had stepped in behind May, made an attempt to say something, but both women glared at him.

Ella got out from behind the counter. 'Let me help you to the front door, May. You are not well.'

May wrenched her arm from Ella's grip. 'I want the money you owe me for all those cakes you sold.'

'I have not sold any cakes of yours.'

'You have and you know it. Do I have to bring in the law?'

Ella grabbed hold of May's arm again. 'Do you want to know what I did to those rotten cakes, with the fruit in them so old it was furry? Do you? I gave them to the hens, and even they got mightily fed up of them.'

May Dorkin, her cheeks pink, stared at Ella. 'Thank you for your time. You won't be seeing me again,' she said, pulling herself free of Ella's grip and making for the stairs. Chuck Winters ran after May, calling out to her as she whipped down the avenue.

★

Ella was wiping down the outside tables when Muriel Hearty led her posse from the second morning Mass up the avenue.

'We met poor May Dorkin and she is in bits. What happened?' Muriel asked, almost out of breath after pounding up the stairs.

'I don't gossip, Muriel,' Ella snapped.

Muriel Hearty rubbed her hands in excitement. 'Ella O'Callaghan, what have you been up to? We want a blow-by-blow account.'

'I don't know what you are talking about, Muriel. What will it be today?'

'Come on now, May is in floods of tears. Don't tell me you had nothing to do with it.'

'Oh, *that*. I am sorry she is upset. I am afraid it was all of her own making.'

'Tell us.'

The women standing behind Muriel nodded their heads enthusiastically.

Ella's face was distorted with discomfort. 'There is nothing to tell.'

'Well, she is spitting fire between the tears. Mark my words, there will be more.'

Muriel Hearty and her party settled in across two tables in the centre of the upstairs café.

'Ella, I was just telling the girls, Fergus Brown only has eyes for the O'Callaghan sisters.'

'God forgive you, Muriel Hearty; the man is married and his wife is very ill.'

'Well, the story is he is sweet on ye.'

'You should know better than to spread gossip, Muriel Hearty.'

'Don't take it so seriously, Ella.'

Ella did not respond. When the women were finished, she decided to close the café early, pushing the big bolt of the front door into place.

She went straight to her room. By now, May Dorkin would have badmouthed her to the whole of Rathsorney and Muriel Hearty would have added her bit of spice. Opening the silver jewellery box, she felt the hard grip on her heart melt slowly. She skimmed over to the small, blue half-moon pin, set in clear blue and sparkling stones. She had worn it only once. This brooch had never been her mother's. Tracing her finger along the crescent, stopping at the azure rectangular crystal, she felt her heart flutter at the memory of receiving the gift.

It was two years after Michael Hannigan had died, and yet she had still felt guilty at accepting a gift from a man she found attractive. Stephen Kenny was a pen pal. They corresponded for a year, letters going back and forth. At first, they spoke of their faith, because that was what they had in common. Slowly, they gave little details of each other and became friends. When Stephen said he would be in Ireland for a few days and asked if he could call on her, she declined but arranged to meet him in Dublin. The only fancy place she knew grand enough for the occasion was the Shelbourne Hotel.

Ella dressed with understated elegance and got an early train from Rathsorney, making sure to sit on the box pleats of her skirt, to keep them in place. She gave herself plenty of time, arriving an hour early.

When Stephen Kenny came up and introduced himself, she was both embarrassed and proud to be having tea with the tall, broad American in the tan suit. He ordered coffee and spoke loudly in a musical voice Ella found attractive. They had chatted for several minutes when he reached into his inside pocket and took out a small box wrapped in gold paper.

'I would like you to accept this gift,' he said.

Flustered, she did not know where to look. 'There was no need to bring a present.'

He reached out, holding it so she could see the delicate black ribbon, tied in a perfect bow. Slowly, she stretched out her hand and accepted the package.

'Go on, open it.'

'It seems a pity to upset this beautiful wrapping.'

'I think you'll like it.'

Delicately, she picked at the sellotaped sides, managing to release the little box without tearing the main part of the wrapping. Examining the brooch, Ella felt again the flutter of delight and panic when she saw the blue, crescent-moon-shaped pin.

'I thought it would be nice to pick up one of the brooches at Weiss for you,' he said. 'Please, I would love to see you wear it.'

She self-consciously pinned it to her jacket, sure that others were watching her.

'Just lovely,' he said.

Ella straightened before her dressing-table mirror, pinning the brooch to her cardigan. It shimmered like it had done at the Shelbourne and she felt a rush of giddiness.

There was a moment as he sat smiling at her when she indulged in a hope for the future. When he made to get up, she was going to follow.

'Please stay where you are. It's Connie, my wife.'

Confused, Ella slipped back into the chair at an awkward angle so that when the other woman put out her hand she could only manage a feeble handshake.

'I just love the way you write. You have a gift. Stephen here loves getting your letters. We show them to all our friends.'

Ella could hear the piercing pitch of her voice and see the sugary smile. Her words hit her like missiles.

Betrayal swept around her: to think that her words were babbled over and commented on by people she did not know. That her letters were passed around was too painful to bear. Even now, all these years later, she felt her breath catch at the memory. She tugged the brooch off.

She had stood up and excused herself in the Shelbourne, and the Americans stood back, thinking she was going to the bathroom.

At reception, she asked for a sheet of paper and penned a short note, explaining she could not accept a gift from a married man. Her mouth was dry, her back wet with perspiration, as she asked for the note and the brooch in its box to be delivered to Mr Kenny and his party. Hurrying to the railway station, she realised she had been a fool and sat to wait for two hours for her train home. Only when the train had pulled away from the city and she was in a compartment on her own did she allow tears to bubble up.

When a package was delivered to Roscarbury Hall a few days later, Ella knew what it was. A letter accompanied it.

Shelbourne Hotel,
Dublin
3/6/1961

Dear Miss O'Callaghan,
I am so dreadfully sorry for having given you the wrong impression and I ask your forgiveness for my crass stupidity.
Please take this brooch, as a token of my friendship and esteem. I hope you will find it in your heart to forgive me and that we may continue to correspond.

Yours sincerely,

Stephen

Ella never replied to the letter.

Fifteen

Debbie rounded the rhododendron to see the house sombre, asleep and grand in the morning light. The birds were shrill in full chorus and a fox flitted past the fountain. There was no hint of anybody inside being awake. Treading lightly, she crossed the gravel courtyard by the fountain, the stones crunching under her step. Up close, she could see the stonework on the house needed pointing and the paint on the windows was falling off in wafer-thin slices.

She mooched into the back yard. In the walled garden, some beds were tidy and had been recently tended, but others were still floundering under a blanket of weeds. She did not see the person wrapped in a wool coat sitting on a wooden bench near the pear trees at the high stone wall.

Unable to sleep, Roberta had put on her warm coat and hat and set off for the kitchen garden, where she sat holding her hip flask by her side. She liked the early mornings, when the blackbirds called out loud and the robins hovered nearby, hoping for crumbs. She had a slice of bread in her pocket. As she sat and worried, her fingers scrunched and broke up the bread until it was time to throw the crumbs out, near the ter-racotta pots.

Debbie watched as a flutter of small birds descended on the shower of crumbs, picking, jumping and squabbling over the tiniest specks.

Roberta saw her stroll along the shingle path, engrossed in the layout of the beds. Stuffing her hip flask into her handbag, she stood up.

'Hello. You couldn't sleep either.'

'Did I wake you, when I left the house?'

'Will you walk with me to the pond?' Roberta said, casting a glance at the kitchen window, where soon Ella would be getting her cake mix ready for the oven.

Debbie hesitated.

'I don't bite, Miss Kading. It is lovely by the pond in the early morning, though the ducks do make a racket. They have got quite greedy because the local children throw them bread.'

Roberta led the way across the field, heavy with dew, to a bench at the side of the eucalyptus grove. She patted the seat beside her. 'Sit, please, Miss Kading.'

Debbie began to shiver with the cold.

'I know why you are in Ireland. I imagine the whole country does, but please tell me why you are so taken by Roscarbury Hall?'

'What do you mean?'

'What do you think you are going to gain?'

'I don't mean to gain anything.' Debbie jumped up. 'I don't mean to be rude, but I have to shower and get the café ready.'

'Roscarbury Hall is not for sale and it is never going to be for sale.'

'I don't know what you mean.'

Roberta stood beside Debbie. 'You might think you are all pals with Ella, but not one blade of grass, not one china cup will be yours; I will make sure of that. You think you can ingratiate yourself into my sister's affections. I am telling you, I am watching you and I will not let that happen.'

Debbie turned and walked away, leaving Roberta to shout that it was time she booked a flight.

Ella, on the way to the kitchen, feigned surprise when Debbie pushed in the front door.

'You should not be going out so early with so little on. You look frozen; you will catch your death.'

Debbie made to go up the stairs when Ella called after her.

'Next time, don't be so polite and tell that sister of mine where to go.'

'How did you know?'

'Don't I know my own sister? And I have a good pair of eyes in my head.'

'For somebody who hasn't talked to you in so long, she is so protective.'

Ella guffawed, throwing her eyes upwards as she turned to the kitchen. 'More protective of her interests in Roscarbury, more like,' she grumbled.

★

Muriel Hearty waved the newspaper frantically as she scurried up the avenue.

'She is in a dither. Let's see what gossip has tickled her this morning,' Ella said, polishing the tables.

Iris, who was about to wash her mug, poured another cup of coffee. 'I might stick around for this,' she said, settling into a table near the counter.

Muriel Hearty burst in to the room, her perfume so strong it made Ella and Iris rub their noses. 'Is Debbie here? She has got to see this.'

'Is there something wrong?'

Muriel rustled the paper noisily. 'Those nuns have done it now; they only had two sets of books going all along, conning every poor thing looking for information, including Debbie.'

Iris grabbed the newspaper and began to read out sections.

'A full inquiry has been ordered after it emerged the Order of the Divine Sisters of Ballygally ran two sets of record books. Every person who called attempting to trace a birth mother was told that there was no record of the birth. It also emerged that every adopted child who wanted to have contact with the birth mother was told the mother did not want anything to do with them. The same applied to birth mothers looking for their children. Sources said it is likely the investigation will be extended to other convents in the coming weeks.' Iris crumpled the paper onto her lap. 'I don't want to read any more.'

Ella sat down, her head in her hands. 'It sucks the energy out of you, for sure,' she said.

'We have got to tell Debbie. It might mean she can trace her mother. Can we sit together and have a coffee?' Muriel said, flopping down beside Ella.

Without waiting to be asked, Iris poured three cups of steaming coffee and brought them to the table.

'Where is she anyway?' Muriel asked.

'What does it matter? She is a Trojan worker when she needs to be,' Ella said firmly.

Muriel seemed disappointed that she could not impart the news directly.

'I will go up in a while and tell her; let her read the paper in peace.'

'Whatever you say, Ella; it is your house,' Muriel said, stirring her coffee so fast some splashed over the side. 'I am sure Roberta isn't happy at all about the American staying here.'

'Is she ever happy, Muriel? Where are all the other ladies? Don't tell me they have given up on the Ballroom Café.'

Muriel laughed nervously. 'I am afraid I skipped Mass, I was so excited.'

'There is nothing wrong with that,' Ella said, rising to greet ten other women who had begun to block up the hall. Some had left directly after communion, hoping to get the tables in the centre of the floor, because there you could join in all the conversations. Only strangers to the Ballroom Café rushed to take up the window seats, giving a view priority over gossip.

When Debbie walked into the room soon after the first gaggle of women placed their orders, there was a hush as each woman sat back and smiled at her. Muriel Hearty made to stand up, but Ella pushed her down gently on her chair.

'Debbie, love, there has been a bit of a development. It might mean you get to find out who your mum is after all.'

Debbie saw the happy, expectant faces of the women and she laughed. 'I feel like I've won the Lotto. Is someone going to tell me?'

Iris handed her the newspaper. Debbie sat down and began to read. Anger swept up through her. Jumping up, she scrunched the newspaper and let it fall to the ground, like a discarded chocolate wrapper. Tears of frustration sprayed out. 'When is it ever going to end?' she snapped, before making a dash for the door.

A woman, her arms outstretched, made to stand in her way, but Debbie pushed past.

'Well, I never have seen the likes; talk of ungrateful,' Muriel muttered, but the woman beside her snarled at her to hush.

Ella stepped into the centre of the café. 'Ladies, I am so awfully sorry. This is all so intense and emotional for Debbie; none of us knows what she has been through. Why doesn't everybody have a free cuppa on the house,' she said, motioning Iris to take over.

'I've had my fill of hot drinks; no thank you,' Muriel told Iris when she approached, a coffee pot in one hand and a teapot in the other.

★

Debbie stumbled along the gravel path past the pond. The warm wind sprayed the pink petals of the cherry blossom across her; the sun pushed its rays through the trees. Trudging slowly along, she could feel the anger slip away, leaving a loneliness weary in her bones.

She sat on a wooden bench under the cherry blossom; the branches whispered overhead and watery-pink petals skated past her, some attaching to her top. Clouds leaned on the trees and it began to rain on far-off hills. A rabbit ran for home; the crows flew low.

She saw Ella skirt past the fountain, the eucalyptus grove and the old oak tree. When she was within spitting distance, Ella called out her name softly and asked to join her.

'I see you have found Carrie's bench.'

Debbie made to stand up, but Ella pressed her down with her hand.

'It is nice to see it being used. Usually it is a lonely old bench looking across at a sad, grey house.'

Ella sat down with a sigh. Shoulders almost touching, they sat looking across the sweep of land to the far-off mountains. A blackbird sang out loud above them. At the pond, one duckling was pecking another fiercely on the back.

'I hope the rain holds off or we will get drowned,' Ella said, flicking petals off her cardigan.

'There was no need to follow me.'

'I couldn't see you upset.'

Debbie jumped up and began to kick small tufts of grass. 'I just don't understand why it has to be so complicated. I never intended to cause all this trouble.'

'I know that, but we can't always pick the set of circumstances we live in; we just have to deal with it.'

'Like you and your sister.'

'In a way.' Ella stood up, flapping her hands across her clothes to dislodge the petals.

'You don't like them?'

'I planted this tree in memory of Carrie and I find I can never come here. There is no comfort in the petals as soft as a baby's touch, the beautiful flowers that remind me of her innocent smiles. There is no comfort in seeing the way the wind can ravage the beauty of the tree, like the sea destroyed my daughter. I never knew when I planted it, it would cause me so much pain.'

'Can't you knock it down?'

Ella stamped her feet and took a deep breath. 'That is the greatest pain: I cannot bear to think of it not being here. I can't bear not to be reminded.'

'I didn't know. I'm sorry.'

'It was a long time ago, but the pain is as hot as ever.'

'What happened to Carrie?'

Ella looked alarmed. In all the years, nobody had asked her that question. Nobody mentioned Carrie: it was like she never existed; the daughter she had brought into the world and brought home was treated as a child nobody ever knew. She felt Debbie's arms come around her and she moved in and let herself collapse into her, sobs wrenching through her, snorts of pain breaking from her across the grass. Pushing her head up, she said she was a show, but Debbie hushed her.

'I will be all right in a while. It just comes over me.'

Sitting up, she clasped her hands together on her tweed skirt.

'Carrie drowned at the harbour; a gust of wind blew the pram into the water. An accident. She was out for a walk with my sister and my husband.'

Debbie reached over and squeezed her hand. 'You don't need to say any more.'

Ella sighed loudly. 'I don't think I can.'

Sheets of grey rain advanced on them.

'We'd better hurry back or we will get soaked.'

They got up and walked at a smart pace across the grass. When they got to the fountain, Ella faltered.

'I am going to my room for a while, just to get myself together. Why don't you do the same? Most of the women are gone anyway.'

'I think I should go back and apologise for my outburst.'

'Suit yourself,' Ella said, as she made for the back stairs. She waited until she got inside her bedroom to buckle like an old soft toy discarded on the floor.

Sixteen

Mother Assumpta stirred an extra sugar into her tea. After the visit of the Order administrator and solicitor, she needed something an awful lot stronger, but extra sugar would have to do. She had been told very sharply to sort this mess out, and she had no idea how she was going to do it. Every day brought new and ludicrous rumours. She knew she had to take measures to quell the rising hysteria that had attracted so much comment. Consuelo, the last time she interviewed her, was both aggressive and belligerent.

Assumpta cursed the competitive drive in her, which had seen her push for this position against more senior members of the community. She was paying the price for her past naked display of raw ambition, for sure. To think she turned down a transfer to the Italian house three years ago because it did not fit in with her long-term goal. Curse her stupidity, Assumpta thought, because it had landed her in this very hot water.

The civil servant leading the inquiry was unhelpful and even turned down an offer for tea in the drawing room. The administrator's final words as she made her way through the hallway were ringing in her ears still.

'Assumpta, you have let this get way out of hand. You need to come up with something fast, to limit the damage being done to our sisters all over the world as a result of this nonsense. There are rumblings in the Bishop's Palace: be warned.'

A slight tap on the door and she rose to ready herself, even though she had not even touched her tea.

'The car is here, Mother.'

'Thank you, Marguerite. Tell the others to keep a low profile while I am away.'

Mother Assumpta buttoned up her raincoat and, carrying a small handbag, she slowly made her way down the curve of stone steps to Gerry O'Hare's car.

'It is a nice day for an outing, Mother,' he said, and she nodded, smiling that Gerry O'Hare should think this trip was one of leisure. In her handbag was the letter she had got in yesterday's afternoon post. She tried not to dwell on the contents, but she knew it was very troubling.

Sea Road,
Malahide,
Co. Dublin

Dear Mother Assumpta,
My name is Frances Rees, née Murtagh, from Bridge Street, Rathsorney. My sister was Mary Murtagh of the same address who gave birth to a baby on April 15, 1959 at Wicklow General Hospital.

I write to you on a matter of serious concern. My sister was told her baby had died and she never recovered from that loss. However, she insisted the baby did not die but was stolen from her. She died in a mental institution, almost twelve months to the day after the birth. She always insisted her baby had been taken from her, and now that I hear Deborah Kading on the radio, I am wondering was she in fact correct. We were never told where the baby was buried; Sister Consuelo said she would take care of everything.

I wonder even at this late stage, would it be possible to unravel this mystery. I intend also to try and make contact with Deborah Kading. I hope you can help.

Yours sincerely

Frances Rees.

Gerry O'Hare knew better than to put talk on her and she nodded off for most of the journey to Moyasta. When he pulled in to the old convent, O'Hare coughed loudly, so she woke up with a start.

'I am going to get a sandwich in the village and have a doze in the car,' he said, and she nodded, saying she would get the sisters to send out a pot of tea.

Consuelo had spent the morning in the cellars, rummaging through boxes of files in what was once the old pantry and grain store. Sweat pooled on her temples as she heaved box after box onto a table and emptied out files contained by thick brown elastic bands. The Kading file was in the fourth box. She remembered Agnes Kading well; pushy and insistent. That baby was one of the luckiest; the Kadings' income alone guaranteed a cushy life and more than likely a university education. Who could say she had done the wrong thing? The young mother was loud, screaming for her baby, but they all thought that would pass. Was it her fault that the parents could not make her see sense and grab a second chance at some sort of life where nobody knew her?

A flutter of nervous excitement ran through her when she heard Assumpta's cold voice. Straightening her skirt and checking her blouse was tucked in, with no gaps showing between the buttons on the front, she grabbed the Kading file and made her way upstairs.

Consuelo rushed into the hall to help Mother off with her coat. 'You need not have come all this way, Mother. I would have gladly come to you.'

'We both know that could not be, Consuelo.'

For a moment, Consuelo stopped what she was doing and looked at Assumpta. 'My conscience is clear, Mother. I won't be told I did not do right for those children.'

'Let's leave it at that, until we are in private,' Mother Assumpta snapped.

Consuelo did as she was bid, leading the way to the drawing room overlooking the rose garden, which normally reserved for receiving important visitors.

As they sat and waited for the tea to arrive, Consuelo attempted some conversation. 'Has it caused a lot of disruption at the convent in Ballygally?'

Assumpta shifted uncomfortably in her seat, conscious

Consuelo was attempting to lead the conversation so she could have the upper hand. 'Quite a bit, as you can imagine, with the world press practically at the gates.'

Her tone was deliberately stiff and sour, so that Consuelo sat back on her chair and folded her hands on her lap.

Sister Angela, when she brought the tea tray into the drawing room, felt the disagreement between the two women and as a result flapped unnecessarily, offering Mother sugar and milk and a plate of rich tea and chocolate biscuits. Her polite enquiry as to whether Mother had enjoyed the car journey was met with a one-word answer. When Sister Angela self-consciously bustled out of the room, Assumpta placed her cup of tea on its saucer.

'First things first: have you the Kading file?'

Consuelo waved the folder in the air. 'I got a fine home for that child; the papers prove it.'

Assumpta moved to the edge of her seat and stretched to take the brown folder. 'I have decided in the extraordinary circumstances we find ourselves in, we will help those who come forward to us: mothers who have given up their children for adoption and those children who wish to trace their birth parents.'

Consuelo elaborately folded her arms across her chest.

'Deborah Kading will have a long wait; the birth mother is dead.'

'Mary Murtagh?'

'Killed herself a year or so afterwards. Tell me I did not do the right thing for that child. I gave her a loving family environment; she was never going to get that from young Mary Murtagh.'

'Mary Murtagh's sister has started asking questions, says

the girl insisted all along the baby was stolen from her, that she was only told it was dead.'

The statement had the devastating effect she hoped for: Consuelo looked stricken. 'Holy divine Jesus, you don't believe her. Tell me you don't believe her.' Consuelo crossed herself several times, muttering a Hail Mary.

'I don't know what to believe,' Assumpta said.

Consuelo jumped up. 'Mary Murtagh's father was very clear: the baby was to go for adoption and she was to be told it died. The poor man only wanted to save her the longing. As God is my witness, I did the right thing, helping a desperate father with a wayward daughter.'

'It may be viewed differently today.'

Consuelo snorted. 'Hindsight is a great thing. Her own father handed the child to me; tell me what I should have done.'

'It is a bit late for that.' Assumpta clicked her tongue impatiently. 'We have to deal quickly with this sorry mess. The file and all the others will have to be handed over. This thing about two sets of books, it is not going to go away. Bishop Lucey is furious.'

Assumpta walked to the window. Outside, two sisters were weeding and pruning, chatting as they worked. No doubt discussing the purpose of my visit, thought Assumpta, as she turned to face Consuelo.

'I will take all the files you have. Tell the sisters to put them in the boot.'

'You should have brought a lorry; I helped a lot of children.'

'Consuelo, do you give me your word it was all above board?'

'You don't expect me to dignify that with an answer, do you?'

'They are saying there were two sets of books. We have one set of records at the convent. Will it be different from what I find in those files?'

Consuelo sighed loudly. 'Mother, look at the end result. Isn't it the bottom line that always matters? These children got wonderful homes and lives the rest of us could only dream of. I did everything to protect both sides, and if that meant telling people who came nosing for information there was none, then I am guilty.'

'What of birth mothers who had requested contact?'

Consuelo snorted loudly. 'I ran an efficient system, the same as every other convent. Best that the files were closed and no contact encouraged.'

'You know I have to hand over these files to the inquiry.'

'I know they are looking for a scapegoat; it might as well be me. I hope that the inquiry asks how these children were given passports and visas, if the adoptions were not above board.'

'That is not our concern.'

Consuelo fiddled with a lace doily, her fingers pushing into the small holes of the crochet. 'It was not so long ago, Mother, when you did not want to know the details.'

'Unfortunately, Sister Consuelo, the situation has shifted considerably, and if we don't revise our strategy, we may find ourselves unable to extricate ourselves from the soup.' Assumpta flicked through the Kading file. 'We will have to deal with each case as it comes up; it is not going to be easy.'

'I can stand over everything I did; I don't mind telling anybody that.'

Assumpta snapped the file shut. 'You will do no such thing.'

'You are treating me, Mother, as if I did something wrong.'

'Let's face it: we never treated those young women right

and we seemed to find homes based on the income of the adoptive parents and nothing else. It smacks of selling children for gain. If I can see that, as sure as God is in heaven others will come to that conclusion as well.'

Consuelo jumped up, her face blotching red with anger. 'All the work I put into finding good homes for those ungrateful children; tell me what should I have done: let them stay in institutions to be the playthings for all sorts?'

'Consuelo, quieten that tongue of yours.' Assumpta stood up, tucking the Kading file under her arm. 'I will send Gerry back for the rest of the files in the morning. Please do not discuss this situation with anybody, not even the other sisters.'

Consuelo nodded, her face pale.

'I will be in touch,' Assumpta said as she made her way to the hall, where Sister Angela was loitering, hoping to take away the tea tray. 'Sister, get the car around please.' Assumpta's voice was sharp and urgent. As she walked to the front door, she turned to Consuelo. 'I will meet Miss Kading; she must know of her mother.'

'And the rest?'

'We will see.'

Seventeen

Ella was grumpy. When the phone rang she at first ignored it, but when after five rings she did not hear Roberta's shuffle in the hall, she rushed down the stairs. Spinning quickly across the tiles, she picked up the heavy old receiver.

'Ella, is that you? That bastard husband of mine has made me homeless.'

Iris was shouting so loud, Ella had to hold the phone a distance from her ear. 'What? Just get away from there and come here.'

'My three-piece suite is in the front garden and my walnut bureau has been chipped on the side.'

'Get somebody to keep an eye on things and come here. Gerry lives down the road. I will get him to mind the place for you. You come here until we can work it out.'

Iris, she knew, was crying, because her voice was extra high-pitched and slobbery, like she was trying to pretend everything was all right.

'Come now. You can stay at Roscarbury until you get sorted.'

'Are you sure?'

'Yes, the sooner you get here the better, and we will have tea and a chat.'

'Ella?'

'Yes?'

'Thank you very much.'

'Not a bother, just come as soon as you can and we will get a room fixed up for you.'

When Ella got off the phone, Roberta was standing beside the hall table, staring hard. She screwed up her nose and sucked in her cheeks, but she did not say anything. Instead, she whipped a page from her red notebook and wrote furiously. Ella pretended not to notice and walked past, up the stairs to her room, so she could watch out for Iris. After all, she did not need to read the note; she knew what was in it.

An hour later, Ella watched as Iris struggled past the rhododendron; a holdall in one hand and a large suitcase in the other. Maybe she should have sent a car to pick her up. Kicking another big suitcase in front of her, Iris slowly made her way up the gravel drive. The dog, on a long lead, snapped and growled at the case every time it rumbled past. Iris, muttering, was grumbling, stopping every few paces to massage the palms of her hands and kick out at the dog. Ella hurried to open the front door. Hearing the bolt go across, Iris dropped her load.

'Goddamn taxi would not come up the avenue. Ella, grab something,' Iris snapped, her face red.

'Come in, you look upset.'

Iris clapped her hands in exasperation. 'Of course I am upset, Ella. The house was supposed to be mine. When that good-for-nothing husband of mine walked out three months ago, it was decided I could have the house. He said there was no need for solicitors; like a fool I trusted him.'

'I am sure it can be sorted.'

Iris walked over to the eucalyptus tree and kicked it; a slice of bark fell off. 'Ella, I have nowhere to go. A woman my age: homeless. Turns out the house we settled he would give me was not even his, it was his brother's, and no mortgage was paid for two years, so the bank has thrown me out. Upstanding Iris O'Callaghan, who has paid her bills all her life, has been evicted. They threw my furniture out in the garden, flattened all my good shrubs.'

She stopped to gather herself, fiercely shaking away the tears, which were making her shoulders shake and her knees wobble.

'Ella, I am homeless. If I ever set eyes on him again, I will kill him. Get rid of a bad egg, and get a roof over my head and three square meals a day in one go.'

Ella laughed and Iris sniggered.

'We will send you food parcels and books, plenty of books.'

'Ciggies. That is all I need.'

'Come on, let's get you inside and put a whiskey down the hatch. I will ring O'Hare and tell him to arrange to collect your furniture.'

She waited for Iris to raise an objection, but if Iris heard Gerry O'Hare's name, she did not react.

The Jack Russell ran into the field and squatted down for a crap.

'Sorry about the dog. I had to bring him. Stupid dog.'

'Of course you did. Let's get you inside and sit down,' Ella said.

'Roberta is going to have a conniption. I don't blame her. I would not like somebody walking in on top of me either. And there is the dog.'

'Leave Roberta to me.'

They left the cases where they had dropped them, in a pile inside the front door, and went to the kitchen.

'You will have to bunk down on the drawing-room sofa for tonight, but tomorrow we will see about getting you a bed.'

'You should have set up a guesthouse instead of a café. I have an appointment with a solicitor in a while, so hopefully this arrangement won't be for too long.'

Ella did not answer.

Afterwards, when Iris banged the front door on the way to meet the solicitor, Ella went upstairs to open the café, stopping to read the notes Roberta had slapped down in quick succession.

Iris struts about like she owns the place. We don't want her or her stinking problems. You have some nerve, bringing her here and letting her stay. R.

The husband has left her. I bet she did not tell you that. This is my house too and I won't have her here. R.

It will be a field day for the gossips, this. You have turned Roscarbury in to a dosshouse. R.

Ella tore the notes into little pieces, letting them flutter onto the table, before thumping down a hastily scribbled reply with her fist.

Iris O'Callaghan is family, or had you forgotten?

She can stay here as long as she likes. Leave her alone or she will be told exactly the sort of person you are. One harsh word to her and your secret will be out, to be picked over by the gossips. E.

Roberta picked up the note and brought it to the drawing room. She sat at the brass coffee table and took out a box of matches. She struck a match and, holding it over the cut-glass bowl, set the note alight. She watched the flames dissolving the words as the paper deepened black. It sank into the bowl, blackening the sides, the ash lodging in a heap at the bottom.

Eighteen

Debbie managed to doze for two hours towards the start of morning. Her skin was dry and a bit flaky, and around her eyeballs was showing brushes of yellow. Nancy would probably notice the most change, she thought. The disease was beginning to devastate her. Soon she would have to go back to Bowling Green to wait out the end.

Ella got up extra early. Switching on the ovens, she decided she would need at least two batches of biscuits to get through the day. Multiplying the lemon cake and the chocolate cake recipes by three, she cracked the eggs, threw in the sugar and forced herself to weigh the self-raising flour, because too much would make her lemon cakes heavy and stodgy. Slicing the lemons, she pushed them onto the squeezer, locking it tight to extract as much juice as possible, and decided she would be better off investing in a machine to do the job. The eggs for the chocolate cake she separated, flinging the yolks from side to side until the whites had dripped away into a big mixing bowl, where Ella let them whisk away until stiff. She sliced open the packets of ground almonds and broke up the chocolate to melt into a big bowl over a pan of boiling water. She wasn't too sure where she had got the other recipes, but this one was her mother's: the Good Cake she called it, because they always made it when they were trying to put on a show for visitors.

Bernie O'Callaghan took great pride in the fact that the cake, made with the darkest chocolate she could find in Gorey, looked sinfully rich and decadent but was light and moist to taste. She took greater pleasure when her guests fought over the last slice or tried to guess the secret ingredient, which gave this cake an intense chocolate fluffiness. Bernie straightened on her seat and waited for a hush in the room before saying in a high and mighty voice: 'This is such a simple cake I don't know what the fuss is all about. I am sure anybody can guess the ingredients.'

She sat looking for hands up, smiling broadly when all sort of wild suggestions were made and clapping when one woman triumphed with almonds.

'Well done, but it is what is missing in this mix that is most important.'

Ludicrous ingredients were bandied about, until Bernie gave in.

'Flour: there is no need for it; I will say no more than that.'

When the time came to reveal the recipe to her daughters, Bernie O'Callaghan had made such a big deal of guarding her methods for the Good Cake that the girls felt rather cheated to find that only egg whites, whisked to resemble snow, gave the cake its magical lightness.

Ella stacked the cakes in two ovens, rattling the racks to even out the mixture.

She had got out the lemon cakes and put the biscuits in

the top oven when Debbie put her head around the door. Breathing in the warm aroma of chocolate and almonds, it made her feel cosy and safe and she managed to smile brightly.

'You should have called me; I could have helped.'

Ella shook her head. 'Don't you have enough on your plate today, going to the convent to inspect the books? Get a bit of breakfast inside you. Gerry will be here in half an hour.'

'I can't eat; my stomach is sick.'

'Strong sweet tea it has to be then. It will settle you nicely.'

She ignored the protests and poured a mug of tea, stirring in two heaped spoons of sugar. Debbie accepted it and sat at the window, sipping slowly, the steam from the mug causing a small cloud of fog to blot out the view.

Ella finished and shot upstairs to change into her good clothes. She chose a flecked tweed skirt with a soft blue cardigan under her black swing coat. Sitting at the dressing table, she rummaged for a brooch.

The sun flowed across, highlighting favourites in the myriad of colours in the silver box. Reaching into the right corner, she picked out the smallest Weiss brooch. She could hear Iris greeting customers in the café. Taking her time, she angled the pin so it looked as if a fragile and colourful moth had taken refuge on her shoulder.

Looking down at the front gravel, she saw a stranger photographing his companion in front of the house. Gerry O'Hare was leaning against the fountain again. Ella saw he was wearing a suit. When Debbie had said she could not face driving herself, he came straight away. She knew he had made the effort for Debbie, so she would not chastise him this time for leaning against the stonework.

Debbie tugged at her hair and flattened her raincoat when she saw Ella. 'I didn't know we were supposed to dress up.'

'Overdressed, more like; I am cursed by an obsession with dressing to the nines every time I encounter officialdom.'

They were both giggling when Iris, followed by May Dorkin, came upstairs.

'I found May leaning on the door, wanting to wish you luck,' Iris said.

May stepped forward. 'I have had my arguments with Ella here, but I hope it is in the past. I want to wish you luck and tell you, no matter what you find out today, you have done your mothers proud.' Reaching into her pocket, she fumbled her words. 'I have a few buns; the hens must be missing my sweet ingredients.'

'May, you are one big bird yourself,' Iris said, snatching the bag of buns.

May laughed shyly.

Debbie reached over and squeezed her hand. 'I am very touched by your kind gesture.'

May glowed with the pride of appreciation. 'I will have a tea while I am here,' she said.

'And a slice of cake,' Ella instructed. 'The new lemon drizzle, on the house.'

The two women nodded to each other.

A woman sipping tea at a central table elbowed her friend. 'Ella O'Callaghan is going soft,' she muttered.

'We had better get a move on,' Ella said, and they left, May and Iris waving them off from the upstairs café window.

★

It was quiet at the convent when the Mercedes pulled up the

driveway, except for a gardener raking cherry-blossom petals from the grassy patch at the front. The front door was opened immediately by a man in a suit.

'Deborah Kading? Come in,' he said, leading the way to a small front office. The desk was pulled out in the middle of the floor, a number of high-backed chairs placed around it.

'I am Bernard Morrissey, appointed by the Minister to supervise the viewing of the records by those women who wish to come forward and check the information. I will tell you at the outset, I can't myself immediately see a record of your birth.'

'Is that the right book?' Ella asked.

Mr Morrissey sighed. 'Everybody who comes asks that question. Yes, it is.' He opened the book for April 15, 1959. 'According to your letter, you say you were born on April 15, 1959 at the convent and adopted by Robert and Agnes Kading, then of New York. As you will see, on that date two girls were born and one boy. One girl was adopted by a couple in Philadelphia. The other unfortunately died at birth. The boy was adopted by a couple in Ireland.'

He continued to talk, while showing her the record for the previous and following days; Debbie saw the names and addresses all over the East Coast of America, but none for Agnes and Robert Kading.

By the time he had finished and closed the book, she could not speak. Her brain was whirring; her head was pounding. She felt she was an observer from a distance, removed and remote, all emotion sucked away.

'What does this mean?' Ella asked.

Mr Morrissey took off his glasses. 'I am afraid there is no record of Miss Kading's birth in the official record of the convent. I am sorry to impart this news; I know your hopes must have been built up as a result of this appointment. However, Mother Assumpta has been most helpful and supplied me with additional files, which we are currently examining.'

'What does that mean exactly?'

'Yours is by no means the only case. We have several men and women who were adopted, yet no record of their birth appears. It is a mystery we will only be able to solve after careful investigation.'

'That sounds like it could take a long time,' Ella said.

'How long is a piece of string?'

Still Debbie could say nothing, a humming rising inside her, a loneliness seeping through her.

'Where do we go from here?' Ella asked.

'We will be in touch when we have any new information.'

'Is that it then?' Ella said, her voice tight, anger bursting up inside her.

'I am awfully sorry; there is nothing else I can do at the moment. We are hoping on the full examination of hundreds of extra files that it will yield further results.'

Debbie pushed her hair back from her eyes and inched to the edge of her seat.

Mr Morrissey straightened his cuffs and quickly checked his watch.

Debbie stood up and put out her hand. 'Mr Morrissey, thank you for your time,' she said, shaking his hand too vigorously before leaving the room.

Ella hesitated. 'Is there nothing you can do for her now?'

'I only wish I could,' he said, shaking his head.

When they got outside, Gerry O'Hare beckoned Ella.

'Is everything all right? She has not said a word since she came out of that place.'

'It is not all right; it is far from it. Take us home, Gerry, please.'

There was silence in the car as they turned around in the courtyard in front of the convent and headed for Roscarbury. Gerry O'Hare deliberately took the long way round, to allow Debbie time to gather herself. She sat in the back seat, the sound of her breathing heaving through the car. As he indicated to turn in the gate at Roscarbury, Ella placed her hand on his arm.

'You don't have to drive up to the house. Just drop us at the gate please, Gerry.'

'Are you sure? It is no bother.'

'I am sure.'

She patted him on the shoulder, whispering thank you, before climbing out of the car and marching across the wet grass towards the cherry blossom. Stopping after a few paces, she waited for Debbie. Above them, the clouds scampered across the sky and the branches of the tree creaked in the cold wind sweeping across the parkland, hitting Roscarbury Hall full on, rattling the windows and sneaking in the big keyhole on the front door.

'Don't be disheartened; we don't always win the first time.'

'Or ever,' Debbie said.

'We will think of another way. Maybe make another plea on the radio.'

'What do you mean?'

'Directly to your mother.'

'I don't think so. She wanted secrecy and she did a mighty

fine job of keeping it secret. I guess there's a message in that. I need to go home and give up this silly wild goose chase.'

'What about following up on Consuelo? She is in the convent in Moyasta, they say. Maybe we could go there.'

'To have another door slammed in our faces and the sympathetic media at hand to listen to my story for the umpteenth time.'

'We could do it together. Nobody need ever know.'

'Isn't that what is wrong with this damned place? Secrecy. Everything's such a big goddamn secret!' Debbie shouted, taking off across the grassland, making for the overgrown rhododendron path.

Ella followed her, but chose the nearby shingle track, which was wet and dirty but not so overgrown. Debbie struck out at a fast pace; she did not hear the birds rustle in indignation as she whacked the sprawling rhododendron out of her way. Not caring that the track was mucky and wet in places, keeping her head down she stayed on the route to the old icehouse and the lake. It was overgrown in places, but she pushed branches and briars out of her way, her hands firmly in her pockets.

In one place, pallets had been thrown over a sodden piece of ground in an attempt to maintain the walkway; these too were submerged by mud. Making no effort to dance between the curled-up, stagnant waves of muck and rainwater, Debbie waded through. She felt the thickness of the pallets underneath her shoes. Her trouser leg was snagged, sticking to her. The water made her cold; the mud slowed her down. The first surge of adrenalin faded. Plodding on, elbowing old briars left over from the summer out of her way, she trampled nettles.

The lake was overgrown with reeds in places, but the jetty was still there. She stumbled on, her feet sinking into the soft bank near the water. A heron screeched loudly and skimmed the water, its wings swishing rhythmically, like sails in a good offshore wind. At the old wooden jetty, there were big holes in places where the wood had given way and fallen through.

Stopping by a low stone wall, slicing a bunch of dead leaves out of the way, Debbie sat down. Her socks were ripped and she could see small cuts around the top of her ankles from where she had been whipped by the briars.

All the times she had wanted to look in her face, to know the colour of her hair, to know her likes and dislikes. All the times she had hoped to sit and sip tea, to be comfortable enough with each other, not even to talk. All the times she had simply needed a mom. She did not hear Ella walk up behind her, but when engulfed in a strong, tight hug she let go inside, letting the howls of tears blow across the lake, where the ducklings zipped happily together in circles.

Nineteen

They sat, the two of them, surrounded by the noise of the lake, the water sloshing against the jetty supports, the air cooling as rain drifted nearer.

'We'd better get back,' Ella said eventually.

They trudged up the shingle path together, both slower this time, their steps heavier.

'Go on up and rest. I will bring you up some supper. You will always have a home here, Debbie. I mean it. I really do,' Ella said, making her way to the kitchen.

'I know.'

'Promise me you won't give up on it yet.'

'I wish I had half the fight that's in you.'

Ella grimaced. 'Too much tragedy has made me bold; don't wish for that.'

Idly, she picked up the red notes on the table and scanned them, as if they were of no importance, before scrunching them into her coat pocket.

Is she planning to die here? R.

What are you hoping for: to surf on the wave of sympathy the Yank is getting? You are a fool. R

'There are some things that never change. Unfortunately, it is the bitterness of my sister which remains my constant in life.' Ella flicked the tap on and watched the water whoosh into the kettle. 'I will bring up a cuppa,' she called after Debbie, who was plodding up the stairs.

Spotting Fergus Brown loitering near the back door, she fixed her hair and walked over to him.

'How are you, Fergus?'

'Ella, I had almost given up on you.'

'There has just been a lot going on.'

'Roberta said you were not expected back.'

'I would not believe everything my sister says, Fergus. We don't get on very well, you know.'

'I detect a certain frostiness in your voice when you speak of her. She does seem rather stressed and bossy.'

'An understatement; let's not talk any more about Roberta.'

'Do you want to talk about it?'

'I wish I could, Fergus, but I can't,' she said, patting him lightly on the shoulder.

He caught her hand and squeezed it gently. 'I understand that sometimes there are things in families you cannot speak of, not outside the household.'

'Fergus, it is so lovely to have you around.'

He felt giddy, like a schoolboy with a crush. His mouth dry, he licked his lips before speaking.

'There is no impediment in us getting to know each other more, Ella, becoming good friends. I would like that very much.'

'Me too,' she whispered. She felt safe, almost happy and content to be here, beside Fergus Brown.

A thrush pecked at the scraps saucepan outside the back door, and two magpies hovered, watching the chaffinches jump from tabletop to tabletop at the front of the house. She forgot about the tea, until Fergus said he had to leave.

'I am so glad we can be friends, Ella.'

She smiled and he noticed she had a small dimple on her right cheek. He made to get up from the chair, but turned, an uncertainty across his face.

'I was wondering would you be free to join me next Friday.' He stopped and steadied himself, as if he could not manoeuvre out of the seat and ask her on a date at the same time. 'There is a recital in the old Protestant church in Gorey; I would be delighted if you would do the honour of accompanying me?'

Ella felt herself blush. 'Won't people talk?'

He stamped his feet in exasperation. 'Aren't we too old to be worrying about that?'

'But Margaret?'

'Ella, we are two friends enjoying an evening out. There is no shame in that.'

She stroked the revere of his blazer. 'I would love to.'

She led the way to the front door. They moved a little closer, their hands almost touching, until they parted and she rushed back inside to make the tea.

Ella set a tray with a china cup and saucer to match the small china teapot with the blue ivy design. Heart-shaped chocolate-chip biscuits she placed on a small plate, before walking to Debbie's room and knocking on the door.

'I am sorry about the delay,' she said, letting the cup slide and clink against the teapot. Changed into her pajamas, Debbie opened the door wide.

'I had forgotten.'

'You are looking better.'

'Maybe, but I don't feel it.'

Ella sat down on the bed. 'You're not giving up now. Are you?'

'I'm not, but unfortunately my body is, Ella. The specialist says I have to come back.' Reaching behind the bedside chair, she pulled out a bottle of Baileys. 'Do you mind? I don't feel like tea.' She poured some into the china cup for Ella and filled a glass for herself. 'I can't think of a toast.'

Ella raised her cup. 'To friends.'

They banged the china cup and the glass, so they looked a bit like two farmers with pints of stout after a good day at the mart. They took long, deep swigs, making Debbie reach to refill.

'I shouldn't; I won't be able to tidy up the café,' Ella said, but she did not pull away her cup from the bottle.

'How do you do it, Ella?'

'Do what?'

'Stay so nice, even though you lost your daughter and husband and have a sister who doesn't talk to you. Where I come from, that's a lot of baggage.'

'I would prefer to travel hands-free, for sure. Seriously, it is this place. I love every brick, every broken window and dirty bit of glass; I love the gardens and the rickety old jetty. My memories are Roscarbury: good ones and terribly sad, but they make up my life, and this house is the backdrop to all my loves and tragedies, my good and bad moments, my quiet moments and the intense pain of loss. There are plenty of nooks and corners around here to hide baggage.'

'Tell me about Carrie.'

Ella smiled. 'You know the worst? People avoid even saying her name, thinking because she was only a mite she was insignificant, had no time to leave her mark.' Slowly, she pulled a small leather wallet from her pocket. 'We didn't get a chance for many photographs in those days. A cousin from Cork snapped the two of us on the front steps of Roscarbury. Pretty as a picture, she was, in that lemon dress and little coat, her best outfit.'

She handed the wallet to Debbie. A small black and white photo of a mother sitting and her little one beside her, pointing at the camera, was pressed behind thick plastic. They were both laughing.

'You look so happy.'

Ella sighed. 'We all were back then. Roscarbury Hall was a happy place to be. John, my cousin in Cork, sent me that picture after the accident. Would you believe she was wearing that same outfit the day she died? When I dressed her that morning, I thought the whole town will be looking at her, she is so bonny.'

Ella stopped to tip more Baileys into her china cup.

'There is nothing worse than losing a child: the touch, the smell, the trust embodied in the hand that slips into yours, holds tight on your finger, the tender touch that will never be replicated, the tinkle of the laugh. I was never just Ella O'Callaghan after that. I was poor Ella who lost her baby. People tried to help me by being normal, not talking about Carrie, but it left me even more isolated. Eventually, I played it their way; I did not talk about her either, and I took part in life not because I wanted to but because it was expected of me. You see, I am not like Roberta. She does not give a goddamn what people think; I worry all the time.'

They could hear Iris clearing off the outside tables and stacking the chairs in a side porch so they did not get wet overnight.

Decades had passed, but time did not matter. The pain of loss abated, but the intensity, when stirred, remained the same. She felt the heaviness of Carrie's lifeless body, her eyes still open but unseeing, her arms and legs dangling as Michael Hannigan held her, her head thrown back, forever to look upwards. It had happened as quickly as it takes a cat to race across the avenue, the water to fill up the rill after a storm of rain, or a thrush to smash a snail shell.

They told her later she came running, calling out like a madwoman. Roberta rushed to her, babbling, trying to explain, to apologise, but Ella pushed her out of the way.

Carrie looked cold and wet; her blonde curls were straightened and heavy with sea water, her outfit sodden and lumpy.

'I suppose you know all about it,' Ella said.

'Iris may have alluded to something,' said Debbie.

'That is when Roberta stopped talking to me. We have never really moved beyond it. That is a story for another time.'

Debbie made to refill the china cup, but Ella put out her hand to stop her.

'I have had more than enough.' Ella stared at Debbie. 'I see it in your eyes at times: the loneliness of losing somebody you loved, the loneliness of not understanding.'

'I didn't know it showed so much.'

'You are in the club, Debbie; only members can recognise each other.'

'My mother . . . she went missing. . . . She came home, but died.'

'Dear Lord in heaven. What age were you?'

'Eight, almost nine.'

'You poor thing. To lose a mother at any time is so hard; to lose her when you were still so young, and in that way, must be torture.'

Pain consumed Debbie's body, so that she buckled. Ella reached to her.

'Don't go back to the States just yet.'

'Ella, I have to go.'

'Give us time to think. There must be something else we can do.'

'I don't know if I want to do any more.'

Ella patted her on the head. 'Have a bath and sleep on it.'

Debbie sank down onto her bed. A sick exhaustion was creeping through her. Flashes of her mother's funeral were running through her head. . . . Even when she really tried, she could not remember her mother dying: only that she came back and then she was in the coffin.

There were a lot of discussions as to whether Debbie should be allowed to attend the funeral, but Rob was firm.

'Of course she has to be there. Debbie, more than anyone, needs to say a proper goodbye.'

Agnes, she was told, was dressed in the blue taffeta suit she had made for the flower-arranging festival. Debbie saw only the closed wooden casket laden down with flowers. When she was sure nobody was looking, she quietly slipped the gold star, which she had carefully and slowly snipped from her homework notebook, among the white flowers they had sent in her name.

'I got the gold star for you,' she whispered, before she was ushered away.

Ella held herself together until she got to her own room. Collapsing on her bed, bawling, she felt under her pillow for the little black and white cow. Grubby and matted, it had been coarsened by decades of dried-in dirt. Carrie had liked to stuff it under her chin and chew the ears. They had only been gone a few minutes when Ella saw it on the ground by the fountain. Scooping it up, she ran down the rhododendron side path, the shortcut to the gates.

She got there first and was behind the large elm tree, leaning to catch her breath, when she heard the pram wheels on the stony avenue. Michael Hannigan was walking fast, as if he was upset; Roberta was trying to keep up. He slowed down at the gates and she put her hand on his shoulder, asking if he was all right. Shrugging, he smiled and reached out, running his hand down her cheek. Ella, the cuddly cow tight in her hand, felt a coldness creep over her heart. She could not see her husband's face, but she took in Roberta's shy smile, the softness in her eyes.

Punching her pillow, Ella cursed over and over she had not stepped from behind the tree to confront them. Carrie saw her and waved bye-bye, but Michael Hannigan, caught up in his own grumpiness, did not even notice. Letting the cuddly cow slip from her hands, Ella stumbled back to the house. She started baking, the flour dropping between her fingers bringing calm thoughts and clear thinking on the next step she must take.

When there was a quiet and hesitant knock on the door, she had considered not answering, but the young lad rapped next on the window, gesticulating extravagantly.

'What is wrong with you, Sean McHenry?'

'Mrs Hearty in the post office sent me. You had better come quick. There has been an accident.'

'What?' A shadow blurred her eyes and cold seeped through her. Leaning against the door, she barely heard the words he said next.

'It is the child. They are trying to get her. She fell in the water.'

She took off her apron, folded it and left it on the dresser, checking the oven was off before getting into the car. Young McHenry did not say another word, but he drove too fast, beeping cars out of his way on the Main Street. When she saw the crowd gather at the mouth of the harbour, she could not stay sitting.

'Stop the car,' she shouted, opening the door and jumping out even before it had finally come to a halt.

Later, they spoke of how she came thundering, screaming her daughter's name, falling to her knees beside her, afraid at first to touch her cold, soaking-wet body.

Ella remembered the cold and the way her hands shook as she reached across to the pudgy cheeks and the mouth, covering her girl in kisses, pleading with her to wake up for Mummy. She was so still, showing what the older child may have resembled.

Pain seared through her, and anger: a torrent of anger. Michael Hannigan blubbered, falling on his knees, begging forgiveness. She told him to be quiet as the crowd moved back to make space for the ambulance. When he tried to get in the ambulance, she pushed him back. That night she lay beside her daughter in the morgue, to keep her warm, before a taxi came to bring her home.

Roscarbury Hall was in darkness, the life sucked from it.

When she walked into the kitchen, her husband was waiting, his head in his hands.

'Will you ever forgive me?'

'You will have to ask God to forgive you.'

'The wind came all of a sudden. I tried to catch the pram. I just missed it.'

'Why didn't you have your hands on the pram, and it so near the water? Tell me that!'

She was shouting, kicking a chair out of the way, fisting the table in front of him.

'I, I don't know.'

'You do know. You do know, you coward; you must know.' She reached over and slapped him hard. He did nothing to defend himself. 'You bastard, tell me the truth. I deserve it.'

When he got up and walked across the room, she thought he was leaving, but he was putting space between the two of them.

'I was kissing Roberta.'

She barely heard him.

'We were kissing: just a small kiss. My hand was off the pram for a second, just a second.'

Ella slumped into a chair, staring at her husband as if he were a stranger who had intruded into her kitchen.

'I saw it straight away. I just missed the handle. Carrie thought it was fun.'

Ella rose up. 'Is that supposed to give me any comfort: my baby daughter was laughing on the way to her death?'

'No. I didn't mean it like that.'

Ella stood up. Her voice was flat. 'Make yourself respectable to receive the coffin tomorrow. I don't want you falling apart on me. You will not let me down again.'

She climbed the stairs slowly to her sister's room. Roberta, her eyes raw red from crying, let out a yelp when she saw her sister.

'Ella, I am so sorry.'

Ella heard the fear in her voice, saw the tearful trembling, the shoulders convulsing in shivers. She reached out with her hand and she saw Roberta relax a little.

In a sharp, quick movement, she raised her hand high, bringing it down across her sister's face. Stunned, knocked back in pain, Roberta shouted, but her words were lost in the spitting rage of her sister.

'Don't even look at my husband again.'

Roberta stumbled back into the room, her face throbbing. 'Hit me; do anything you like. Nothing matters.'

'Shut up with the self-pity: if you had not been batting your stupid eyelids at a married man, my daughter would not be in the morgue now. Cold, lifeless and alone; there is nothing left of Carrie; the sea water has soaked it away.'

Roberta attempted to rally, put her hands out as if seeking calm. 'Michael Hannigan is no innocent in all of this . . .'

Ella lunged forward, this time catching Roberta by the hair and tugging so hard some came away in her hands. Beating the hair from her hands as if it was loose dirt, Ella stepped further into the bedroom.

'Stay away from my husband, you interfering bitch. I will let you stay in the house, I have to, but I do not want to hear your voice ever again.'

Roberta made to speak, but Ella raised her finger to her lips.

'Not a word: ever.'

Ella could say no more, so she left and moved her clothes from the bedroom she shared with Michael Hannigan to the front room, where she settled into the single bed, but not to sleep, the dark waves of emptiness pressing on her until morning.

Roberta stayed away from Ella the rest of that night, only appearing the next day as the undertaker arrived with the coffin.

'Tell her she is not wanted here,' Ella snapped at her husband, and he did.

Roberta sank to the back of the crowd gathering outside the front door, tears chiselling a channel through her face.

Several weeks went by at Roscarbury Hall, but not even the change from spring to summer could change the mood in the big grey house. Roberta took to buying her own provisions and labelling them. She spent the afternoons sipping cheap sherry. Ella and Michael Hannigan sat together but did not speak; it was an uneasy silence they both grew accustomed to.

Two weeks in, Roberta knocked on Ella's bedroom door and handed her a small box wrapped in black tissue paper. Ella ignored her, moving away to the window, watching the rain shower sweep across the parkland, not looking around until she heard Roberta put the box on the dressing table before leaving the room.

She had not looked at it since that day. An urge to locate it, where she had carefully stored it in the attic playroom on the top floor, came over her.

The knob of the playroom door was stiff; she had to twist it hard for it to give way. The room was gloomy and smelled musty and stale. Thick cobwebs ran across the ceiling and down the walls in a wavy pattern, accentuated by the fading light of the evening. Rita, the old Crolly Doll, watched Ella, as she tiptoed across the room to the shelves in the fireplace alcove. A mouse skipped behind an old Meccano set when she stretched in for the red leather musical box. Gently sweeping away the heavy dust and mouse droppings, Ella opened the clasp. The lid creaked and the musical box, which had once played 'Twinkle Twinkle Little Star,' was silent as Ella picked out a small black box.

She slipped it into her pocket and left the room, stopping to pick up an old fire engine from the floor and put it on a shelf.

Back in her room, she pulled the box from its packaging. She did not read the gift tag, which said, 'To Ella. With profound apologies and sorrow. All my love, Roberta.'

Inside lay a Weiss pinwheel brooch, each spoke covered in black rhinestones, their glittering darkness reflecting the heaviness inside her, each spoke like a dagger that was aimed at her heart by her sister and Michael Hannigan. She still could not forgive them for what they had done.

A blackness enveloped her, as dark and deep as the stones on the brooch. She lay down on her bed, staring at the wall, the floral wallpaper dancing in front of her.

She must have slept, because when she woke it was dark and the house was quiet. Her head ached, but her mind was clear. She took the pinwheel brooch and walked over to the window, pulling her cardigan around her against the night chill. Opening the window, she threw the brooch with as much force as she could muster. It must have landed in the rhododendron, because she heard a faint swish of the broad, shiny leaves as they bounced the brooch to earth.

Twenty

Debbie was already in the kitchen eating breakfast when Ella made it downstairs the next morning.

'You look as if you need a strong coffee. My dad swore by it after a bad night.'

'Did he drink?'

'There were bad nights, I guess, when he couldn't get my mother out of his head.'

'I think I will have that coffee after all.'

Ella took out her mixing bowl and took down the self-raising flour.

'I have booked the flight.'

Ella, who had been tying up her apron strings, stopped, her hands suspended behind her back.

'Maybe we could go to see Sister Consuelo first.'

'I don't want to, Ella. I had a long think about it last night. I want to end the search. It's time to concentrate on what's next.'

She pushed a mug towards Ella.

'I don't feel up to the coffee. It is a waste after you went to the bother to make it.' Ella shovelled her hand into the bag of flour and took out a huge scoop. She let some of the flour drift over her fingers as she watched it slip into the baking bowl.

Debbie switched on the ovens; the low humming sound filled the kitchen.

'I was thinking of a different cake for every day of the week.'

'You should have an Internet presence.'

'What we are doing is more than enough.'

'Do you know that many cake recipes?'

'Variations on a theme, I suppose.'

'I've upset you. I didn't mean to.'

Ella would have told her she had not, but Iris burst in the back door, letting a cold breeze whip at the tablecloth and around their ankles.

'Ella, I have to go. The solicitor rang. He gets the impression that bastard husband of mine is going to give in, so I have to hightail it to Gorey.'

'But it is likely to be busy this morning.'

'I have to go, Ella; I have got to get him to agree to a settlement before he changes his mind. Seemingly he has hammered out something with his brother and the bank. I could get my house back.'

'But—'

'Ella, you might be getting rid of me. Don't tell me you don't want that.'

Ella smiled. 'Give it a few days and it will be just myself and the quiet sister again,' she said tightly, standing up and reaching for the white bag of sugar.

Iris did not answer but ran off to change into her good clothes. Debbie went out the front to set the outside tables. She was hauling two chairs at a time across the grass, wet with dew, when her phone rang.

'Miss Kading, it is Mother Assumpta from the Order of Divine Sisters, Ballygally Convent. I hope I am not disturbing you.'

'No, not at all.'

'Miss Kading, I know how pressing your situation is and I wonder could we meet in private. Would tomorrow suit?'

'I suppose so.'

'Two p.m. If you don't mind, could we meet somewhere other than the convent? I was thinking maybe the Valley Hotel on the N11.'

'That sounds good.'

Ella was standing at the front door, beckoning to her.

Debbie put away her phone. For the moment she wanted to keep the meeting to herself; she was not ready to have the reason why Assumpta wanted to meet picked over and analysed. Ella's fussy nattering gave her the perfect excuse not to tell her.

'Is there something wrong? We are way behind this morning. I don't know what has got into us all. It is lemon and poppy seed cakes today. I am sure Muriel will have plenty to say about it when the seeds get stuck in her dentures. Will you set up the coffee machine and set the tables upstairs?' Ella whipped inside to pull her cakes out of the oven before Debbie had time to answer.

For the next two hours, each was busy with the chores that had to be completed before opening. The smell of baking wafted through the house and the coffee machine gurgled, so that when the first customers came the Ballroom Café was functioning normally. Roberta came to the door twice and peered in as if looking for somebody, but she said nothing to Debbie. When she came across Ella in the front drawing room, where she had retired to sit and compose herself for ten minutes before the café opened, she walked across and handed her a note.

I have arranged for the sale of the Roscarbury Hall painting. A man will come to collect it today. Maybe then you will stop this nonsense and close down the tearoom. R.

Ella felt like laughing, but she knew if she did she would also start to cry and there would be no stopping her. Roberta was at the door when Ella caught up with her and stuffed a hastily scribbled reply in her hand.

Don't you think I have thought of all these things? The painting is only worth a few hundred, if that. Tell the valuer not to waste his time and petrol; the café brings in more in a day than that painting will ever be worth. E.

Roberta did not bother to answer but walked out front, where Gerry O'Hare was waiting to drive her to Molloy's.

Ella was rather glad the painting was not worth a great deal. She was probably the only person in the world who liked the heavy oil on canvas, but that was because she did not see the sad darkness of Roscarbury Hall and the sheets of grey rain but the story behind it.

The artist had struck a deal with Great Aunt Becky where he would have food and lodging for as long as it took him to complete the painting. Rebecca O'Callaghan had reckoned on a week, or possibly two, but when it ran to two months, she stood over the artist, forcing him to finish the canvas before she threw him out. That was why some of the finer architectural details were missing on one side of the house and several of the shrubbery did not appear on the canvas at all.

Rebecca despaired that the house in the painting would never be as grand as the one she lived in. She was also very angry, because in a fit of pique the artist had coloured in sheets of grey rain, which gave the scene a cold, foreboding look.

Ella's mother threatened to throw the painting on the fire countless times, but John O'Callaghan was having none of it. He consented to its removal from the drawing room but kept it safe in sight of his reading chair in the library. It was a dull Roscarbury scene with the charcoal-grey house, which looked sad and neglected. Ella liked to have it in the Ballroom Café, though nobody seemed much taken by it.

Ella saw a gaggle of young girls come up the driveway and she made her way to the café.

'There is a right lot coming in now. I don't want them crowding up the tables at the windows; it will put off the older set.'

'Aren't you happy that the Ballroom Café is regarded as rather cool?' Debbie laughed.

Ella grimaced. 'I just never imagined that lot coming here. I hope they don't break the china. Loud, and no life experience. I would have thought Molloy's was more their thing.' She stopped, because she heard them screeching and laughing, thundering up the stairs. 'I suppose they help towards keeping the bank manager happy,' she said.

A girl swung in the café door but stopped short when she saw Ella.

'Come in, dears; we have only just opened up,' Ella said, smiling sweetly. The girls trooped in, taking over three tables, dumping their bags around them, their mobile phones taking up most of the spare space on the tables.

'You've changed your attitude,' Debbie said, digging Ella in the ribs.

'Money is money. Now, don't keep the customers waiting,' Ella muttered, pulling a severe face. She watched as Debbie took their orders, the girls giggling and pointing to various ornaments and bits and pieces, texting as they conversed, happy in their worlds, where nothing threw them. She felt a well of envy that she had never felt that way.

Muriel Hearty spilled into the room, her face red with excitement. 'It is about Fergus Brown.'

'What is wrong?' Ella shook her head and shoulders to compose herself and began to cut some lemon cake.

'Fergus Brown's wife has died. Fell down the stairs. Something about thinking she was on a cruise ship and dancing along the deck.'

Ella stopped, the knife suspended over the plate. 'This is terrible for poor Fergus.'

'Of course, but at least now he can begin to enjoy life. This is the best bit. He is a millionaire several times over. Now, won't he be a good catch?' she said, pulling a face at Debbie.

'May God forgive you, Muriel Hearty! That is no way to be talking. The man loved his wife and is no doubt heartbroken. Do you know the funeral arrangements?'

'Burial after eleven o'clock Mass on Wednesday,' Muriel answered, without looking at Ella.

Ella felt a weakness come over her. Fergus Brown had loved his wife; she could not bear to think of him so sad, so alone. She waited until the women from Mass had been catered for before asking Debbie to keep an eye on things.

Ella sat down at the kitchen table. When Fergus had held her hand, she felt a warmth course through her, the sound of his voice reassuring. For a while, something had been possible. The sunlight squinted into her eyes and she got up and fussed about tidying the worktop.

Ella thought the gossips were proving to be right: the O'Callaghans were bad luck. It was Muriel Hearty who had blurted it out a long time ago, tried to make light of it. It hung in the air between them, like washing on the line, heavy and cold on a day without a breeze.

'You girls seem to grow it, don't you?'

'Whatever do you mean?'

'Tragedy, loss . . .' Muriel Hearty shifted in her seat.

'We have had our fair share, if that is what you mean.'

'It is not me, it's others saying. I don't take much notice of it.'

'Good.'

Ella remembered Muriel's discomfort and she smiled at how she had concentrated on buttoning up her sheepskin coat so that when she walked, she waddled, tight and stiff, like a toy soldier.

By the time she got back to the café, the rush was over and Debbie was sitting by one of the windows.

'Are you ready to kill me?'

'No, Ella, I figured you were upset about Fergus Brown.'

'I am going to call on the house; I feel I should. I can close up the café if you like; we have probably got everything we are going to get today anyway.'

Debbie stretched out her feet in front of her. 'Chuck and May are due in soon. I don't mind holding the fort.'

Ella ran her hand lightly over Debbie's hair. 'You are a star. I honestly don't know what I am going to do without you.'

Debbie looked out the window. 'I think I'm going to miss this place an awful lot.'

★

Ella wore her black wool coat and purple scarf. A young man who looked like Fergus opened the door, his eyes red from crying.

'I am sorry, we are keeping the house private,' he said quietly.

Ella felt a flush of embarrassment rise up her neck. 'I am so sorry; I had no idea. I am only here to pass on my sincere sympathy.'

The man looked uncomfortable. 'Do you know my father?'

'Yes, and I knew your mother a long time ago.'

The man, who was wearing jeans and a sweatshirt, stepped out onto the street. 'I don't mean to be rude. It is just my father is so overcome with grief. He can't talk to anybody. This has been such a terrible shock. He found her at the bottom of the stairs when he came back from his early-morning walk. She usually slept until after nine, you see.'

Ella put a reassuring hand on the man's shoulder. 'Tell him Ella O'Callaghan called. Will you?'

He nodded, retreating quickly, closing the door gently.

Twenty-One

Debbie was early, so she sat where she could watch the door for Assumpta. Outside, a woman called to her young daughter to follow and the little girl tumbled after her mother, her little face anxious lest she lose her in this strange place.

Debbie remembered she had liked to swing on the gate as a young girl. The kitchen clock ticked out Mommy's name; the fridge gurgled in the kitchen; the oven stayed cold. In the sitting room, Agnes's sewing machine was covered, as if she were away on holiday. The sunshine streamed through in the same spots, but lacked warmth. Sometimes Debbie wet her pants because she could not hold any longer and she could not face struggling up the stairs, waiting for her heart to tighten as she passed the second landing. Sometimes she peed at the back of the potting shed, but she was always afraid Helena Long, the nosey next-door neighbour on the right, might spy her.

Sometimes she wished she had been knocked down by a car on the run home from school that day or that Gainsborough's wicked dog had got over the fence and savaged her. Then she would not know her mother had come back not to be with her family but to die.

Mommy was back two full days. She slept a lot and the doctor came. Debbie did not get to talk to her; every time she lingered at the bedroom door, she was ushered away. But that morning, Agnes got up. It was almost a normal morning. Debbie only wanted to remember that morning, when she had left for school with a warm, fuzzy feeling, that maybe Agnes loved her.

When she got downstairs, Agnes had a stack of blueberry pancakes and maple syrup ready.

'Eat up, darling; you don't want to be late,' she said, and kissed her daughter on the top of her head.

As she stuffed her mouth, she saw her mother watch her and she grinned a happy grin. Agnes sat down opposite with her muffin and tea.

'We never go to the playground any more,' Agnes said, pushing her fingers into the muffin on her plate.

In her eagerness to please, Debbie did not think to wonder why Agnes was mashing the muffin with her fingers, flickers of agitation crossing her eyes.

'Maybe we can go after school?'

Agnes guffawed loudly. 'Not today,' she said, getting up to get the lunch bag ready. 'You make sure you do well in your spelling test, sweetheart. We can't be the only people on the street who don't have a 100 percent score on the refrigerator door.'

They did not say much more to each other, until it was time for Debbie to leave.

'Bring home a gold star, darling. Make me proud,' Agnes said, kneeling down beside her daughter to fix her cardigan and straighten her skirt. When Debbie gave her a hug, Agnes laughed.

Debbie could still feel the warmth that rippled through her, when she heard her mother laugh and Agnes told her she loved her.

'I promise I will get a gold star and run all the way home with it to you.'

Agnes hugged her tight. 'Do that, darling. Have a good day.'

Her mother did not step out on to the veranda to wave, but Debbie did not mind and walked down the street, practising her ten spellings over and over in her head, to make sure she would bring a gold star home to Mommy.

She recited the ten spellings now, one after another, swinging the gate in rhythm with the rhyme so that the old hinges squeaked loudly.

★

Debbie, fiddling with the fronds of her silk scarf, saw Mother Assumpta glide towards her, and she stood up, not sure if she should extend her hand in greeting.

'Miss Kading, I hope you are well today. I am sorry about the secrecy. I wanted this to be a private meeting between the two of us. Off the record, so to speak.'

'Is there something further you can tell me?'

Mother Assumpta eased herself in to a velvet armchair and arranged her skirt carefully around her knees. 'I hope you do not think any the less of us, as a result of your experiences in trying to track down your birth mother.'

Debbie did not answer.

'I may have been a bit harsh previously, but you have to understand I was going on what I saw in the record book. I had no idea of and do not condone the practices of the past.'

She paused, hoping the other woman would talk, but was forced to continue as Debbie stayed silent.

'I have spoken to Consuelo and she has given me your file.'

Debbie edged out on her seat. 'Can I see it?'

'I can't of course show it to you, but if I were to read parts of it aloud, it would not be my fault if you were to hear the information you are looking for.'

Solemnly, she opened the file and read out the names and addresses and income of Rob and Agnes Kading. When she came to the details for the birth mother, she read the name slowly and deliberately: 'Mary Murtagh, with an address at Bridge Street, Rathsorney, Co. Wicklow. Aged nineteen.'

Debbie's head began to whirl; she could only see a wave of colour swirling in front of her. The back of her neck hurt like hell and her brain felt like it was swelling.

'That is her name?'

'Yes, it is.'

'Why was it not in the book when I inspected it?'

'I don't know.'

'When can I meet her?'

'What I am about to tell you may be difficult to hear, but your mother has not made contact and I understand the Murtaghs moved from the area soon after the birth.'

Debbie pushed her head into her hands and attempted to breathe deeply. Pain shot through her and she felt suddenly weary. 'Why couldn't you have told me this before?'

'I did not know any of it.' Assumpta reached to take Debbie's hand, but was forced to retract when Debbie shrank back, the tears spilling down her face.

'How do you know all this now?'

'I have spoken to Sister Consuelo.'

'Could I talk to her?

'She is not well. It is not possible.'

Debbie swiped her hand across her cheeks.

They sat, neither knowing what to say next, until Assumpta pulled herself out of the armchair. 'My car has arrived. Can I offer you a lift anywhere?'

Debbie shook her head.

'Goodbye, Miss Kading. We will pray for you.'

Debbie nodded, not bothering to stand up.

She wanted to throw up. Her mouth watered and she cupped her hands in case she had to vomit. She saw Assumpta chatting lightly to a woman on the front steps, laughing heartily, before she made her way to the taxi.

Mary Murtagh: it was a simple name.

Her head was heavy with pain, so she closed her eyes. She should be rushing off, trying to trace the Murtaghs, but she felt exhausted. There was only one certainty: she would never know Mary Murtagh as a young woman or Agnes as an older woman.

Agnes floated by. It was Friday: the day to test drive her latest outfit. At the start of each week, Agnes set herself a challenge. Chairs were pushed back in the sitting room, a Butterick tissue pattern pinned down on fabric and a shape cut out with thick, heavy shears. Agnes would hide herself away, pumping the foot pedal of the machine and stitching into the night. By Friday she was usually finished, so she paraded around the garden and sat on the porch, to break the dress in, she said, before she wrapped it in plastic and placed it in the wardrobe with all the other dresses, stitched in a desperate attempt to keep busy.

Debbie loved to be among the outfits her mother had

carefully created. Often, when Rob was asleep on the rocking chair, she stole to the spare room and rummaged through the plastic covers, breathing in the sweet smell and style of Agnes and marvelling at the frills, flounces, satin and silk details that her mother had laboured over. If she had a bad day, she would disappear for hours, wedging herself into the wardrobe so that Agnes enveloped her, the soft caresses of the flouncy summer dresses like comforting kisses on her cheeks, the heavy brocade jackets holding and supporting her.

She never tried on the dresses, never wanting to upset the careful arrangement and symmetry of a dead woman's wardrobe. As she got older, she did not need the comfort of visits to the wardrobe so much, until one day when she was somewhere around fifteen years old and Johnny Thompson had been a nasty bully to her. When she got home she bolted upstairs, but when she pulled open the wardrobe doors, it was empty.

'Daddy, where are all of Mommy's dresses?'

'What dresses?'

'In the spare-room wardrobe.'

'Oh, that old stuff, I threw that out ages ago. No point giving it to a thrift store; nobody would wear it,' Rob said.

He did not even take his eyes from the newspaper he was reading.

★

Iris moved out late in the evening and within hours of securing her house keys.

'I am going to take a few days, Ella, to straighten the place out,' she said, as she piled the last of her stuff into a taxi.

'What about the café? Debbie is leaving, you know.'

Iris swung around. 'I will be back before she goes, just a few days. I need to do this, Ella.'

Debbie came out on the front steps to wave goodbye to Iris.

'You are all leaving me.'

'At least Iris got what she wanted.'

'Stay longer, Debbie? We will look after you here.'

'All the arrangements are made, Ella.'

'Is there any way of persuading you?'

Debbie put her arm around Ella. 'Do you fancy a Baileys?'

Ella smiled and they linked arms as they walked to the drawing room together. She took down her mother's Waterford Crystal glasses, while Debbie nipped upstairs for the bottle; she wiped the insides of the rims lightly with her skirt.

'You should start serving lunches as well as tea and cakes,' Debbie said, skipping back into the room.

'Well, if you stick around I might have a stab at it. Iris's heavy hands are only good for gardening.'

'I have to go, Ella.'

'I know. I just wish it were different.'

'Don't you think I wish that too? That I was not going to die, that Agnes and Rob were not dead, that somebody knew where my mother Mary Murtagh moved? For all we know, she was in the States all along.'

'Mary Murtagh?'

'That was my mother's name; the family moved away soon after she had me. Assumpta finally told me.'

'Mother Assumpta? When did this happen? Were you ever going to tell me?'

'I was waiting for the right moment, I suppose. She only told me yesterday.'

'At least I know before Muriel Hearty,' Ella sighed.

'Ella, you've been so good to me; of course I was going to tell you, but I'm still trying to take it all in myself.'

Ella put down her glass and walked over to put her arm on Debbie's shoulder. 'Don't mind me; I am a selfish, jealous old cow.'

'There is not much to tell, Ella.'

'Did they live in Rathsorney itself?'

'Bridge Street.'

'There was a lot of chopping and changing in those houses over the years.'

'It's not the ending I hoped for,' Debbie said quietly.

'I know,' Ella replied.

They sat in the big fireside chairs sipping their drinks, not needing to say more. Ella refused a top-up.

'I am up extra early on account of Iris being away.'

Ella pulled herself out of the chair; Debbie followed her up the stairs, afraid to be left on the dark staircase on her own.

Twenty-Two

Ella was cleaning out the coffee machine the next morning when Chuck Winters rushed up the avenue.

'What brings you so early, Mr Winters?' Ella said, taking in his red cheeks and his coat flying open.

Unable to catch his breath at first, Chuck stood in the middle of the café, panting like an old dog after chasing a rabbit. 'Forgive the intrusion, Miss O'Callaghan, but is Debbie here by any chance?'

'She is having a cuppa in the kitchen, before the rush starts.'

'I will wait for her.'

He took a seat at a window table, drumming his fingers as he kept his eye on the door.

'Do you want me to call her?'

'No, no need.'

'Would you like your coffee while you wait?'

Slightly agitated, Chuck nodded. When he heard Debbie on the stairs, he jumped to his feet. 'Miss Kading, I have come with important news.'

Debbie, who was tying her hair up in a chignon, smiled at Chuck. 'And before Muriel. Not many people manage that.'

'Is there somewhere we can talk in private?'

Ella came out from behind the counter. 'There is nobody due for another twenty minutes at least. Why don't you go to one of the window tables?'

When Chuck hesitated, Ella added, 'I have more to be doing than eavesdropping on your conversation, Mr Winters.'

Embarrassed, Chuck protested that the thought never crossed his mind, but he picked the table furthest away from the counter and kitchen.

'My apology for the secrecy, Miss Kading. A friend of mine who is close to the inquiry has given me some valuable information.'

'About me?'

Chuck dropped his voice. 'I think you will find it important.'

Debbie looked over at Ella, who was making a big deal of polishing the glass on the old painting.

'What is it?'

This time he edged his chair a little closer, so that his back was turned to Ella. 'My source informs me that a woman has come forward with important information.' He paused for effect. 'The woman, who worked in County General Hospital, says women at the hospital as well as the orphanage were told their babies had died when in fact they were smuggled away for adoption by American couples.'

Debbie sat back. 'Are you saying my mother thought I was dead all along?'

'I don't know, Miss Kading, only that they are going back on the records over a fifteen-year period, 1954 to 1969, and that the Little Angels plot at the orphanage, where all those babies were buried, is to be dug up.'

'Mr Winters, I'm not sure this concerns me.'

Ella's stomach began to churn. She rushed downstairs to gasp in some air, while pretending to check on the outside tables. Muriel Hearty was pounding up the avenue.

'They have cordoned off the convent. The word is they are going to dig up the graves,' she said, her face flushed with excitement.

'I know.'

'How do you know?'

'I have my sources, Muriel.'

'Tell us what it is all about then. Has this got something to do with Debbie?'

Debbie appeared in the doorway. 'I know nothing about it.'

Muriel looked disappointed.

'I should be there. I am sorry Ella, but I don't think I could face coffee and cakes, knowing the little graves of those poor babies are being dug up,' said Muriel.

Ella waved off Muriel, shutting and locking the gate before quickly propping up the closed sign in case anybody came looking for a café. Her head thumped. What would they find when they broke the compacted earth holding those little remains? There were a lot of women who would not sleep a wink until this whole mess was sorted. She could not bear them all talking about it non-stop, as if it were some big scandal instead of the tragedy it was stirring up to become. She wrapped plates of cake in tin foil. If she plopped on enough cream tomorrow, nobody would notice the cake was a day old.

She laid out her best navy coat and matching scarf on the

bed for Margaret Brown's funeral. Opening her big silver box, she picked out the Weiss silver and blue starburst brooch and pinned it to her lapel. She liked that it blended in with her coat, silver rays moving out from one central blue stone. Little blue stones trimmed the edge, aurora borealis stones wedged between the rays.

She set off early, walking into town and to the church at the far side. She sat halfway down the aisle.

Flanked by his son and daughter, Fergus looked frail. In a suit and a long black coat she did not know, he looked every inch the gentleman.

They must have complemented each other well at one time, Fergus and Margaret, she thought, and she felt a pang of jealousy rise inside her. When it came to her turn to sympathise, Fergus kissed her on the cheek, which made her feel both happy and embarrassed. She was in no doubt that that particular peck on the cheek would be ruminated on when the ladies of Rathsorney had time.

'Ella, it was so good of you to call at the house. I am so sorry Michael here turned you away.'

'Fergus, I am so dreadfully sorry about Margaret.'

She saw a tear slip from him and he clenched her hand tighter.

'We are going to bring her home, to bury her with our eldest son, Miles. I am going to stay in Dublin with my daughter after the funeral.'

'You do the right thing, Fergus,' she said and gripped his hand a little tighter.

By the time Ella got home, Roberta had placed two notes in different colours on the hall table.

That American has started big trouble, and whether we like it or not it will catch us in its net, thanks to you. R.

Don't think Fergus Brown is going to put his feet under our kitchen table. I won't have it. R.

Ella did not have the energy to throw them away, so she ripped them up, leaving the pieces on the hall table, before rushing upstairs to look at the news.

'The dig was ordered after a midwife in County General Hospital, Wicklow, between 1954 and 1969 came forward with information. It is claimed that in some cases women were told their babies had died when in fact the babies were taken away for adoption without the knowledge or consent of their mothers. Gardaí are also waiting to interview a nun who was in charge of the home for unmarried mothers at the time.

'A spokesperson said records are being examined and each woman involved will be contacted in the next few days and kept informed with developments . . .'

Ella switched off the television. Not wanting to go to sleep, she went back to the café and sat in the window seat, watching the moonlight travel across the sea. When they were young, she and Roberta used to steal into the ballroom and pretend to have grand evenings, dancing, sitting and chatting until, almost asleep, they sneaked back to their beds. Sometimes they saw their father's car turn up the avenue, the lights beaming across the room as if searching for them. They belly-flopped like soldiers.

Those were the happiest days, when the sisters had no secrets. They formed the Ballroom Club and swore allegiance to Roscarbury. Roberta cut both their hands and they pledged their faith to each other in blood. Bernie O'Callaghan had later seen the cuts and got so angry at the girls she slapped them three times each on their bottoms.

Debbie stuck her head around the door. 'Do you want anything before I go to bed, Ella?'

'No, dear, you sleep well.'

Debbie dithered at the door. 'I don't think I could imagine it: finding out the baby you thought was dead is alive.'

Ella did not answer. She felt a twinge of pain up her arm, so she sat a little longer in the café.

What if they came looking for her? What if her baby was not dead? How could she have believed them? What did he look like now? A chap with strange clothes and a hairstyle she did not like, no doubt. Would she speak to him?

Would she feel anything for him? God, she hoped they came looking for her, because even in the middle of the tragedy of it all, wouldn't it be amazing to meet her son? She was afraid to feel excited; the awfulness of it clouded her head, pushing in on top of her. She traipsed up to bed, though she knew she would not sleep.

She had wanted him so much: a reprieve from grief after losing Carrie. She could remember every detail, except him; she was never allowed to even look in his face, never allowed to hold him, marvel at him. She did not know his smell. She had turned to the wall, back in County General Hospital.

Sweat lathered her face, sweeping across her eyes, blinding her, so she could make out ridges of grey. She reached out; her hands were brushed aside, like she was a madwoman in a crowd.

'I want to hold my baby,' she shouted. Nobody listened.

Sister Consuelo told her to hush, that it was all over. Pain pressed down on her. She heard them clicking with their tongues, as if she were creating an unnecessary fuss. She asked again, stretching her fingers to try to reach her baby; they ignored her. Attempting to sit up, she was pushed back roughly.

'Leave it. It is for the best,' Sister Consuelo snapped in her ear, her breath hot and short.

Her arm was held rigid; a fog blanketed her; ghosts hovered over her. Her head was heavy, her neck thick with pain; she could not lift her hands, could not talk. She sank away into a river of tears.

Sister Consuelo's snoring woke her up. The nun, her head on her chest, her arms folded over her bosom, was slumped like an old sack of flour on the pantry floor. Scanning the room, she searched for the cot. She tugged the nun's starched uniform hard.

'The baby? Where is my baby?'

Consuelo massaged her eyes slowly with her knuckles. 'Dead. We tried everything.'

'I heard it cry.'

Consuelo stood up. 'Only that breath. Go back to sleep.'

'A boy or a girl?'

'Does it matter? A dead baby is a dead baby.'

She tried to sit up, get out of bed, find her baby, but was gripped by the shoulders as Consuelo rang the bell.

'The most unlikely ones cause trouble. She needs to quieten down,' she said as she pressed her weight onto her chest. Someone gave her an injection. She stayed drugged in a heavy sleep.

On the third day, Consuelo, anxious to have the room for the next admission, marched in and pulled back the curtains so that the spring sunshine needled Ella's eyes.

'You are going home today, dear. Time to get up and get your things together.'

Smelling the sharpness of the starch, she shrank back.

'Now, no point feeling sorry for yourself. It was only a baby.'

'Can I see it, hold it?'

'Don't be so silly. What good would that do you?'

'Was it a boy or a girl?'

'A boy, I think. Don't be worrying yourself; we have taken care of the burial.'

'Can I say a prayer at the grave?'

'And upset yourself and everybody else. You go home and forget about it. It is for the best.'

Ella sat up; she must have fallen asleep. Unfortunately the nightmare which made her clothes wet with sweat was a reality she could never get away from. . . . She was shaking with cold as she fumbled in the dark to switch on the light. She did not even know where he was buried. She hadn't asked, did not think she could. Sister Consuelo had told her to move on. She remembered she had met her six months later and had begun to cry.

'Dear, it is in the past; leave it and move on. You are still a young enough woman to meet a man and marry, have another child. You are one of the lucky ones. What about all those women who have lost the chance to have a baby? Toughen up.'

She had no choice. Everybody told her to move on. She went back to talk to the midwife, to ask about him, but she could not help.

'Miss O'Callaghan, I help deliver a lot of babies; some live and some die. I don't have time to be counting the hairs on their head.'

'I never got to see him. I just wanted to know if he had any hair. My daughter had a soft, golden little thatch.'

'I can't help you.'

She had nothing to hold on to, only the night he was born and died. The starch, the only smell that came back to her, smothering her, blotting out her brain. She dared not think he might be alive; there was too much sorrow stored there, waiting to encompass her. She might as well be baking.

The kitchen was cold and she turned on the ovens first thing to warm up the place, before making a cup of tea. No doubt there would be a right crowd in the café in the morning, looking for clues that she was one of the women waiting for news.

Twenty-Three

Debbie stood outside the small terraced house. Lifting the latch on the front gate gently, she walked to the front door, edging past the rose bushes blistered with rainwater. Junk mail clogged the letterbox; a telephone directory was propped against the doorway. She knocked loudly on the glass panel of the door, but there was no sound from inside.

'Are you looking to rent the place?'

A woman stuck her head over the roses.

'I was looking for the Murtaghs.'

'Never heard of them. The place has been rented for years. Are you sure you have the right house?'

'The Murtaghs are from way back, distant relatives.'

'You should go to Mrs Messitt at Number 22. She has lived here all her life.'

'She won't mind me knocking at the door?'

'I am walking that way anyway. I will do the introductions. Aren't you the woman from the café?'

'Roscarbury Hall.'

Debbie waited while the woman locked her hall door.

'You can't be too careful these days. Time was when we would only lock the door if we were moving out of the county.'

She fussed with her shopping bags as she walked slightly in front of Debbie to the far end of the street.

'How is Ella doing?'

'Just fine.'

'Tell her Martina Cleary was asking after her.' She walked up the neat footpath of Number 22 and knocked loudly. 'You will need to speak up: Betty is a bit deaf.'

A small, thin woman with a shy smile opened the door.

'Betty, this woman is looking for a local historian and I told her you know everything there is about this street and the scandal of all its inhabitants.'

The old woman laughed nervously. 'That's a nice way of saying I was always a busybody.'

Debbie put out her hand and noticed that Betty Messitt, though frail, gave a vise-like grip of welcome. Martina waved goodbye, but neither Debbie nor Betty Messitt seemed to notice.

'I wanted to know about the Murtaghs.'

'Are you family?'

Debbie dithered. 'A distant relative from the States.'

'Welcome, come in. I remember the Murtaghs; they had two good-looking girls. They were always up here trying out the hairstyles. My sister was friendly with them.'

Debbie felt her chest tighten. 'What can you tell me about Mary?'

'There was a Mary and a Frances: Frances was very tall; Mary was younger, a little bit quieter.'

Betty fussed with the kettle and took down her china cups and saucers.

'This is a treat, being able to share a cuppa. Most people these days are too busy to stop for a chat. What relation are you to the Murtaghs?'

Debbie shifted uncomfortably in her velvet seat. She noticed a jug of roses on the table contained the same tea rose as the bush outside Murtaghs.' 'Our mothers were related.'

'They did not live long here, you know. Left in the middle of the night; some said they emigrated, but I heard afterwards they only went as far as Dublin.' She stopped and eyed up Debbie carefully. 'I don't want to say anything untoward.'

'Please, anything at all you tell me would be most helpful.'

Betty poured the tea and fussed over the milk and sugar. 'Let me put it straight. I will be honest with you, if you are honest with me.' As Debbie flustered, she continued. 'I heard you on the radio. Age has not stolen my good sense yet, you know. Do you think Mary Murtagh was your mother?'

Debbie felt her face flush pink. 'I do.'

'Well, you look like her: same long, glossy hair, though she always had it in some elaborate hairstyle. Before they even named it the beehive, Mary Murtagh was styling her hair up on top of her head like that.'

'Did she go to school locally?'

'Not at all; her sister helped out at a hairdresser's in the next town, but Mary stayed at home: the mother was not well, so she looked after her mainly. She had a bit too much time on her hands, that one.'

'What do you mean?'

'She was young and really lovely-looking with a yen for the very short skirts. She used to wear them with very high shoes. My father said he did not know how her parents let her out, wearing clothes like that. There were rumours.'

'What do you mean?'

Betty fiddled with a doily on the table. 'They were only rumours spread by people who had nothing better to do with their time.'

Debbie reached and took the old woman's hand. 'Please, don't spare me.'

'You don't know any of this?'

'None of it.'

Betty reached for a handkerchief as she felt the tears rise inside her. 'You understand I can only tell you what I know and what I heard. I can't distinguish between fact and fiction.'

'It's bad news, isn't it?'

'Straight out: I heard she died, went off her head after the baby was born.'

Debbie's head began to thump. The sitting room, with its patterned wallpaper and carpet, made her feel claustrophobic.

'Will I continue?' Betty asked gently.

'Please.'

'There was word that young Mary was expecting and that it could have been any number of men. Her father took to locking her in the house while he was at work, and when he came back she was only allowed out the back garden under his supervision, though the harm was done by then.

'He never stopped her when she was out walking the roads, meeting up with different men and hanging around street corners. There was a lot of rowing in the house; Felicity Feighery, who lived next door, used to hear Mary sobbing after the father had reared up at her. It was always the same thing: he wanted to know who the father was, and she would not tell. From the time she told them she was having a baby, she was treated like dirt.

'It affected Frances too: they married her off to a young man from Wexford, who had no idea of the family history, and we never saw her in Rathsorney again.'

Betty stopped when she saw Debbie start to cry, and she reached into a drawer in the china cabinet, taking out a box of tissues. 'Help yourself. Will I continue?'

'In a minute.'

Betty got up, saying she had washing to hang on the line. 'You take your breath.'

Debbie blew her nose. There was a pain somewhere under her chest. Any chance of a happy reunion was gone now, because Betty was surely right on the key fact that Mary was dead, and had been for a very long time.

She looked around the sitting room. On every spare piece of wall there were photographs: graduations, weddings, christenings, Betty standing tall among the children she loved.

Debbie jumped up and followed the old lady to the back garden. 'You are very good to let me take up your time like this.'

Betty did not turn from the line, where she was pegging out towels. 'Time is the one thing I have to spare. I am just sorry it is causing you so much pain.'

'I hate to think of her so alone.'

Betty gathered up her empty laundry basket. 'We will go inside; the wind has a knack of carrying your words from this garden, and next thing Muriel Hearty will be spouting it out at the post office.'

Inside, she poured a fresh cup of tea and opened a packet of chocolate biscuits. They sat quietly for a moment, until Betty was ready to begin again.

'It gave you a jolt, didn't it, to find out she was dead?'

'Is there any chance you're wrong in that?'

'I was thinking out at the line that that was what must be going through your head. I should not have broken off like that. I met her sister Frances; I think it was ten years ago. It was at my middle grandchild's graduation at UCD; she was there for the same reason. She had not changed a bit: still tall, with the hair done to the nines; you could see she had done well for herself. It was only a few minutes we had, but I asked her was it true Mary had died and she said it was. I could see it upset her to even to talk about it. Neither of us wanted to spoil the day, so we chatted on about stupid things. She said she lived in Dublin, but for the life of me I can't remember her married name. He was a businessman.'

Betty stopped talking and reached over to pat Debbie on the knee.

'I have not been much good to you.'

'You have filled in the gaps; without you, I would not know she is dead. It means a lot to me.' Debbie stood up to leave, but immediately a pain stabbed through her and she flopped down again.

'Are you all right?'

'Just give me a minute.'

'It has all been too much for you. Will I call someone?'

'I'll be all right.'

'I will make some more tea.'

Betty flustered around the kitchen, watching her charge keenly.

Debbie sat slumped, knowing this pain would pass. The rattling of the china cups was loud inside her head; the kettle boiling sounded more like a ship's whistle. Through the fog of pain, she heard Betty fussing, placing a blanket over her, talking on the phone. Fatigue washed through her and she tried to close her eyes, images of Agnes in her ball gown floating past, Blue Grass perfume resting in the air, cloaking Debbie in its sweet softness. Agnes always wore Blue Grass. Even if she were going to the mailbox, she would sit first at her dressing table, check her make-up and dab her perfume on the wrists, the neck and finally an extra spray on the hemline. A lady, she told her daughter, was not properly dressed if she did not wear her perfume: never too sweet or strong, but pleasant.

When the phone rang at Roscarbury Hall, it was Roberta who answered it.

'Mrs Messitt, it is very kind of you to ring, but what do you expect me to do? I hardly know the woman; it sounds to me like she needs a doctor.'

'Maybe I had better talk to Ella.'

'You will have to hold; I think she is in the café.'

Betty Messitt, who was in her hallway, pulled up a chair and waited.

Roberta scribbled a quick note.

There is somebody on the phone—something about that Yank being ill and in the town. R.

She stopped three women as they made to ascend the stairs. 'Ladies, my leg is not good today; would you mind giving this note to my sister Ella, most urgently.'

Turning back to the phone, she spoke again to Betty Messitt.

'Mrs Messitt, my sister will be down shortly; I am sure she can sort out this mess. I will leave you now.'

Betty threw her eyes to heaven. She never liked that Roberta: always a bit of a snooty toots.

Agitated, Roberta pulled a notebook from her pocket and rushed another note, propping it beside the phone.

I told you that woman was trouble. Maybe now you will finally get her out of my home. R.

Ella tore down the stairs.

'Betty, what is wrong?'

'The poor thing came asking about the Murtaghs and we were having tea and I don't know; it is like she is sleeping. She seemed to have pain.'

'I will send Iris over and she can bring her to Dr Carthy. I thought she looked drained the last few days.'

'All this is too much for her.'

'You might be right. Were you able to help her?'

'That's for her to tell you; I don't work at the post office, Ella.'

'You never were like that, Betty, and it is much appreciated.'

It was only ten minutes before Iris pulled up on Bridge Street.

'Betty, is she all right?'

'Sleeping, but she does not look too good.'

They trooped into the sitting room and stood looking at Debbie.

'She is doing too much,' Iris said.

Betty was about to answer, when Debbie stirred; they withdrew to the hall.

At first Debbie was not sure where she was, staring at the wedding photograph, wondering why Rob and Agnes looked so strange.

'I am so sorry; I must have dozed off. I didn't sleep well last night.'

'That is all right, dear. It was a lot to take in. Iris came to bring you home.'

'I thought the doctor first,' Iris said.

'No need, I feel fine.'

'But Betty said you seemed in pain.'

Debbie smiled. 'Iris, I have cancer; pain is part of the package.' She turned to Betty. 'Thanks for being so kind and so frank.'

'I wish I could have told a happier story.'

'The truth was all I wanted; you gave me that.'

Iris clicked her tongue impatiently. 'Ella says to bring you to the doctor.'

'No need for that; I will be glad of a lift to Roscarbury, though.'

Betty waved them off, until they had rounded the bend before Main Street.

'Has the cancer got worse, do you think?' Iris asked gently.

'Stage 4, as bad as it gets.'

'You are sure?'

'I am.'

They reached Roscarbury's avenue.

'I need to talk with Ella. Do you think she could meet me at Carrie's seat?'

Debbie paced slowly across the grass, stopping every now and again to catch her breath and take in the view.

Her two mothers were dead; the only family she had left was Nancy, who had worried and fussed over her all these years. It was time to ask Nancy to pack her bags and come to the hospice. Her quest here was at an end.

She saw Ella hurriedly pull on a coat at the front door and

salute a group at one of the outside tables before heading across the parkland, buttoning her coat as she moved. When she came closer, Debbie saw the deep frown on her face and her hands clenched inside her pockets.

'I couldn't face meeting any of the women. I'm sorry to drag you away.'

'You forget about that. How are you?'

'Mary Murtagh is dead.'

'Good Lord in heaven; how did you find that out?'

'Betty Messitt remembered her, and met her sister a few years ago.'

Ella sat down and put her arm around Debbie. 'That is desperately sad news. I am so sorry.'

'I came looking for answers, and now I know. Maybe I always knew it wasn't going to end with a tearful reunion.'

'We all prayed it would.'

'I know, and you have made me so welcome. I loved working in the café. It has been the best fun.'

Ella turned Debbie's face towards her. 'It is time for you to go, isn't it?'

'I have a hospice place arranged.'

Ella felt her heart wrench inside her. 'Stay, and we will be with you.'

'I know you mean that, Ella, but my aunt Nancy will be with me; she stepped into Agnes's shoes and has always been there for me. I can't deprive her of this drama.'

Debbie managed a giggle and Ella slapped her lightly on the wrists.

'I am glad you have not lost your sense of humour.'

'Not yet, anyway.'

'I am not sure I knew Mary Murtagh very well.'

'They only lived here for about a year. At least I know her name. That's something.'

'You started something huge over here. You are some person, Deborah Kading Murtagh.'

'You make me sound important, Ella.'

'Are you going to tell the others you are leaving?'

'I think even if I was in my full health, I couldn't cope with Muriel's reaction.'

'She will be disappointed.'

'Which is something I can live and die with, Ella.'

'You are sure about going back?'

'Yes.'

They sat quietly, watching the wind rustle through the high grass at the far side of the parkland, the trees swaying as the wind grew.

'It is getting blustery; time to get you back inside.'

They walked arm in arm, avoiding the front door, making for the back.

'It was a lucky day when I met you, Ella.'

Ella snorted loudly. 'Not at all: you are the one who has woken up this old house. Would it be all right if I planted a tree beside Carrie's for you? It will make that corner of the land a pleasant spot, for sure.'

'I'd like that.'

Twenty-Four

Iris pulled back the big gates as the squad car turned in. Garda Martin Moran saluted her and continued up to the house, driving around to the back.

Roberta, who was sitting in the walled garden, began walking towards the house. 'Is there something wrong, Martin?'

'I was looking for Ella.'

'You will find her up in the café. What is it, Martin?'

'I need to talk to Ella.'

'Go in by the back door and up the stairs. First landing.'

Martin Moran took off his cap and threw it on the front seat before knocking on the back door.

'She won't hear you. Just go on up,' Roberta shouted after him. She was hanging back, waiting to follow once there was a bit of distance between them.

Iris came puffing around the back. 'What's wrong?'

'It must be the baby, something about the baby.'

'That couldn't be,' Iris said, pushing past Roberta.

Martin Moran knocked on the café doors and waited. He

heard somebody working inside, so he knocked louder. Ella slapped down her tray and wiped her hands with a tea cloth.

'My God, what will it be next? An all-night café they are looking for,' she grumbled, as she went to the door. 'I am sorry, we are closed,' she shouted out.

Martin Moran felt uncomfortable. 'Ella, it is Garda Moran; I need to talk to you.'

The stench of starch surrounded her, creeping across her heart, seeping into her, strangling her so she could not say anything. It went up her nose, the pong of it hurting her and making her eyes water. She knew why he was here; he did not need to say it.

'Can I come in, Ella?'

She opened the door and stood back, letting him step into the café, his broad frame taking up the space between the tables. Iris shot in behind him. Roberta lingered at the door-way.

'Is there somewhere private we can talk?'

Ella looked to Iris. 'Just let me talk to Garda Moran here.'

Iris retreated, pulling the door gently behind her. Ella could hear her whispered warning to Roberta to leave them be.

'Iris is very protective of me,' Ella said. She sat down at a table, clenching and unclenching her hands, in an effort to remain calm. She motioned Martin Moran to join her. 'You are here about my boy?'

'The baby you had in County General Hospital on December 21, 1959.'

'Oh God, he did not die, did he?'

'We don't know, Ella. The midwife, Alice Kearney, has come forward with information on about fifty cases; yours is one. This morning we intend to dig up your baby's grave.'

'In Ballygally?'

'Didn't you know?'

'God forgive me, I didn't. They never told me. Was he given a name at all?' Her hands were clenched on the table in front of her.

'We have a reference number. He is called Baby Hannigan.'

She nodded her head to show she understood. Raising her fist, she bit into a knuckle. To feel pain meant she was still alive, and that at least must account for something.

'You have a hard job, Martin.'

'I am sorry, Ella. What do you want to do? You can wait for word in the garda station or, if you like, go to Ballygally. I will warn you there are a crowd of press and hangers-on there.'

'I will stay here at home. When will you know?'

'By noon. We will need to take a statement, when you are ready.'

'You don't think you will find the body of my baby, do you?'

'We honestly won't know until we open the grave, Ella. I promise you will be the first to know. I will give you a mobile and I will ring you the minute we have anything definite.'

'If he is not dead, where do we go from here?'

'We will cross that bridge when we come to it. It could take a long time.'

'So we could face the relief that our children are not dead, but suffer the pain that they are missing?'

'Let's get through the next few hours and days first, shall we?'

He sounded so strong, and she trusted him.

'Sister Consuelo told me they looked after the burial.'

'Ella, we are going to get to the bottom of this. What you must do now is wait. I know it is devastating, but we will help you through it. Have you somebody who can stay with you?'

'The whole of Rathsorney will be here in the café.'

'Have you got somebody who can run the café?'

Ella stood up and straightened her apron. 'You are a good man, Martin; your mother is a lucky woman.' Carol Moran had her baby two days before her; her son and Martin might have been friends, gone to school together, dances. 'Are you married yet?'

'A few years now, Ella.'

'Good. Don't worry about me. I will wait and you will ring me when you know.'

'You will be all right then?'

'As all right as I can be.'

He walked out and left her sitting, the mobile phone on the table in front of her. She heard him talk quietly to Iris and Roberta before he went downstairs. The squad car would be well gone by the time Muriel and her friends made it to the café.

'Are you all right, Ella?' Iris, followed by Roberta, walked into the café.

'Tell her to leave. I don't want her around me. Not now.'

Roberta turned on her heel and marched out of the room.

'That was a bit harsh, Ella. She is concerned about you.'

Ella stood up and went behind the counter. She started to slice the carrot cake. 'It's her shenanigans that lost me my daughter and left me vulnerable to those witches who took my baby. They knew I was a woman without a husband.' She stopped, knife in mid-air. 'Imagine all these years lost; will he ever even want to talk to me?'

'Ella, leave all that; we will organise the café. You need to sit down. Have a whiskey,' Iris said, taking the knife and gently directing Ella away from the counter.

'I have to keep busy; I can't sit, Iris. What am I going to do?'

'You will wait, Ella, and we will wait with you.'

'What will we do with the café?'

'What do you want to do?'

Ella walked to the window. 'There are three hours before I can expect any news. Best to keep busy.'

Iris made to protest, but Ella ignored her and began to set the tables. 'He is Martin Moran's age now. I wonder what job he has. Do you think if we ever met, would we have felt something? Surely we could not have passed in the street without some stir of recognition.'

Debbie, her hair tied back and fresh from the shower, walked in. 'Is everything all right?'

'Everything has changed,' Ella said, pulling the tops of the sash windows down to air out the room.

Iris pulled Debbie in behind the kitchen partition. Ella heard their hushed, urgent whispers. She had no energy to resist when they came and told her to take it easy; she said she would go to her room.

'I will call up in a while, once the rush is over,' Debbie said.

Ella stopped at the door marked private, opposite the ballroom. She had notions before he was born that it could be his little hideout, when he was older. She had been painting it a fresh lemon. Turning the knob, she pushed the door with her shoulder to open it.

In all the years she had not come in here, had passed it by, because the room contained too many hopes for the future. She left it a mess to lie down that sunny Tuesday and never came back in, because by the end of that week her baby was dead and she could not bear the little room facing the busy backyard.

She was going to call him Little Michael, though as he got older he might have resented the prefix in front of the name. She knew it was a boy; God knew she could not cope with another girl.

The paint was peeling on the walls, and there were blisters of damp across the ceiling towards the window. The paint bucket was rusted, a slick of dried-out oil and a hard brush all that was left of her decorating. The air was heavy with cold and damp. In a brown paper bag were the folded curtains she had had Mrs Murphy run up; she was dead ten years now. She had paid extra to have a row of cars hand stitched above the hem. Mrs Murphy said it was tempting fate to be so certain it would be a boy.

Scraping the mouse droppings from an armchair, she sat down. The cold rose up from the floor; not even the warm sunshine through the glass could heat the room that had been empty so long.

She heard Muriel rush up the stairs. She knew by the pounding on the steps, the seconds taken to catch her breath, followed by the loud voice and the charge as the ladies in the entourage jostled for position at Muriel's elbow.

'Where is Ella?' Muriel screeched.

'Not here this morning. You only have us beauties,' Iris said, tying an apron around her waist.

There was a murmur of disappointment in the group and Ella sank back in the old armchair damp with dirt, glad she was hidden from view.

'Is she gone to Ballygally?'

'No, no shopping there. Took a day off and went to Gorey.'

Ella, in all her pain, smiled. Iris would boast of this tall tale for many years to come.

'Does she know what's happening?'

Iris, who had begun serving out the teas, ignored the question. Muriel sat down, her mood deflated. When Debbie came with her coffee, she pulled her on the arm.

'You know they are digging up her baby's grave. Ella should know.'

Debbie looked to Iris.

Iris bustled down the room.

'We all deal with things in different ways. Ella has gone shopping.'

'Well, I never heard the like,' Muriel snapped, and the ladies around her murmured in agreement. 'When will she be back?' Muriel asked Debbie.

'I think she has a long list. Sometime this evening, I suppose.'

Muriel clicked her tongue in annoyance. 'I will have to cut short this morning; it is going to be a very busy day in the post office,' she said, making sure to drain her cup before rising to pay.

Ella shrank back as she heard Muriel and three other women leave.

'I have never heard the likes. Those O'Callaghans were always as odd as two left feet and this proves it. I thought today of all days would be a great day at the Ballroom Café,' she snorted.

Over the next hour, the café remained busy. Ella listened, sitting in the cold, damp room that no amount of sun could heat up, the mobile phone on her lap. When she closed her eyes, she could think back to when the room walls were like lemon icing, when there were no cobwebs and brown fly spots, no wet patches and damp blisters of paint. She used to sing and paint, ignoring the protestations of the other women that she should not work so hard. She locked herself in and painted, pretending that life was as normal, Michael away on manoeuvres. She only stopped when she became so fatigued her arms ached. It was as she lay on her bed at night that tears overwhelmed her and she worried how she was going to cope with a child on her own.

She only told people she was pregnant after Michael died. After the birth, she agonised that her frenetic painting and constant maudlin thoughts had killed her baby. She hated herself for all her grieving, which meant her baby had not possessed the will to live. She blamed herself, locking the door to this room and to her heart. She did not allow herself to snatch any future happiness; she never thought she deserved it enough. Sitting in this freezing, dirty room, Ella knew that not only had she lost this baby but her life too had been taken away, by the person who had decided another was to mother him.

She imagined she should feel angry, but there was only a lonely numbness, like a thick fog on her brain.

'Do you think I should bring a coffee up to Ella?'

'She is not in her room; I saw her go in the small room opposite.'

'Would you rather go?'

Iris, her elbows deep in the sink, washing up, laughed out loud. 'I am not into all this emotional stuff. I will keep things going here.'

Debbie poured a coffee and walked across the landing, knocking lightly on the door. 'It's me, Debbie. Can I come in?'

Ella rose from the chair, the mobile phone falling out of her lap. 'Hold on. I am coming,' she called out, scrabbling for the phone among the old newspapers on the ground, scattering big black spiders and earwigs as she did. She opened the door carefully, in case some of the old paint fell on Debbie. 'You don't want to be coming in here; it is cold and musty. Do you think we can get down to the kitchen without meeting any customers?'

Debbie walked across the landing and looked down the hall. 'The coast is clear.'

Ella hurried downstairs, followed by Debbie. In the big kitchen, she sat beside the old Aga, even though it was not on.

'Drink the coffee,' Debbie said, pushing a little table towards her and setting a place.

'You are good to look after me.'

Debbie sat opposite her, her face troubled. 'I have caused a lot of unnecessary trouble.'

'For God's sake, girl, you are the last one who should apologise; if you had not been so dogged in seeking assistance, I would have gone to my grave thinking my baby had died.' Ella cupped her hands around the warmth of the coffee cup. 'He is alive. I feel it, but I can't understand why I never could feel it before.' She sat, the warmth of the coffee cup radiating from her hands up her arms, and she smiled to think he was alive. 'You would be about the same age. Isn't that something?' she said, but Debbie knew she did not expect an answer.

They sat quietly, the kitchen clock ticking away the seconds. In the back yard they could hear the old hen clucking, the geese flocking about searching for slugs among the dug-up beds under the window. Every now and again there was a din from the hall as a group on the way in and out of the café met up.

'Who would have thought the café could be so busy?' Ella said, and Debbie nodded.

'What time did the officer say he would call?'

'When they open it up. I wonder will he ring if he finds remains in there? It is nearly noon now.'

'Muriel said they opened two graves yesterday and there was nothing but old newspapers and cloths.'

'She does not really think I am shopping, does she?'

Debbie smiled. 'I think she did. Maybe she's on the way to Gorey as we speak.'

'More like telling all and sundry I am off gallivanting as my little one's grave is dug up.'

'Do you want me to stay with you when you take the call?'

Ella leaned over and patted Debbie on the arm. 'Please, please do; I don't want to be on my own.'

They sat together waiting, neither needing to talk further.

Twenty-Five

Roberta paced up and down in the small library. From here, she could see the pear trees had been pruned and tightly fastened onto the stone wall with steel wire. A stone seat forgotten for decades underneath the briars and nettles had been uncovered last week, after Iris attacked the patch with a slash hook. Roberta reached in behind the world atlas and took down her sherry glass and bottle. Not bothering with the glass, she took a slow swig of sherry from the bottle.

The night Ella had been rushed to County General Hospital, Roberta had woken up to her moaning on the landing. She rang for the ambulance, but when it came she let her sister travel alone. She stayed up through the night, but no word of the birth filtered through. When she rang they would not tell her, so she called Gerry O'Hare. Consuelo came to her in the hospital waiting room.

'Are you here about Ella?'

'How is she?'

'Very tough birth, we will keep her in a few days.'

'And the baby?'

'Died.'

Consuelo took off her headdress to flatten her hair, thick, dull black hair held back with heavy grips.

'The baby is dead?'

Consuelo went to the mirror over the fireplace to fix back her veil. 'Isn't she better off? Sure, she will never get another husband with a baby in tow.'

'How is she?'

'She does not know yet. Best that she sleeps it off.'

Consuelo turned around and took Roberta's two hands. 'You go on home. We will look after everything, bury the mite.'

'The cost?'

Consuelo laughed, as if the very thought was a joke. 'Not at all, dear. It is the least we can do. We all know you two have been through your fair share of tragedy in the past while.'

Roberta, who had been reaching into her handbag to gather a small contribution, stiffened.

'Don't even think of it, Roberta O'Callaghan; we went to school together, we are friends.'

'You will look after Ella?'

'Like she is my own family.'

Consuelo swept out of the room, and soon after, Roberta got a nurse to send word to Gerry O'Hare. As she waited at the window of the waiting room, watching for his car, a tall, well-dressed lady came in. She sat down, tapping her heels against the tiles in an absentminded sort of way. She smiled at Roberta but did not say anything until a man in a raincoat came in.

'How long will it be? Have they said?'

'Not long, just another bit of paperwork and we should be there,' he said, smiling indulgently at his nervous companion.

'I would have preferred to be in the delivery room,' she snapped, and he sat down and put his arm around her shoulders.

They were still there waiting when Roberta saw Gerry O'Hare's car swing in to the front of the hospital and she walked out to meet him.

She did not cry until she got home, a newly opened bottle of sherry on the kitchen table. She wanted to see his child; she wanted it to be a boy and see him grow up to be like his father. She could not talk to Ella, she accepted that, but she knew her sister would never risk the confusion it would cause for the child, to ban him talking to her. She had planned to be a very indulgent aunt and there was nothing Ella could do about it.

She had loved Michael Hannigan; she still did. She met him first, though Ella would no doubt dispute that. It was at the dance in Gorey. He asked her out on the floor and she liked the way he moved. He didn't talk much, but when the band called the slow waltz, he pulled her close. They talked. He wasn't thinking of being a soldier then but was going to join in the family fishmonger business. She remembered she had given great attention to her appearance the next week, but he wasn't there, or the week after. She went to the fish shop in Gorey, but there was no sign. Her head and her heart were sore from thinking of him.

Ella, meanwhile, headed into Dublin city on a Friday night for the dances and sometimes stayed over. She was very coy about who she met, but one Saturday evening she came off the train, her face pink with excitement.

'I have met the man I am going to marry,' she announced, and they had to rush home to tidy up the house, because he intended to drive down and visit the next day.

Ella was in a dither, up since early, baking. When the Morris Minor pulled up the avenue, she whipped off the apron and reapplied her lipstick before running around to the front of the house. Roberta followed, happy for her sister.

'This is some pile. Is it all yours?' Michael Hannigan said as he jumped from the car and grabbed Ella in a tight hug.

'Don't be taken in by the looks of the place. It is a money pit,' she said, pushing him away so she could introduce her sister.

Sitting in her father's old leather chair, Roberta fancied she could hear his voice, see the twinkle in his eye when he complimented the sisters for being so lovely.

'I am a very lucky man to be in such company,' he said, making both women giggle.

Thinking back, he had a brass neck, but at the time she was taken by his bravado, the way he made both of them feel so good. Ella had no notion that behind her back he blew Roberta kisses, making her blush, and once he rubbed up against her as she fed the hens.

They had many Sundays like that, and in the summer they went for picnics by the lake. Sometimes he persuaded Roberta to get in the water and they played like schoolchildren. She heard Ella steal away with him to the old icehouse when they thought she was asleep, and yet she believed he loved her, because he said so. Once he persuaded her to get a train in to Dublin for the day; they walked around hand in hand. He brought her to a grotty guesthouse, where he made love to her on an iron bed with a patchwork quilt. She told him she loved him beyond anything.

As they lay entwined on the lumpy mattress, he told her he was going to marry Ella.

'I am in the Army now and it makes sense for me to have a

wife. I am too old for you, Roberta; me and Ella, we fit nicely together.'

'You only want the big house. There is only five years between us,' she said, getting out of the bed and pulling on her clothes.

'I won't deny it. I love you, Roberta, but I am going to marry Ella.'

'Do you love her?'

'I think I love both of you. Nothing needs to change, you know.'

She whacked him over the head with the handbag that only contained her train ticket and her lipstick. 'She loves you, everything about you. You are a bastard and I am a slut.'

She ran from the guesthouse. She had no idea where she was. Holding her handbag tight under her arm, she walked as if she knew her way until she saw an old lady waiting at a bus stop and got directions.

'Watch yourself, love; they would rob you blind around here,' the woman said, pointing her in the direction of the railway station.

When she got back to Roscarbury Hall, Ella bounced out of the house. 'Roberta, Roberta,' she shouted, so that her younger sister, afraid she had been found out, stopped in her tracks.

'Are you all right?' Ella asked, but before Roberta could answer she blabbed on, filling the space between them with words.

'Michael rang me up and proposed. He said he has a few days off and he wants me to go to Dublin to pick the ring.'

Roberta gasped, Ella taking her reaction as astonishment.

'I know, I can hardly believe it myself. I will be Mrs Michael Hannigan.'

She took off across the grass, skipping, and Roberta thought she had never seen her so happy.

'You will be bridesmaid, of course. Will you wear pink? It will go so well with your colouring.'

Ella skipped off again, jumping over the bed of dahlias.

'Do you think we can have a drinks reception here at the hall? Wouldn't it be marvellous? Are you all right?' Ella walked over and put her arm around her sister. 'There are plenty of nice fellahs out there, Roberta; you will meet one soon enough. You have a few years before you get to my stage. Where were you, anyway?'

Roberta turned and looked at her sister. 'I was in Gorey meeting up with a few girls.'

It was the first of many lies. It was not long before Michael Hannigan persuaded her there was nothing wrong with them continuing to meet. She went to Dublin twice a week, even the day before the wedding. After that, they met down at the ice-house.

Sometimes he grabbed her on the stairs and kissed her, or came up behind her and pushed against her, and she enjoyed the excitement. When Ella became pregnant with Carrie, she was ill for a lot of her confinement. Unwittingly, she threw the pair together as she asked her sister to look after Michael.

Roberta smiled, remembering lazy days with picnics, lying on a check rug down by the jetty, Ella at home, her feet up in bed, dozing over a book. They sang and smoked; at times they went in to the icehouse and he made love to her.

The birth of Carrie brought a new guilt to Michael Hannigan and he suggested they take a break from each other, so that he could concentrate on being a good father and husband. She agreed, because at that stage she would have agreed to anything he said.

Believing it would be like other times he tried to resist her, she acquiesced, thinking it would last just days or weeks. But Michael Hannigan had tired of the delights of the two sisters and often chose to spend his evenings off in the city, where he leaned against the bar, his tall bearing and twinkling eyes a draw to any woman. Ella, caught up in her young daughter, was too preoccupied to wonder what her husband got up to, but Roberta was deeply upset. When he did come home, she spent her time trying to cajole him back into her arms.

'When I am at Roscarbury, Ella has first call,' he said, pushing her away.

She thought of him now and wondered what she had ever found so exciting; he had grown peevish over the two years of his marriage and resented his wife pushing them together. Slugging sherry from the bottle, she tried not to remember the day at the harbour as the pram slipped away, Carrie squealing in delight.

Twenty-Six

Ella jumped up when the phone rang, making it fall off her lap to the floor. She snatched it, but her hands were trembling so much she could not press the button.

'Ella, is that you?'

Her hands shaking, she pressed it to her ear. 'Yes, Martin.'

'It is like all the others: only rags, no remains.'

She felt the room spin around her: her baby was crying, she heard it; she could smell strong starch. 'Are you sure, Martin?'

'The pathologist is here and there are no human remains.'

Her mouth was dry. She sat down. She did not know what to say.

'Ella, are you all right?'

'Yes, yes, I am. Where is he, Martin? Where is he?'

'I don't know. Do you have somebody there with you?'

'Debbie is here. Debbie Kading.'

'Do you want me to outline to her what happens next?'

Ella did not reply but handed the phone to Debbie, tears streaming down her face. Ella heard Debbie talk to the garda as she reached inside her pocket for her hankie and buried her head in the linen and lace. She would never know him as help-less and dependent, but only as the man.

Debbie left the phone on the table and put on the kettle. 'He says he'll call in the morning to take your statement of what you remember of the time of the birth. They have to look into it further, because there's no record yet of where the children ended up.'

Ella stood up. 'What do you mean "no record"?'

'They've seized all files at the convent and they have detectives going through them, but so far there is nothing.'

'So we don't know where my boy was sent.'

'I am sure they will find him, Ella. We just have to be patient. They have a team combing the hospital files as well.'

Ella fisted the table. 'I have waited decades; I thought there was nothing in this lifetime that could return my son to me. I want to meet him.'

'Garda Moran said to prepare yourself; it could take weeks, or longer.'

'Do they know what it is like to find out there is a chance of speaking to your child? What I wouldn't have given to get that chance with Carrie, to have her open her eyes as she lay on that quayside, her lungs full of water.'

'It'll come; we'll both have to wait.'

'But we needn't: that bitch Consuelo knows.'

Debbie took down Ella's flowery teapot and poured hot water into it. 'Don't you think we should leave it to the police?'

Ella sat down, her head in her hands. 'I can't sit here and do nothing. I can't do it.'

Iris walked in. 'Muriel Hearty rang and said they had opened the grave.'

'I know. Empty,' Ella said.

'Well, where in God's name is the child?' Iris said, sitting down opposite Ella.

'The man, Iris. The man.'

'Jesus Christ, you are right.'

Ella insisted on closing the café herself. She was busy clearing the tables when Fergus Brown stuck his head in. 'Have I got it wrong again, Ella? I thought Wednesday was the half-day.'

She looked at him. His face was still pale. Automatically, she straightened her dress with the palms of her hand and attempted to smile.

'Fergus, it is so nice to see you. I am afraid we are closed; something urgent has come up.'

'Nothing is the matter, I hope.'

He saw distress in her eyes, and her forehead was lined, as if she was worrying and thinking too hard.

'It is hard to know where to begin. You have heard the news about Ballygally?'

'Yes, an awful business.'

'They dug up my baby's grave this morning.'

Fergus reached her in two strides. 'I had no idea. I am so dreadfully sorry.'

'My baby is a man now, and alive. Somebody else has mothered him, loved him, advised him. Now I don't even have the memory of him in my head, because he was never dead. Isn't it strange I have gained him and lost what I had, in the space of minutes? And they say it could take weeks, maybe months to locate him; so far there is no record . . .' She was babbling, but she could not stop.

Fergus led her to a chair and made her sit down. 'Isn't there somebody who can do this work for you?'

'It keeps my hands busy.'

'Will I get you a coffee?'

She nodded, and he went behind the counter to get some cups. Consuelo had hatched it; she was sure. Hadn't she held her down, told her to forget about it? They had sat beside each other in secondary school, Ella always telling her to buck up or she would never make anything of herself. She was a right one for the boys as well, until her mother started forcing her to Mass every morning.

Ella knew Consuelo secretly liked being in the convent church, often sneaking in during break. It was not a surprise when she did not return to the classroom after the Easter holidays and word went round she had entered the convent. Ella did not see her for another five years. When they did meet, Consuelo, who had put on a lot of weight, was bossy and full of herself.

Fergus came back with a tray and two cups of tea.

'I thought hot sweet tea might be best,' he said, placing a cup and saucer in front of her.

'You are a kind man, Fergus. How have you been?'

'Strange, I lost Margaret to Alzheimer's a long time ago. I have got to say I was not prepared for the pain I would feel in her passing.'

'You loved her so much.'

'I did, but in truth, these last years have been so hard. I don't miss her recriminations or her wanderings; she could walk for miles, you know, and refuse to come home. I should have put her in a home, but in one of her more lucid moments at the start, she made me promise I would not.'

Ella stretched out her hand and cupped his tight. 'You did your best, Fergus; that is all any of us can do.'

They sat holding hands, each heavy with their own thoughts for a few moments, until Fergus spoke.

'Ella, I came for a reason today,' he said, his mouth dry with emotion. He coughed lightly and swallowed hard, before continuing. 'I wanted to say how much I have missed you, this past while. Losing Margaret has been an awful blow, but to be honest there is a relief that this section of my life, looking after her, is over. I want to start over, and I want you in my life.'

Ella pulled her hand away. 'Fergus, my mind is full of the child I lost. Please do not say any more; it will break my heart, because there can only be one answer. I let down that baby all those years ago; I know I did.'

'You are a victim here,' Fergus snapped, his voice angry.

'I appreciate your defence of me, I really do, but tell me what I did to locate my baby? I never asked enough questions. For God's sake, I did not even know where he was supposed to be buried.' The tears spouted from her eyes, but she brushed them away, digging her fists into her eyes. 'I like you Fergus, a lot, but I don't deserve any happiness after what I have done. I have to concentrate on finding him, if only to say sorry for letting him down.'

Fergus got up and pulled Ella to her feet. 'Let me show you something,' he said, guiding her to the window. She resisted, but only a little. 'Look out there. What do you see?'

'I see the garden, that Iris has not dug out all the rills fully, and if she doesn't soon they will silt up more, and if it rains as much as last winter we will be flooded in the parkland at the front.'

He put an arm across her shoulders and gently whispered

in her ear. 'There are the fields and the sea, the road leading to other towns, there is the wide-open sky. There is a whole world beyond Roscarbury, Ella, and when you are ready, I want to show it to you.'

'Fergus, now is not the time.'

He pulled away, his face sad. 'Ella, we both have seen too much of life. What you are going through now is gut-wrenching. I know you will meet your son. When you are ready, we will take the next steps together, and only then.'

Placing her hands on his chest, she felt his heart thumping. 'Margaret was such a lucky woman, and I am too, to have made such a good friend at this late stage. I thank you, but I can't say more, even if you want me to. My son is my only priority now. It has to be that way.'

'I understand, Ella,' he said, his voice low and tired.

He told her he was planning to sell the house in Rathsorney.

'I have always liked Italy; I fancy I will buy there.' He stopped talking, because he saw in her face the strain of trying to maintain politeness when a far greater thing was eating her up inside. 'I am rambling on, Ella, and you have much to do.'

'No, Fergus.'

He stood up and she did not protest. Reaching over, he pecked her on the cheek, saying he would let himself out.

She saw him drift along the avenue, never stopping to look back at the window. Iris came tramping up the stairs.

'What was Fergus Brown doing here?'

Ella shook her head and closed two buttons on her cardigan, to regain her composure. 'He just dropped in. He is thinking of selling the house.'

'Oh, that's a pity.' Iris gave her a look, checking closely for her reaction.

'He might buy an apartment in Italy.'

'That is what money does for you: it gives you freedom,' Iris replied, starting to stack the dirty dishes in the sink.

'Leave them, Iris,' Ella said, her voice wobbly.

Twenty-Seven

Debbie could not sleep, so she stole to the drawing room to sit quietly in the musty gloom, a small table lamp spotting a soft light around her. The house was dark, the only sound the mice scrabbling in the walls. She tucked up her feet under her on the velvet couch, after pouring a large Baileys.

She dozed and was almost asleep when the drawing room door opened and Roberta walked in.

'I saw the light and thought it had been left on by mistake. I am sorry to disturb you,' she said, her face betraying her disappointment that the room was not empty.

'There's plenty room for the two of us. Won't you have a Baileys?'

Debbie stood up and took a crystal glass from the cabinet. Roberta watched, unsure of what to do next.

'You know I'm leaving?'

Roberta relaxed and sat in the leather armchair, fitting the rug around her knees. 'It is for the best.'

'Maybe,' Debbie said, handing the glass to Roberta.

They sat, an awkward silence between them, the mice scrabbling louder as they moved up the walls and into the ceiling, making their way to the kitchen.

'Has there been any news about the child?' Roberta asked, fixing her handbag on her lap.

'No. It is terrible for Ella.'

'Terrible for all of us.'

Roberta sipped her drink and enjoyed the change from the sharp, cheap sherry she had to buy these days.

'In the village, they say you are a nice person.'

'That's good to hear.'

'I wondered, then, why you did not leave when I asked you.'

'I stayed while there was still hope of tracing my birth mother.'

'You have not done so?'

'No.' Debbie drained her glass and got up. 'I'd better get to bed. It's been quite a day.'

'Thank you for the drink.'

Debbie smiled and let herself quietly out of the room, her arms and legs tired and aching.

On her own, Roberta took down the battered *Complete Works of Shakespeare* from the top shelf of the bookcase. Turning to Act One of *Hamlet*, she lifted the envelope from its hiding place. Pressing it to her nose, it was damp and musty, but still she fancied she could smell him. It was addressed to her, but it was a father's letter to his son. If Michael Hannigan's son was to come back to Roscarbury, then she must fulfil his father's wishes, whether her sister liked it or not.

September 4, 1959

My dearest Roberta,

What I am about to do is going to let you all down, especially Ella and our unborn baby. I feel it must be a boy and that brings with it such terrible joy. In her grief, Ella is going to be extremely angry with me, so I ask you, please, to represent me to my child. I want him to know I could have been a good father, but circumstances have brought me to this place and I see no way back.

I caused the death of beautiful Carrie and for that I will never forgive myself. I do not have to forgive myself for loving you, because in truth, I loved both of you, Roberta and Ella. I regret deeply the hurt I am about to cause.

Please, Roberta, tell my boy I loved him but I just could not stay. Tell him to be good to both of you and to grow up to make his mother proud. Tell him she is a strong, loving woman and he must respect and love her always. Stay strong, and keep each other strong.

May God bless the three of you, and I hope some day in your hearts you will be able to forgive me and remember me fondly.

Roberta, please stay with Ella and help her when she needs it. She is a proud woman and I know she values your company. I have not been a good husband or a faithful lover. In time, you will know how weak I have been and how I have wronged you all. I humbly ask your forgiveness. I am a coward and a weak man. I am deeply sorry. When *the time comes, look kindly on me. In time, I hope you both can forgive me.*

All my love,

Michael.

He gave the letter to a private who was going home on sick leave. Tardy about posting it, the private only remembered to throw it in a postbox on his way back to barracks two weeks later, when Michael was already seven days buried. Roberta rushed to show it to Ella, but Ella would not talk to her. When she tried on several more occasions, Ella screamed until the spit flowed out of her mouth. After that, Roberta kept it in the book, returning to it from time to time.

She placed the envelope carefully in her handbag before leaving the drawing room and turning off the light, because the first curls of sunrise were forming and the birds were mooching, getting ready to greet the day.

It was only an hour later when Ella made her way downstairs to turn on the ovens. Her head thumped and she wandered outside to breathe in the cool air. A hedgehog, surprised in the herb bed, snuffled slowly away as Iris's dog watched it, afraid to move closer.

Two magpies took up position by the henhouse, in readiness for the scrap bucket. She had nothing to offer a child: only this place, which sapped every bit of her money and energy. The café, too, would only always be just that: a tea and cake house to help make things meet.

She made biscuits again this morning, because she liked the

feel of the butter and flour pressed through her fingers, and rolling out the dough and stamping out the different shapes.

Maybe she should have sold up when there was good money to be had for an old place like this. Where would she and Roberta have gone? They could never live in a small house or get on with neighbours; they were both too set in their ways now.

She had four cakes in the oven and was sitting having her first cup of tea of the morning when Garda Moran pulled up in the squad car. Squaring back her shoulders so that she felt brave, she opened the back door before he knocked.

'You are here early, Martin. Is there anything wrong?'

'Ella, can I come in?' He stepped into the kitchen, his wide frame taking up the door space.

Ella felt sick; her knees began to buckle. When she heard Consuelo's name, her stomach twisted. She counted four shrivelled lemons in the bowl on the kitchen table, and an apple, which was bruised. She thought she would throw it out later. She felt his hands take hers and lead her to the table, where she sat down, her mouth dry.

'Please listen, Ella.'

A pain shot up her neck, flaring across the side of her face.

'Files were hidden under her bed in old suitcases. Yours was on top. Your boy was sent to New York.'

As simple as that, she thought. He is in New York. Her heart began to flame; pain ran up her arms and legs; she wanted to get excited and yet she felt exhausted, a sense of desolation thumping across her head, a well of loss drowning her.

She placed her head in her hands and Garda Moran thought she was crying. She heard him rummage and take some mugs from Roberta's cupboard. He placed a tea, too white with milk, in front of her, but she did not sit back until the steam fluffed past her face.

'Did he go to a good family?'

'The documents show they had plenty. Ella, we have to talk about what happens next.'

'What?'

'It is not as simple as just giving you the details. An expert is going to take over the cases and contact the families involved.'

'More waiting.'

'Ella, the same rules apply. It will be up to your son whether he wants to make contact and up to you if you want to meet.'

'Even though he was stolen from me.'

'All you can do now, Ella, is wait.'

'I suppose I am good at that.'

Roberta walked into the kitchen and put her kettle on the ring.

Martin Moran pushed back his chair and stood up. 'I will ring you.'

'What about Debbie?'

'We are going through the files; there are a lot of them. Ballygally Convent gave us a pile and we found more in searches at the convent in Moyasta,' he said as he rinsed his mug out under the kitchen tap.

He tapped Roberta on the shoulder and beckoned her to follow him. Outside, Garda Moran moved quickly to the car, so he was out of earshot of the house.

'I know you don't get on the best, but she needs you now, Roberta. Maybe try and talk to her.'

'What is it, Martin? Have you found the child?'

'Something like that,' he said, getting into the driver's seat before she could ask any more questions.

Roberta returned to the kitchen, scalded the inside of a mug and stirred in a heaped spoon of coffee and sugar. She sat at the table, picking at the tablecloth edge, watching her sister. She did not feel able to say a word. The tick of the clock sounded louder than usual. She stuttered out a sentence.

'Where is he?'

Ella heard Roberta's question, but there was no fight left in her.

They sat, the only sounds the clock ticking and the hens outside clucking, waiting to be fed.

Roberta picked tiny balls off her dressing-gown sleeve, her head down as if in deep concentration. Ella watched her snag a small ball and pull it hard.

'In New York.'

Roberta stopped, her fingers still on her sleeve.

'Not so far; I am glad,' she said.

They did not know what else to say to each other, the chasm of decades too wide between them.

'The café won't open on its own,' Ella said, loud enough for Roberta to hear. Jumping up to turn off the ovens and scoop out the cake tins, Ella began to knock the cakes out. Roberta brought her tea to the drawing room.

Twenty-Eight

Debbie pretended to be very busy and flitted about the café so that even Muriel could not pull her into conversation. The postmistress made several attempts to engage her, calling her over to her table and asking aloud where Ella was, but Debbie answered quickly or waved in a frantic gesture to show she was under pressure.

'There was a time they would linger to chat, but since this place started being mentioned in the national press their heads have swelled somewhat,' Muriel sniped to the woman beside her, from behind her hand.

Chuck Winters enquired after both Debbie and Ella.

'I don't know, Chuck; sometimes I wish I'd never come here.'

'Don't ever even think it; after all, you have been a lifeline to Mrs Hearty,' Chuck whispered, touching Debbie's arm lightly.

'The service around here has gone to the dogs. Maybe we were too hasty in abandoning Molloy's,' Muriel snapped, but the other women ignored her tight, jealous tone. Muriel hated more than anything not knowing what was going on behind the scenes at Roscarbury. She jumped up of a dash. 'I don't have time to sit around and gossip all day,' she said, leaving the price of her cup of tea on the table. Without even a sideward glance to the counter, she left.

'I always think she is like a spoilt child, adorable in so many ways,' Chuck said, gathering up his cup and saucer and making for the window seat.

With Muriel gone, the noise level in the café went down and Debbie had time to sit at a table and rest. That her coming to this country had caused such a furore was difficult to comprehend. If Ella's son did not want to meet her, Ella would surely blame Debbie for raking up old embers and setting a fire alight none could put out.

Soon, she was alone in the empty café with the tables not cleared. When Garda Moran tapped on her shoulder, Debbie jumped, making the little vase holding a tulip fall over, spilling water across the tablecloth. Garda Moran stepped back, apologising profusely.

'Miss Kading, is there somewhere private we can talk?'

Sweat prickled on her back. Debbie swept her arms across the span of the room. 'There is nobody here, officer.'

Garda Moran took off his cap and carefully placed it on a chair. 'Did Ella tell you we have got access to new files?'

'Yes.'

Her throat was painfully dry, her head throbbed; she found it hard to concentrate.

'We have only started to go through them, but we have found a reference to your adoption.'

She could not look in his face but zoned in instead on the parkland, where a golden retriever was running in circles around its owner and barking.

'I was one of the babies taken from my mother, without her consent?'

She sat watching the dog evade its owner and she wanted to be out in the grass, still wet with dew; she wanted to be in a day where there was no worry, only everyday niggles that could easily be forgotten.

'Is there somebody I can call, to sit with you?'

Debbie sat up straight. 'There is nobody. Please, let's get this over and tell me.'

She saw him swallow hard before he launched into his explanation.

'We know you were born on April 15, 1959 and adopted several days later by Agnes and Rob Kading, but it appears only after the baby they had intended to adopt died unexpectedly at birth. Mrs Kading was distraught and Sister Consuelo arranged for another baby to be brought to her.'

Debbie put up her hand to tell him to stop. She could see Agnes making a scene, telling them how far she had travelled and how she was not leaving without a child. She had seen her do it often enough in Bowling Green when she did not get her own way, insist with her marbles-in-her-mouth voice, placing her bag primly on a counter, her body stiff with determination.

'Will I continue?'

Debbie nodded.

'Sister Consuelo arranged for a baby who was born two days later to an unmarried mother to be taken instead for adoption. We believe your actual date of birth is April 17. The mother was told the baby died.'

'My birthday isn't even real.' Debbie stood out onto the floor.

He looked directly at Debbie. 'You know Mary Murtagh was your mother?'

'Yes.' Debbie got up from the chair and straightened the painting on the wall. 'I had better get the tables cleared or Ella will have something to say about it.'

'I don't think Ella is going to mind today,' he said, watching Debbie as she over-stacked a tray. He made it to her just as the china cups slipped to one side, managing to catch a blue thistle-patterned cup in mid-flight. 'Sit down,' he said, guiding her back to her seat. 'A baby that young would have needed a passport to leave the country. It is possible Agnes Kading pretended you were their natural child and had you registered at birth, putting herself and her husband down as the natural parents.'

'Could they do that?'

'Quite a few Americans did, those stationed or living in the UK; we will have to wait and see.'

Debbie slumped into her chair. The pain in her chest prevented her bolting, so she sobbed, her tears gushing down her face, seeping into her silk scarf, making it look thin.

'I will make some tea,' Garda Moran said, and he went off in search of cups, as Debbie sat facing the window. The woman with the dog put it on a leash and headed towards the lake. No doubt the dog would soon begin to strain and sniff the air as the ducks swam to the centre of the lake to stay safe. Only last week a cocker spaniel had romped into the water and nabbed a duckling as all around it adult ducks squabbled ferociously. The sun was shining, highlighting the bench under the branches of the cherry blossom. Grey clouds waltzed across the sky; Debbie knew that soon the lake would be obliterated by sheets of rain.

'I have grown too attached to the place,' she said half aloud, so that Garda Moran stopped what he was doing and asked if she was all right. She did not answer. 'This is the end of my journey,' she said, as Garda Moran set a china cup and saucer and a small teapot for one in front of her. Debbie poured her tea and stirred in a sugar. 'Ella said you were nice, and she is right.'

Garda Moran coughed, to hide his embarrassment. 'I had better get along.'

She shook herself and stood up and extended her hand. 'Will you promise me something?'

'If I can.'

'Please find Ella's son and tell him he has to come here.'

Garda Moran smiled. 'I don't think there is anyone in Rathsorney who would want it any other way.'

He left her and she listened to his heavy step on the stairs and how he stopped to have a quick word with Roberta before driving off. She watched the squad car bump along the avenue to the gate, sweeping to the left into the town.

She was not sure how she felt: disappointed, for sure, but more angry that after kicking down a huge brick wall there was now an even bigger one in front of her. Mary Murtagh might have known Roscarbury Hall, walked along the avenue, stolen down to the old icehouse.

She felt strangely empty and very, very tired. She got up and had begun to clear the tables when Roberta stepped into the room.

'I can do that for you.'

'I'm good.'

'No, really, I want to.'

Debbie put down her tray and took in the older woman.

She was smiling, telling her to take a break. Debbie did as she was told, too numbed to ask why. She wanted to be alone, to wonder if Mary Murtagh liked jewellery at all, to shut her eyes and be in the dark.

Twenty-Nine

Ella tried to imagine the man, but that was impossible when she had not even known the child or the baby. She could only hope he would want to meet her. Almost afraid to think of him and what he might be, she turned to the jewellery box. She should be happy and yet she was so worried. What could be worse than to discover he was alive and have to put up with the pain of his rejection? Reaching down to the bottom layer, she scrabbled until she felt the light tissue holding the happy brooch.

If he wanted to meet her, she would wear it. There never had been an occasion joyous enough to wear the last brooch her mother had received from her father.

A glorious pink flower, the domed brooch was small in her hand. A pink rhinestone was at the centre, navettes of rhinestone radiating from it. There was no special occasion when her father presented it to her mother, which heightened the excitement. John O'Callaghan had surprised them all on a very ordinary day. His wife, Bernie, was busy in the kitchen, her hands covered in flour as she pummelled the brown bread before throwing it in the oven. Sweat formed along her temples and she pushed up her sleeves roughly when her husband walked in.

'I am a bit behind; get yourself a cup of tea and a biscuit, to keep going,' she snapped, without looking around.

'I am all right,' he said, and placed the small box beside her.

She quizzed him about the contents and chided him for handing her any such thing when she was up to her oxters in flour, but he refused to back away, forcing her to wash her hands and towel them dry quickly, to open the box.

Ella remembered the smile that transformed her mother's face; the strain of her labours faded away as she took in the delicate pink flower.

'It is the most beautiful of them all, you mad fool,' she declared, reaching up, kissing her husband on the lips: a show of affection so unusual that Ella and Roberta stopped what they were doing and stared. Quizzed on the occasion being celebrated, John O'Callaghan simply answered 'because she makes me so happy.'

Known as the happy brooch after that, it shone on Bernie O'Callaghan's lapel on those special occasions she decided were so imbued with happiness that they deserved such a signal.

Ella kept the brooch wrapped in tissue, carefully storing it at the far corner at the bottom of the big silver box. Never daring to even consider wearing it, she promised herself now, if she were to meet her son it would surely be the happiest day, deserving of such a significant brooch.

Ella sat and examined her reflection in the mirror. He would never know her as a pretty young woman. Her hair had been rich auburn once, like her mother's. Her eyes, though still hazel, had lost their glint. She had weathered well, she thought, but what he would make of the old woman who had spent her life grieving for a child who was dead and for another who was not, she simply did not know.

She paid extra attention to her powder, because she knew many of the women in the village would be watching for any clue she was waiting for definitive news.

Pinning a small Christmas tree Weiss brooch to her cardigan, for no other reason than it might distract her customers and provide a point of conversation, she combed her hair, pulling it back from her face, pinning it up with a tortoiseshell comb that once belonged to Bernie O'Callaghan. Ella tweaked a few loose curls out, letting them fall down to frame her face.

It could be days before she knew his name; Martin promised he would tell her his first name whenever he found out, no matter what. When she allowed her mind to wander, she was silly in her head imagining all sorts: thinking of walking across the parkland together, walking down the town, teaching grandchildren to bake, letting them run cars on flour mountains. She shuddered in anticipated happiness at the thought, and then the worry came flooding over her, that maybe he would not want to know her and life ever after would be unbearable.

Tidying up stray clothes on the way, she made her way out of the room. Walking into the café, she saw the tables had been cleared. The tables by the window were taken up by people she had never seen before.

'You have been run off your feet, tidying up after the hordes,' she called out, her head down, checking the till.

When there was no answer, she went behind the screen, where Roberta was drying her hands with a tea towel.

'There is a hand towel; you should not be using that,' Ella snapped, her voice low and firm.

Roberta folded the teacloth slowly. 'I am sorry, I was doing my best.'

Ella did not answer.

Roberta fidgeted with her fingers. 'Miss Kading got news. She was upset. I was helping her out.'

Ella attempted to keep her composure, but the old anxiety was seeping through her. 'I am sure she is grateful,' she said, turning back to the counter quickly so that her sister would not see the tears in her eyes, memories of her husband and her daughter flooding her brain, making her unable to say anything else.

Roberta slipped past her and out of the café as May Dorkin and Chuck Winters came in. May took up the last seat by the window and Chuck came to the counter.

'We will have two teas and chocolate cake, Miss O'Callaghan, please.'

He drummed the counter, as he waited.

'Have you something on your mind, Mr Winters?'

'I was wondering, Miss O'Callaghan, could you give me some advice?'

'If I can, Mr Winters.'

'I have asked Ms Dorkin to join me for tea. Do you think she would mind if I asked her for dinner some evening, the new restaurant in Ashford?'

'Why are you asking me, Mr Winters?'

He looked embarrassed, running his hand nervously along his beard. 'I am sorry; I know you have a lot more important things on your mind.'

Ella lowered her voice so she sounded kind. He leaned

across the counter to hear her better. 'Look at her, Mr Winters. Tell me, is that a woman happy to be asked to tea?'

They both looked at May carefully fixing her blouse, a smile on her face, a nervousness about her as she clasped and unclasped her top button several times.

'I hope so.'

'Isn't that your answer?'

★

Debbie packed her bags and loaded her car before going to see Ella in the café.

Ella, who had been arranging biscuits on a serving plate, stopped what she was doing. 'You look well today.'

'In my case, looks are definitely deceiving.'

'Curse that goddamned disease. I wish to God in heaven it was me, not you.'

Debbie put her arm around Ella's shoulder and squeezed tight. 'Never, with the prospect of meeting your son on the horizon.'

'It is an unfair world, Debbie; I won't have anyone tell me different. I can't believe what happened to you and my own son.'

'It's done.'

'But where does it leave you now?'

'I want to go home; this journey is over.' Debbie sat on the stool Ella normally used towards the end of the day when she was tired and had to count out the drawers of the till.

'Ella, I'm so glad I met you.'

Ella blubbered, reaching into her pocket for her handkerchief. 'What have I done, Debbie? If it were not for you, I would not know what happened to my son.'

Debbie squeezed her shoulders again. 'I have a long drive ahead.'

Ella shook herself free and, pocketing her hankie, straightened her dress. 'Of course you do; that is enough of me, feeling sorry for myself.'

'I didn't mean it like that.'

'I know.'

'Ella, I'm tired.' Debbie picked up a lemon biscuit and bit into it. 'You have enough on your plate now. I'm genuinely happy for you, Ella.'

'I know you are, darling, but we don't know yet if my son will want anything to do with me.'

'He would be mad not to,' she said, and Ella saw her eyes were wet with tears.

'I just wish you were not so hasty.'

'It can't be any other way,' Debbie said as she reached and took Ella's hand.

'Did you meet Roberta?'

'I did.'

'Don't let it fester any longer; I think the two of you are quite lonely.'

Ella walked to the sink and began to sluice it out with water. 'There is nothing wrong with being alone; I'm alone, not lonely.'

Debbie picked up her car keys. 'Will you come down to wave me off?'

Ella nodded, unable, at that moment, to speak. Slowly, she patted her hands dry before linking her arm tightly with Debbie's as far as the car.

'You have everything? The brooch?'

Debbie nodded, throwing her handbag in the front seat. She saw Roberta on the old stone seat and ambled over to her.

Roberta quickly stuffed her hip flask into her oversized handbag.

'I'm leaving. I wanted to say thank you for this morning, and goodbye.'

'You are welcome. Have a safe trip,' Roberta said, her hand up to shield the sun from her eyes.

Debbie had already turned on the path when Roberta added: 'I am sorry it did not work out for you.'

Debbie mumbled thanks and continued to where Ella was leaning against the car bonnet.

'You don't have to go.'

'I have to.'

Debbie jumped behind the wheel, afraid if she hugged Ella she would not want to leave. She turned the car, revving it too much, when Ella knocked on the window.

'I am not good at words, Debbie. You know how much I care about you.'

Debbie reached out her hand and Ella gripped it tight, before letting her go.

Ella stood and watched as the small red car made its way down the avenue, stopping when a group of women waved Debbie down. The car swerved past the crater pothole before rounding the rhododendron, to turn out onto the road to Rathsorney. She could not explain it fully, but Ella felt a terrible loneliness creep up through her. She did not hear Roberta approach from behind. Roberta pushed a note to her sister.

Close the place now. Haven't you had your moment of glory? R.

Ella scrunched the note in a tight fist.

'You would like that, wouldn't you? The Ballroom Café

stays open,' she snapped, whipping back into the house, making for the stairs before the next wave of customers came bursting in. Iris was in the door behind her.

'That wasn't Debbie I saw leaving?'

'Yes.'

'Is she coming back?'

'No,' Ella said, cutting slices of chocolate cake too thin so they broke as she transferred them to a serving plate.

'So how are we going to manage?'

Ella put down her knife. 'I have no idea, Iris, simply no idea.'

'You are in a bad way, Ella.'

'I will miss her. She was taken from her mother and sent to America, and look at the life she had. What if my son has been unhappy, or with people who could not love him?'

Iris pushed Ella in behind the screen. 'I will take over; go rest.'

Ella pulled her hands down her face. 'Don't you see there is no rest until I meet him, and even then those lost years will haunt me?'

'Will we close up for the day? There are only a few left.'

'Everybody will guess, then, that I am one of the women involved.'

Iris put up her two hands in exasperation. 'Sure, doesn't everybody know that anyway? You sit there and I will put the signs up at the gate.'

Ella sat on the small stool they usually used to reach the high shelf where she kept the napkins. Her head was swimming with worry for her son, and fear that she would never be able to meet him. Clasping and unclasping her hands, she listened to the low hum of conversation in the café, afraid one of the local customers would come to the counter.

She was in a desperate state; she knew Iris had seen the

signs. She wanted to cry, but she could not; she wanted to scream, and she did, inside her head, her hands clasping her fingers tighter, until the realisation of pain made the scream go away. She wanted to tidy up, but she could not move from the stool; her mind and body were paralysed in the time when her baby was taken from her. How could she have ever believed he was dead? She surely should have known; she had carried him for nine months, talked to him every day.

When she heard somebody go behind the counter, she presumed it was Iris. She ignored the light tapping on the screen.

'Ella, are you there?'

She jumped when she heard his voice, flustered, wanting to answer but not wanting him to see her in this state.

'Ella?'

She stood paralysed, unable to move, unable to utter a word. She wanted him to go away, for Iris to return so she could put talk on him. The screen was slowly inched back and Fergus Brown pushed his head through.

'Ella, are you all right?'

He stepped into the small area around the sink as she tried to wipe her face and take deep breaths to calm down. Placing his arms around her, he spoke in soft tones, as a parent would to hush a distressed baby.

'I heard the news. I had to come.'

She did not answer but placed her head on his chest and let him stroke her hair.

They stood like that for a while, until Iris came back into the café and began the final clear-up.

'Will we go for a drive?' Fergus asked.

'Go, a change of scenery will do you good,' Iris called out from where she was counting the money at the till.

She pretended not to take too much notice of Ella and Fergus. Ella pulled away and slipped from behind the counter to get ready in her bedroom. She slicked on some pink raspberry lipstick and picked her soft purple coat with the black handbag and shoes. She was about to go out the door when she saw her jewellery box on the dressing table.

Reaching in, she took out the Weiss triangular-shaped rhinestone pin. A simple clear-stoned triangle, her mother said it was pure in its beauty and should only be worn on extra-special occasions. 'A mother does not have time for such occasions,' she announced, and the brooch was confined to the little box it came in. Ella pinned it to her lapel. It flashed, reflecting a rainbow of colours when she moved, making her look and feel peacock-elegant.

When she came down the stairs, Fergus was waiting on the landing as Iris locked up the café.

'We'll take a run into the mountains.'

He held the door, as she sat in his Rolls-Royce. She thought if her head were not so full of her son, she would have very much enjoyed the drive through Rathsorney. Even in this quiet mood, she smiled when Muriel Hearty, saluting Fergus Brown as they stopped at traffic lights, nearly tripped on the pavement when she saw his passenger.

'Isn't it nice to know we can cause such a stir by driving through the town,' Fergus said, tapping the steering wheel lightly with his fingers.

There was a companionable quiet between them as Fergus pushed his car up the narrow mountain roads. Ella let her mind wander past the heather and the stones to the clouds, and to wonder if she would ever show these places to her boy.

When Fergus pulled in to a lay-by, she did not comment.

'I took the liberty of packing a picnic basket before I left,' he said, reaching into the back seat. He poured hot coffee in stainless steel cups and they nibbled on smoked salmon and brown bread.

'What if I had said no?' Ella asked.

'I would have been stuck with Iris, or even Muriel Hearty. The air up here clears the head; the view is soothing on the eyes.'

'You heard my boy is in New York.'

'Muriel is always up to date.'

'Maybe she even knew before I did.'

'What happens next?'

'Maybe Muriel knows.' Ella finished her coffee. 'I wait, Fergus. Garda Moran said if I draft a letter to him, they will make sure it is delivered. It will be up to him after that.'

'None of these things happen quickly, Ella.'

'I know. I just wish I knew what to say in the letter. "I am the mother who let you be taken away, believed you were dead, never visited your grave, did not even know where it was, because I never asked." What is he going to think of me?'

'You are being too hard on yourself.'

'Am I?

Fergus Brown did not answer immediately, but he let her compose herself. When he spoke, he reached out and took her hand.

'I am here for you. Maybe I can help in the café, for starters. I am not going to let you go through this on your own.'

She squeezed his hand but could only manage a thank you before floods of tears cascaded down her cheeks, creating wavy channels through her make-up.

Thirty

Fergus Brown was as good as his word. His Rolls-Royce lumbered up the avenue just past seven. Ella, sitting with a cup of tea in the kitchen, heard the purr of the engine and the hens' excitement that the day had begun. She saw him get out of the car, take off his overcoat and throw it on the back seat, and pat the dog before making for the back door.

'You are very early,' she said.

'Reporting for duty.' He saluted elaborately, clicking his heels, standing to attention.

'Come in, you old fool, before you catch your death. There is work to be done.'

'Don't we have time for a cuppa first?'

'When the tables are set, we will both sit down. There is a bank manager to be kept happy,' she said firmly. She led the way upstairs and showed him the sets of china, kept in a mahogany sideboard. 'Mind you don't drop any; we have been lucky, no breakages yet.'

He picked up a cup and turned it upside down, to check its provenance. 'You will find it very hard to replace any of these if they break. Why not go for simple white cups like everybody else?'

'Yes, and bought-in-shop cakes as well; that is what will keep me standing out from the crowd,' Ella guffawed loudly.

Fergus Brown carefully turned up his cardigan sleeves. 'You know best, Ella.' Slowly he made his way from table to table, placing the plates and saucers before returning to the store and taking down six cups.

'Go easy there,' she said, beginning to count out slices of cake.

'Easy peasy,' he snorted, and began to whistle a tune.

Despite her aches from a restless night, she found herself swaying, just enough to enjoy the tune.

'We won't have time for a coffee if you don't get your skids on.'

'No wonder Miss Kading left. You are a slave driver.'

She hushed him because she heard Iris climbing the stairs. 'She always seems to know what time the coffee will be brewed,' she said.

Iris had seen the car parked at the back of the house and thought Fergus Brown must be walking in the grounds. When she saw him sitting down, waiting for a coffee, she turned to Ella and whispered, 'We are not open for another hour; what's with Fergus Brown?'

'Fergus has kindly agreed to help out until I can find a replacement for Debbie.'

'Muriel and the gang are going to think it is Christmas. Has he moved in as well?'

Ella slapped down Iris's mug on the counter. 'Whatever do you mean?'

Iris threw three cubes of sugar in her coffee. 'I think you had better get your story straight before the ladies arrive.'

'Don't be silly,' Ella said, walking over to join Fergus.

He took her hand when she sat down, but she pulled it away quickly.

'Ella, who is the one being silly now? Let them think what they like. We know the truth.'

'I don't like being talked about, Fergus.'

He leaned closer to her. 'Think of it this way: while they are yattering on about us, they won't have time to question you about the other thing.'

Iris, throwing her eyes to the heavens, left to plant some drills in the kitchen garden. Ella stirred her coffee and looked out the window. From here, she could see the women's heads as they walked down the short lane between the church side gate and Roscarbury Hall. Even from this distance, she could see there were more women than usual this morning.

'A mob following the leader,' Fergus remarked. She did not need to reply, but she felt a certain apprehension rise up inside her, so she went behind the screen and pretended to fuss about napkins. Fergus walked around the café, straightening the settings and fiddling with the cutlery as he watched Muriel Hearty lead her team up the avenue.

'They are nearly on top of us.'

Ella came out from behind the screen, flattening her apron over her skirt.

'Play it cool. Muriel will do all the talking, if you let her,' Fergus whispered.

Ella would have answered, but she heard the group in the hallway.

'There you are. I told you, nothing closes the Ballroom Café,' Muriel Hearty trumpeted, quickening her pace on the stairs. Muriel, dressed in her light-green spring swing coat, sashayed into the café, calling out Ella's name. 'Oh, Mr Brown. How nice to see you. I did not know you were back visiting these parts.'

Fergus opened up a small apron, lightly shaking it out before tying it at the waist. 'Not just visiting, Mrs Hearty. Miss O'Callaghan has been kind enough to offer me temporary employment.'

'You? Working here? Whatever next. Where is Debbie?'

'She has gone home, left yesterday afternoon,' Ella said, from behind the counter.

'Without waiting to say goodbye,' Muriel said, making a face to the other women.

'She asked me to convey her best wishes to you all.'

'That was nice of her,' Muriel harrumphed, and turned her back to the counter, calling out loudly, 'My usual please, Ella.'

The women settled themselves down and enjoyed giving their orders to Fergus, who wrote everything carefully, double-checking with everybody whether they wanted cream with their cake.

'You are spoiling them, Fergus. They are not used to such attention. The coffee will go cold with all your chat,' Ella said, lining up the cups of tea and coffee on the counter for collection.

'You are hard on him, Ella. Isn't it great to have a man around the place all the same?' Muriel said, transferring to a stool at the counter.

Ella concentrated on plating the cake as Muriel watched Fergus deliver a tray of coffee.

'Is there something you are not telling us, Ella O'Callaghan?'

'Whatever do you mean, Muriel?'

Muriel leaned over the counter, her two elbows pushing the plates of cake out of her way. 'We all know he is not in need of a job.'

Ella put down the knife and picked up a silver tray. 'He won't have a job here for long if he does not hurry up with the orders,' she muttered.

Muriel waited until Fergus collected the tray and was down near the café windows before she spoke again. 'Go on, Ella, you can tell me. Sure, I am only delighted for you.'

Ella stopped what she was doing. 'He is helping out. What is wrong with that?'

'Nothing at all. It is sweet.'

Ella shook her head. 'One of these days, Muriel, one of these days somebody will . . .'

'Will what, Ella O'Callaghan?' Muriel said, standing up.

'Nothing, Muriel, nothing.'

'Have you heard anything?'

Ella sat down on her stool. 'Not yet, Muriel. It could be months. It might be never.'

Muriel reached over and took her hand. 'We are all rooting for you; you know that.'

Ella made to stand up. 'I know.'

'Debbie should not have left.'

'There was no reason for her to stay.'

'Don't you remember Mary Murtagh?'

'Vaguely.'

'She had the beehive hairdo and the shortest skirt in the county. I think they went to Australia.'

'She was a nice girl,' Ella said.

'We will all miss Debbie, though Fergus is definitely doing his best.'

'He is a good friend,' Ella said, for that moment forgetting she was talking to Muriel Hearty.

Muriel reached over and pinched Ella's cheek. 'Nobody is going to begrudge you this bit of happiness.' Muriel giggled like a child.

Ella, flustered, called to Fergus to start clearing the tables. 'You are going to have to learn to chat less and work more,' she snapped at him as he pushed a tray of crockery onto the counter.

'Sure, we all love the extra attention,' Muriel said, going back to her table to finish her coffee.

Ella stood and watched for the next few minutes, as Fergus lingered at each table, the women giggling and joking excitedly. When he wandered close to her, she noticed he was limping a little. Calling him softly, she beckoned him to come in behind the counter.

'You are doing too much. Take your break now.'

'I am enjoying it, Ella. I am fine.'

'You stupid man; if you don't take a break, I will fire you.'

He laughed out loud and several of the women turned around, hoping to be included in the joke.

'If I didn't know you liked me so much, I would think you were being serious,' he said, throwing his hands in the air and sitting down.

'I can call Iris to take over for the last hour or so.'

'That's more like it. Maybe we can stroll down to the lake.'

'That would be nice,' she said, and began to clear some more tables.

Muriel and her three friends were the last to leave. Each stopped at the counter to chat to Fergus before they went.

'You are a hit with the ladies anyway,' Ella said.

'All in a morning's work. Are we ready to go to the lake?' he said.

'After the washing-up.'

She washed and he dried, placing the china cups and saucers on the counter so Iris, when she arrived, could set the tables for the afternoon.

'Won't Iris mind? She strikes me as happiest with her feet in muck.'

A voice from behind made both of them jump. 'I would not put it exactly that way, but you are right, Mr Brown.'

Fergus Brown, who had begun to fidget with the end of his tie in his embarrassment, made to speak, but Iris put her hand up to stop him.

'You two young things better get going, before I change my mind,' she said, grabbing too many china cups, so they clinked loudly.

'Be careful with the china, won't you?' Ella asked, but Iris did not answer, waving her hand in mock irritation.

They tramped across the parkland, the sunlight on their backs, Ella too nervous to link arms until they were well away from the house.

'When do you think you will hear from America?'

'I have not even written a letter yet. Martin Moran says it could be a few weeks. They have to tell him and his parents. I am sure it will be a blow to them. His name is James. I like that name; it sounds strong.'

'I will wait with you, Ella. We can work in the café together,' he said, taking her hand in his and rubbing it gently, because it looked cold. He slipped her hand into his pocket and they walked on to the water's edge.

★

Roberta was walking past the post office when Muriel called her in.

'How are you, Roberta? You are looking well.'

'What it is, Muriel? You saw me yesterday. What is eating you?'

Muriel called her husband.

'I need to have a chat with you, Roberta. Wait until I hand over the reins to hubby.'

Roberta sighed elaborately and checked her watch several times as Muriel briefed her husband before letting herself out of the small office and locking the door behind her.

'Do you have time for a cuppa? We can go upstairs to the apartment.'

They walked up the stairs, Muriel talking non-stop to cover her nervousness. Roberta walked into the middle of the room and looked around.

'We should let out Roscarbury for thousands if you can get two hundred euro a week for this,' she said, walking to the window.

'Will a mug do? I don't believe in having china cups for tenants,' Muriel said, washing out two mugs and switching on the kettle.

'What is it, Muriel? Why have you brought me up here?'

'You have not heard then?'

'Heard what?'

'The American found out who her mother was.'

'Miss Kading? She has gone.'

Muriel spooned instant coffee and sugar into each mug and poured the boiling water before answering. 'Did you hear who the mother was?'

'I saw she was upset. She said goodbye. I don't know anything.'

'Mary Murtagh. That's who it was.'

Roberta did not say anything.

Muriel grew more agitated.

'Do you remember she was a bit wild? Michael Hannigan was very taken by her.'

Roberta put down her mug on the counter. 'What do you mean, Muriel?'

'Roberta, don't play the innocent with me. We all know what he was like. Sure, Ella was the only one who thought the sun shone out of his arse.'

'I didn't know about Mary Murtagh,' Roberta said, her voice low, her head hurting.

'Of course, if he was the father, Debbie Kading might be related . . .'

Roberta jumped up so fast the coffee sloshed onto the new carpet.

'May God forgive you, Muriel Hearty! Don't you think my sister has enough to put up with, without your incessant gossiping?'

Muriel ran to get a cloth to mop up the spill. 'Will you calm down; we are only talking.'

Roberta gathered her handbag close to her. 'It is loose, hurtful talk, Muriel, and I warn you, if you continue to say things like this I will go to Reidy, the solicitor.'

Muriel stopped scrubbing the carpet. 'I am only saying what every other person is thinking.'

'Stop it, Muriel. Ella is on tenterhooks as it is. Don't you think she has been through enough? This could kill her. Debbie Kading has gone back to the States; let's leave it at that.'

'There is no need to go all legal on me. Sure, I am not one for gossip at all. I can't help it if, sitting down there behind the glass, everybody tells me their woes.'

'I have to go; I have a lot to do this morning,' Roberta said tightly, making her way to the door.

'We must have a proper chat one of these days,' Muriel said, following her, her voice deflated.

Roberta did not answer but swept out of the post office before Muriel reached the bottom of the stairs. Her heart was thumping and she needed a drink. She turned left, as if to walk home, breathing deep in an effort to appear calm. A man tipped his cap to her and she made an effort to smile, but she wanted to run and to scream. All these years she had loved him, believing he had been truly conflicted about the sisters. She remembered Mary Murtagh: she had been such a quiet girl, everybody said, until she started to doll herself up like a tramp.

Passing the cemetery, her pace slowed. The path was little used, but she diverted down, skirting around the graveyard wall, until she came to the clearing. Ella made sure to keep the grave tended. There were fresh flowers in a pot that was inscribed 'Gone, but not forgotten.'

Reaching into her handbag, Roberta took out her hip flask and unscrewed the top slowly. All the times she had stood here and cried for him, begged him to give her a sign he was in a better place.

She slugged long and hard, letting the sherry slip down her throat until she finished most of the hip flask. Wiping her mouth with the back of her hand, she sat on the big old rock they had taken out the ground when they dug the grave. Idly, she pushed at the white marble stones Ella had scattered a few years ago. Some were completely covered in moss, others dirty and stained from rain and hard frost. The sherry made her feel warm, but her leg had stiffened with the creeping damp. She felt the tears flowing; she made no attempt to stop them.

Gerry O'Hare was walking back from visiting his wife's grave when he saw Roberta over the wall. He pretended not to notice and went on to his car. He could still see her between the trees, sitting on the old rock, her shoulders hunched, her head bowed. He walked up the narrow track and called out softly. 'Do you want a lift back to Roscarbury, Miss O'Callaghan?'

Quickly, she pulled her hands across her cheeks. 'Thank you, Gerry,' she said and got up from the rock. 'I don't know what came over me. There has been so much going on these last days.'

Gerry O'Hare stood on the wet grass, to let her go in front. 'I will drop you up at the back door, if you like; get a cup of tea the minute you get in.'

'I will, Gerry.'

Thirty-One

Debbie walked over the grass and up the steps to the veranda. It was wide and bare without the rocking chair. The house was still for sale, a flutter of litter in the corner, the windows grimy with dust. She pressed her nose to the glass and looked in to the sitting room. The burnt-orange couch with the lace backs her mother had crocheted, the low coffee table, which she was never allowed to put her feet on, the glass bowl where Agnes arranged red apples, four the perfect number each week. The gold brocade armchair near the fireplace was angled with its back to the window, as if Agnes were there, hand-sewing delicate buttons and hemming wide satin skirts.

Their wedding photograph was on the wall: Agnes leaning into her husband, Rob laughing, his arm around her waist.

Feeling like she was intruding, she stepped back.

'Debbie, Debbie. What are you doing here?' Nancy Slowcum pulled into the driveway. 'I wasn't expecting you until later, honey. It hasn't sold. Only an outsider will go for a house like this. Somebody who doesn't care about the history.'

'I couldn't drive past.'

They both stood, as if waiting for Rob Kading to emerge from the overgrown side path, a tin cup of coffee in his hand. Nancy stepped onto the veranda.

'You found out about the adoption?'

'You knew?'

'Agnes swore me to secrecy.'

'You knew everything?'

'Not until just before she died.'

'Did you tell Rob?'

Nancy leaned against the veranda post. 'How could I, Debbie? What good was it going to do a man who was grieving so bad to find out his child had been stolen from the arms of her real mother? Rob wouldn't have been able to live with that.'

'Why didn't you tell me?'

'I couldn't,' Nancy said, kicking at the worn paint with her foot so that it fell off in slices onto the porch floor. 'It was easier to hide it, hope it would never come up. I am a sorry coward.'

'Nancy, I don't blame you; I just don't know why you didn't tell me. All these years, I could have known.'

'Debs, darling, I know now, I should have; you had to put up with so much stress over there, and we could have avoided all that. When you told me you were in Ireland, I couldn't say anything, not over the phone. It had to be a face-to-face meeting.'

'I'm here now,' Debbie said, her voice low and firm.

A child whisked by on a scooter; his father waved.

'That's Haussmann's son, moved back here two months ago, three doors down. Everybody wants the house to sell; it's bringing down the street,' Nancy said, flicking dust off the veranda steps with her shoes.

'Aunt Nance, you should have told me.'

Nancy walked down the steps, stooping to examine a rose bush. 'There was nobody to prune it this year. Maybe I should have told you, but it's easy to look back and be wise. Did you want to go into the old place?'

'I don't think I could face it. I thought it was being cleared out.'

'Realtor said to leave it; it made it more homely. We can talk at my kitchen table.'

By the time Debbie followed on in her car to Nancy's, she was already bustling about making tea. There was an agitation about her that Debbie noticed as she piled too many biscuits on to a plate, spilling the milk as she placed a jug on the table and fussed unnecessarily over napkins. When, finally, she poured the boiling water into the teapot and sat down, it spouted onto the table, making her jump up again, snatching a tea towel to clean the mess. Debbie reached over and caught her hand.

'Nance, it's OK.'

'You are skin and bone, Debbie; this goddamn cancer is knocking it out of you.'

'You need to tell me everything. I want to hear it while I still have the energy to deal with it.' Debbie coughed and spluttered, so her aunt got a box of tissues and left them beside her.

Nancy took a deep breath and slurped her tea. 'I never suspected anything. In fact, I always thought you had Agnes's slender nose and Rob's hair colouring. When they moved to Bowling Green, Agnes was the happiest woman. Mrs Haussmann, who had nine, used to say you were the luckiest girl in the world.' Nancy stopped to press her fingertips under her eyes, so she didn't start to cry. She switched on the kettle. 'I think we'll need a hot drop in the pot.'

Debbie smiled, because her aunt was widely known to drink far too much sugary tea.

'You're such a good girl; I was afraid when you went to Ireland you wouldn't want anything more to do with us.'

'That's not going to happen,' Debbie said.

'Your mother: you found out about her?'

'She died a year after I was born.'

'I am so sorry, Debs.'

'Tell me everything you know.'

Debbie stretched out her legs and folded her arms, waiting for her aunt to begin. Even if she was reading her shopping list, Nancy liked to know she had an audience.

'Agnes so wanted a daughter, but I think the reality could never live up to the ideal in her head. Don't get me wrong, you were not a difficult child; in fact, you were the sweetest thing, but for some reason, Agnes never seemed fully happy.

'Agnes was a perfectionist. She couldn't sit in a room if the furniture wasn't just so. She even had Rob return the Christmas tree once, because when they decorated it, it leaned slightly to the left.'

Stopping to take a breath, Nancy reached for a new packet of cookies and poured a few onto a small plate.

'I'm telling you all these extra bits because it is so damn difficult to talk about the rest.'

'I need to know, Nance.' Debbie tried not to sound impatient.

'Switch on the oven there; it'll heat up the kitchen for us.'

Debbie turned the oven dial and opened the door.

'Not yet, Debs, let it heat up first.'

Nancy waited until Debbie had settled back in her chair and she had her full attention once again.

'Aggie came to me. She was missing for months and was home two days. It was all so strange. She wouldn't tell us anything, where she had been, anything. That morning when she came in, she was agitated, but I got her to sit and have tea. She said she had gone to Montana and holed up in a small motel, but now she was sure she was back for good. She wanted to tell me what had forced her away in the first place. She swore me to secrecy, said she had done an evil thing and she was being punished, every second of every day. She said you were adopted, but that you had been stolen from your Irish mother, a young, unmarried mother. She paid extra, under the table, for a newborn; Rob knew nothing, only that she had travelled to Ireland to collect a child. The baby she was due to adopt died at birth and Agnes kicked up a stink, insisting she was not leaving without a child. She offered a huge whack of money. It worked. The nuns said she would have to extend her trip by a week. They fed cod liver oil to the young woman and she gave birth. Agnes waited in another room. You were brought to her straight away. The poor mother was told you were dead.'

Nancy got up from the table and leaned against the sink.

'I told her, look at the life they had given you, what a lovely, happy girl you were. Curse my stupidity. Debs, if I had known what she was going to do I would never have let her go home. She said she wanted to go home and freshen up and be ready for you both when you came home.'

Nancy stopped to take a cookie, the sweet bite taking her mind off the story.

Debbie reached over and patted her on the shoulder. 'It wasn't your fault, Nance.'

'I should have done more for her. To the day I die, I'll regret that I let her go home on her own. I was a fool.'

'What happened?'

'Don't you remember?'

'Remember what?'

'You found her.'

'Tell me, Nance, please. I only know she died.' Debbie clasped and unclasped her hands, drifting from being supremely angry to feeling sorry for her aunt, who was crying quietly.

Nancy began to pace the room. 'Surely you remember something. It was when you stopped talking for six months; it must have been the shock.'

'Remember what, Nancy?'

Her aunt stared at Debbie. 'You ran in from school. You had a gold star for the spelling. You found her.'

'What?'

'Hanging over the second landing.'

Debbie stared at her aunt; she heard the midday freight train trundle through the town.

'I don't remember.'

Nancy reached out and took Debbie's hands. 'Best that you never do. The shock kept you silent for months afterwards; we were so worried.'

Debbie dropped her head, too exhausted to cry.

Nancy switched on the kettle.

'Rob found her after you. You were hiding, shaking to bits in his potting shed. There is something else you might as well know. She left a note. Rob dropped it in the hall. He looked everywhere for it afterwards; he couldn't remember a word of it.'

Nancy's face reddened and she began to pick at the edge of the table.

'You have the note, don't you?'

'Leave it, darling; there's enough here to break your heart.'

'Aunt Nance, you are my only source. If you know any more, please help.'

'What more would I know?'

Debbie reached out and grabbed her aunt's hands. 'You never were good at hiding anything, Nance. I have to have that note.'

Relaxing her hands in Debbie's grip, Nancy began to cry. 'Don't you know enough? There is a lifetime of sorrow in what you know already.'

Nancy roughly pulled her hands away and went to the sink. She could see the red cardinals dip down to the little bird table Bert had made and placed, so she could watch the birds' antics as she did the washing-up.

Without thinking, Nancy turned on the tap and rinsed out their two mugs, leaving them to drain. Debbie watched her. Nancy got a chair, so she could reach the top of the kitchen cabinets. She pulled on an old tin box stuck in at the back. Blotted with rust, the cookie tin was dulled with age and stiff when she tried to open it. She sat down at the table and wrenched the lid.

'I didn't want anybody coming across it by accident.'

The letter was loose, on light, soft, pink paper.

Debbie felt cold; the letter was heavy in her hand. A sea of nothingness lay ahead of her, ready to swallow her, if she let it.

'I think I need to be on my own to read this.'

'Of course you do. You take as long as you like; I have a few chores to finish.'

Nancy made the chair screech as she pushed it back in her hurry to get up.

Debbie heard her fuss about in the basement as she slowly unfolded the pink paper.

Bowling Green, October 1968

My darling Rob,

Remember when we were so happy? If I could have one day like that again, I would trade everything for it. A black fog envelops me. It should be that way. I cannot live as a fraud any longer.

A long time ago I did something unforgivable. I have run away from it, but I cannot escape it.

I cannot forgive myself and I know I can't blame Deborah either, but it is a block to me loving her. I have done a terrible thing and there is no way to right the wrong.

When I arrived in Ireland, the baby assigned to us had died, caught some sort of fever and died. I remember it was like somebody had kicked me in the stomach. The nun in charge, Sister Consuelo, said another child would come along and we were at the top of the list. I did my usual thing and stamped my foot and made quite a stink and they got me a baby.

Rob, I am ashamed to even write this, ashamed to say it now, but I can't love her. It is a terrible thing for a mother to admit. Isn't it?

As she grows up, the hatred I have for myself intensifies. I can see no way out. I am surrounded by blackness. She is a good child and I know you can love her. But I can't stay and watch her grow into a young woman. In her, I see the woman I wronged. She is the embodiment of the great wrong I did; there are days I can't bear the sight of her.

I want the pretense to be over. I falsely registered her birth in Ireland with our names as parents. I don't ask for your forgiveness; I don't deserve it. I merely offer this explanation. It is time to end this pretense.

I made sure we brought that child to the US, but I wronged her and us. I have always loved you and I can only say I did what I did because I knew you wanted to be a father so much.

In time, try to remember me fondly.

With all my love,

Aggie.

Her heart was empty and her knee joints stiff, so when she stepped from the table she looked as if she was in pain. She put the letter back in the box and pressed hard on the lid, to wedge it in place. Nancy she could see pottering about the garden, idly fingering her flowers. Debbie startled her when she spoke.

'Nancy, I was wondering, would you help me settle in at the Marigold Hospice?'

Nancy swung around, tears streaming down her wrinkled cheeks, lodging in the hollow at the base of her neck. 'Darling, I wouldn't have it any other way.'

'It won't be easy for you.'

'Nor for you, my sweet, but I will be with you to guide you and see you off; never fear on that.'

'I put the letter back in the tin.'

'The right place for it.'

Thirty-Two

Order of Divine Sisters, Rathnew, Co. Wicklow, April 2008

The notification of the Bishop Lucey's visit came with just an hour to go.

'His Grace apologises for making a night call, but he has no choice considering the press are practically camping out at the palace,' his secretary told Assumpta on the phone.

'He will stay for dinner?'

'It is not a social call. Your office will do fine. What His Grace has to say shall not take long.'

Assumpta asked for fresh flowers to be placed by the window. A good cushion was plumped up and put on the high-backed chair in front of mother's desk.

Assumpta waited, doodling on a sheet of paper, which she hid in a drawer when she heard the doorbell.

Bishop Ciaran Lucey, a wide man with a fat chin, burst into the room all smiles, his voice jovial and light. Assumpta was not fooled by his demeanour, which she knew was put on for the benefit of the other sisters. He waited until the door was closed to scowl, his wide eyebrows dancing, disturbing the furrows on his brow.

'Mother, you could have handled this sorry situation better, don't you think?' He sat down, spiking his fingers into a church spire.

'It is a very difficult situation, Your Grace.' Assumpta attempted to sound calm, all the time clenching her fists where he could not see them.

Bishop Lucey leaned his ample chin on his spire of fingers. 'The problem is, Mother Assumpta, you have started a forest fire, and because you did not rush to stamp out the first sparks in a proper and firm manner, others have erupted. We will soon be in a situation where we cannot contain these raging fires, and what do we do then?'

'It is surely not my fault, or the fault of this order, if other women are coming forward because their babies were taken illegally.'

Bishop Lucey put his hand up to quieten Assumpta. She felt a stab of pain run across her chest and she fell silent. The bishop stood up.

'We have to prepare ourselves for the worst; it is an intolerable situation. I am not the only one disappointed with such a slack attitude. No doubt your own superiors will also express their dissatisfaction. It has been decided to shut down this convent.'

Assumpta felt an anger rise inside her. 'What will become of us?'

'That is hardly my concern, Mother.'

'We are being blamed for the appalling practices of the past.'

'I would advise you to watch your tongue, Mother Assumpta.'

She straightened on her seat. 'What was I to do, Your Grace, refuse to let them dig up the Little Angels cemetery?'

Bishop Lucey stood up and stared out the window into the blackness of the night. 'Of course not, but to provide so many files—truckloads, I hear—without first contacting the Bishop's Palace; now that was foolish.' He turned to Assumpta. 'Unfortunately, the matter has escalated too far and is now beyond my remit.'

'What do you mean?'

'The matter is now in the hands of the State authorities, and all we can do is what we are asked: cooperate as much as we can. When they put back the cemetery, these lands will be put on the market. I doubt if anybody will want this convent to remain here anyway.'

'But where will we go?'

'I hear there is plenty of room in Moyasta. It might be good for you; you can live a prayerful life without the added responsibility and burden you have had to carry these last months.'

'I have done nothing wrong.'

Bishop Lucey, with a whip on him, marched to her desk. 'Bar opening up the door for legal suits and wayward women to make money out of the church, when all we did was take them in when nobody else would. I will bid you goodnight.'

He swiftly walked from the room.

Assumpta sat in her comfortable armchair at the window and watched Bishop Lucey, highlighted by the light spillage from the open front door, get into the back of a Rolls-Royce. She fingered the band of silver on her left hand, revolving it over and over. She prayed fervently that God would give her the strength to accept with grace the decision made by others and that she may be able to keep her vow of obedience.

★

Unable to sleep, Mother Assumpta remained in prayer until first light, when she went to the first landing and watched the meander of the river. The water flowed, the daffodils were beginning to tinge brown and the grass would soon need cutting. It was a familiar scene that at a time of anxiety calmed her heart, bringing her peace, reminding her of the changing seasons and yet the constancy of nature. Today she looked out on it because it was the only place in all the acres that surrounded this beautiful building which had not been taken over in some way by the band of outsiders and hangers-on. This pastoral scene she would soon have to consign to memory. More than likely, the money raised from the sale of these lands would be used for the compensation claims that were surely going to flow in from women who had lost their babies to forced adoptions.

That her name would be linked with this unsavoury episode in the order's history wrenched her heart and made her intensely angry. Crowds of people, press and various onlookers, had descended on the convent since it had first been made public a week ago that the Little Angels graveyard was to be dug up.

No longer could she risk walking and praying along the garden paths, lest she meet someone who wanted answers she could not give.

The plot, down the far corner of the gardens and behind a bank of cypress trees, was cordoned off, a massive tent over the patch of ground, as if an archaeological dig was taking place. She did not dare think of all the lives not lived, or those lived but begun under a cloud. It was unbearable to think of what had happened and what would become of all of them.

She had done her best. Once informed the investigation was widening, with the potential for a criminal element, she had gathered the sisters together. It was, she thought, probably one of her hardest and saddest moments since becoming a nun.

'It will appear as if we are under siege; in a way, we are, for the possible sins of the past. I want each of you to be as cooperative as possible to the police and state officers charged with this most gruesome task. However, I urge each one of you to be on your guard; loose talk at this time could be very damaging indeed.'

The sisters did not ask any questions, sensing the anger bubbling at the edge of her voice, but she knew they would have plenty to say behind her back. That Consuelo had been sent away was also, she knew, a major worry to the other sisters, but she chose not to address that thorny subject.

Just hours before, Consuelo had been informed that she should get ready for a return to Moyasta.

'Mother, I only ever had the intention of finding good homes for those children; God knows that.'

'It is not for me to decide, Consuelo, the rights and wrongs; my job now is to try to salvage as much of our reputation as possible.'

'And you blame me for this.'

'I don't blame anybody, but I do say that taking babies without the permission of the mothers and forging signatures on permission forms is wrong. What does it matter who came up with the idea?'

'Mother, they were different times; without me, those children would have had no life at all.'

'What makes you so sure of that, Consuelo, what makes you so sure?'

Consuelo huffed loudly. 'That Deborah Kading has a lot to answer for. Before she came on the scene, everybody was happy.'

'You mean nobody knew.'

Consuelo shifted uncomfortably on her seat. 'And wasn't that the best way to have it.'

Assumpta dropped her pen and slapped her desk hard. 'You can't honestly believe that, Consuelo, even now.'

'I know I am being judged by the norms of today. What unmarried mother could keep her child then? Tell me that.'

'That is not the point, Consuelo, and well you know it.'

Consuelo leapt from her chair.

'But it is the point. What family wanted that great shame brought down on top of them? The ones I sent to America were the goddamned lucky ones. God knows how many were born in the corners of fields in the dark of the night and buried straight away.'

Assumpta felt tears of anger well up inside her. 'You don't see you did wrong.'

'You don't see the good I did every day of the week.'

'There is far higher than me making decisions now, Consuelo. I am just following orders.' Assumpta tried to keep her voice firm, but she could not help the shake welling up from her throat.

'What is to become of this little band of women, Mother?'

Assumpta snorted loudly, as she tried to hold back the tears. 'I am afraid I do not know.'

'Tell me, Mother. I need to know what I have done.'

'This order, by its work and uncaring attitude in the past and its refusal to recognise it now, has done it to itself.'

Mother Assumpta shook her head fiercely to shake away the harsh memories of a shameful time she had not lived through but which would forever follow her on life's path. She turned away from the window, tears flowing down her face.

Thirty-Three

Roscarbury Hall,
Rathsorney,
Co. Wicklow,
Ireland.
May 9, 2008

My dearest James,
I am not sure what I should say in this letter, only
that I am overwhelmed with joy to think you are
alive, and overwhelmed with sadness to think I lost
you for so long. I know from everything I have been
told you are a fine man and were lucky to have
Mr and Mrs Spring as your parents. Please tell
them I bear them no ill will and, instead, I thank
them for raising you and giving you the childhood
you deserved.
 The investigator told me you were brought up in a
lovely apartment in Manhattan, and I thank God
that even though you were taken from me it did not

mean a dilution of love in your early years. You must know your mother and father had no reason to suspect they were being told anything but the truth when they were told I had died in childbirth.

That you had a mother to love you is a source of huge comfort to me and that you had a father too is a great joy. I understand you do not have brothers and sisters, so there was no competition for the love of your parents.

James, what is to become of you and me? I gave birth to you. They told me you died. I had so many plans for us. But these plans must be left in the past and we must find a way forward that allows us to become friends.

Do you think you would like to visit? You could stay here or there is a fancy hotel a few miles away. James is such a strong name; I get the impression that your mother, Mrs Spring, was a strong and loving woman: firm, too, I imagine. You are a very lucky man.

I know all of this has caused upset and upheaval in your life, not least the angst and pain it has caused your parents. I would dearly love to meet you, but in your own time. I understand if you need time to think things over; I pray and pray that you will want to meet me as much as I long to meet you.

All my love,

Ella O'Callaghan.

She did not sign it for a whole day, wondering if her full name was a little too formal. Ella did not want either to appear too friendly or to be frostily formal, which could put off the son she did not know.

Her arms were open wide; it was up to him to take a step towards her. She phoned Gerry O'Hare and he drove her into Gorey to post the letter.

'Muriel is a lovely woman, but the less she knows about my affairs the better,' Ella said to Gerry.

He nodded and continued to watch the road, lest Ella O'Callaghan think he was too interested in her business.

'How long does a letter take to get to the States these days?' she asked him, because she was so excited she could not stop thinking about James, and as a result she could not stop initiating conversations that would let her luxuriate in the fact that her son was a successful man in New York.

'These days? I don't know. Who posts letters any more? Why don't you send an email?'

Ella laughed out loud. 'What I had to say ran from the heart to the pen. There isn't a computer I know of that can loop the J in James, to show the flourish of love I feel for the child and the man.'

'Right so,' said Gerry, and he lit up a cigarette, blowing a cloud onto the windscreen. So caught up in her own thoughts, Ella forgot to give out or cough extravagantly to show her disapproval.

★

It was several weeks before Ella got a reply. From the day she posted the letter, she had taken to loitering at the front café tables when the postman was due.

Roberta noticed the expectation in her sister's gait and sat at the library window each morning, watching Ella clean down the tables, fix the chairs and rearrange the candle holders and flower centrepieces.

Once, when a young woman came down the stairs and asked to be served upstairs, Ella sighed loudly and abandoned her post reluctantly. If an upstairs table was free, she sat waiting to see the post van before it pulled into the drive.

Roberta watched the spectacle each day. Sometimes, in her agitation, she poured out a sherry but forgot to sip it, letting it go dry in the glass. Once, she left a note on the kitchen table for her sister.

I have a right to know when you get word. He is my nephew. He needs to know about his father. R

Ella ignored it, screwing it into a tight ball and batting it into a wastepaper basket. She left her reply in its place.

His father left me and him high and dry. This is none of your business. E.

When the letter came, it was in a business envelope: his name, James Spring, and an address on Manhattan bounded by flowers. She was afraid to open it and stuffed it into her pocket as she saw Muriel pushing up the avenue.

'Ella did you get the post?'

'I did.'

'And?'

'And what, Muriel?'

Never deterred by a sharp voice, Muriel persisted. 'Is he coming?'

'Who?' Ella pretended she wasn't interested.

Muriel sat down. 'Ella, we have been friends for years. I want this for you: for you to be happy.'

Ella shrugged and wiped her forehead, as she felt queasy.

'I have not opened it, Muriel. It is not that I am not telling you. I am afraid to open it.'

'Oh.'

'It has taken him so long to reply; there surely can only be one answer.'

'Open it, Ella. Open it.'

'I am sorry, Muriel, I need to be on my own. It will have to wait until I can close the café; Fergus is in Dublin on business, on today of all days.'

'Ella, I can serve the teas and coffees and cut a few slices of cake. You do what you have to do.'

'Do you mean it?'

'Ella, how difficult can it be? Go. The post office is covered, so take your time.'

Ella dithered, her hand over her skirt patch pocket, as if she was afraid she would lose the envelope.

'Go,' Muriel said, and gave her a slight shove.

'I will get my coat,' Ella said, making for the back hall, where she pulled on her raincoat.

Muriel was already on the stairs when Ella came back through the hall.

'I don't how long I will be. I will just find a quiet spot on the land.'

Muriel pooh-poohed out loud and continued up the stairs

to the café. She hung her coat and hat on the coat stand inside the door and slipped in behind the counter. Far better than the post office, she thought, beginning to rearrange the plates of cake. The coffee machine was in the wrong place too, but she could live with it. Standing, her two hands spanning the counter, she viewed the long room. Ella could have spent more money and covered the floorboards and put proper drapes on the windows. If Muriel Hearty were running this establishment, it would be warm and cosy. She jumped when she heard a slight cough at the door.

Roberta, using a walking stick because her rheumatoid arthritis had flared up, was staring at Muriel.

'Don't tell me she has roped you in to help. It is not as if she is overloaded with customers.'

'Come in, Roberta; have a coffee.'

'No, Muriel, I prefer the blend they serve at Molloy's. Thank you.'

Muriel got out from behind the counter and walked over to Roberta. 'Come on, it is only the two of us and we have a good ten minutes before anyone will darken the door. I will be able to sit and chat with you.'

'I don't think Ella would like me to frequent her café,' Roberta said as she made to move away.

'Ella is not here. I am in charge and I am inviting you,' Muriel said, sitting down and patting the chair beside her. 'Don't you want to hear the big news about your sister?'

Roberta dithered, but only for a moment. 'I might do,' she said.

'Will you have a tea? I am half afraid to use that coffee machine.' Muriel pulled down a teapot and threw some tea-bags in. 'I know Ella likes her Darjeeling and jasmine teas, but there is noting like a good plain teabag. Don't tell her I never go anywhere without my teabags.'

'I am hardly likely to be chatting to my sister anytime soon,' Roberta said, and Muriel laughed nervously.

'Do you mind? I couldn't keep up something like that myself.'

Roberta spilled some sugar into her tea. 'Of course I mind, but I did not start this; she told me not to speak to her again and started all these stupid notes.'

'What notes?' Muriel said, leaning closer to Roberta, even though there was nobody else in the café to hear.

'We have to have some way of communicating, Muriel; let's leave it at that.'

Muriel detected a shake in Roberta's voice and covered her hand with hers. 'If only the child had not drowned.'

'Muriel, don't go there.'

'At least there is good news on the horizon,' Muriel said.

Roberta pulled from Muriel's grip. 'Whatever do you mean?'

Muriel look flustered. 'Only that the boy has written to her.'

Muriel rushed to the counter when two women came in, keeping busy getting their orders out. Roberta followed her.

'How is he?'

'I only know what you know. Seemingly, he was brought up by a rich couple in Manhattan.'

'Is he coming here?'

'Ella has gone to read the letter. God, I hope he does; that woman has put up with enough.'

Roberta nodded and slowly made for the door. Muriel barely noticed; she was so caught up with four of her friends who had congregated around the counter, and she had such a story to tell them.

Roberta pushed past the women coming up the stairs and they stood back.

'Roberta, is everything all right?' one woman asked, but Roberta did not answer.

She wanted to follow Ella, read the letter, and discuss the young man they both should have brought up. That this enmity had gone on so long was a huge sadness she tried not to address. Sometimes she sat out in the garden and pretended that Roscarbury was a happy house again, but she was frozen in her heart. Even when Iris came up on her, it was easier to put out the hard word. A weariness seeped through her. A group of women were laughing at the far outside table, but they quietened down as she skirted around them.

She felt in her bag for her hip flask but resisted the urge to take a slug from it. She saw Ella walk across the park and followed her. Her progress was slow, as the walking stick sank into the damp ground, but she persisted. Ella, she knew, would be down by the lake, sitting on the bench Michael Hannigan had put in place one weekend after they married. Roberta sat there too, when she was sure nobody was about. In a quiet corner blocked from view by a hedge of fuchsia, the sitter could view the lake and the mountains beyond without interruption. Once, he had pulled her in there and kissed her, putting his hands up her jumper. She pushed him away, afraid of being found out. He laughed, grabbed her again, pushing his hand between her legs.

'Why do you think I worked so hard getting a long wide seat? It certainly was not for the view,' he said, pushing her roughly back on the bench.

The ground was soft and slippery in parts, so she grabbed at the thick old ferns to steady herself. Overhead, the clouds bustled about and a wind whipped the trees, as if announcing her presence. A small mouse hurried across her path; the ducks were kicking up a racket on the water. She pushed into the fuchsia, the water from the leaves soaking into her light jacket and drowning her skirt.

Ella, sitting holding the letter, did not hear her sister approach from behind. When Roberta put a hand on her shoulder, she jumped.

'Jesus Christ, you frightened the life out of me,' she said, quickly turning back towards the lake, to discourage her sister from attempting to make conversation.

The wind whipped across the water and Ella shivered because she was only wearing a light coat. Carefully, she folded the letter and put it back in her pocket. Fixing her hair, she stood up to leave, but Roberta blocked the way. With a heavy sigh, Ella plopped down on the bench and began to idly fiddle with an old teasel plant, which was brown and tough.

'Is he coming here?' Roberta spoke so softly she did not know if Ella had heard, but she saw a shiver in her shoulders. 'Ella, I want to talk to you, please.'

Ella shifted in the seat, reaching out to pull at some long grass.

'Ella,' Roberta called out louder, moving to sit on the seat.

Ella rose up. 'Why after all these years do you call on me now? Why now, Roberta?' Ella shouted, making to move past her sister.

Roberta pushed out her walking stick to stop her. 'Please, Ella, please.'

Ella yanked the stick. 'Let me pass.'

'Can't we talk?'

Ella guffawed out loud. "'Can't we talk?' Pardon me if I ask why. Why now?'

Roberta shifted on her feet.

'Why? Have you run out of drink money?

With a fierce push, Ella knocked the walking stick out of the way, forcing Roberta to grip the bench in case she fell.

'I have a café to run,' she said as she stormed through the fuchsia. Roberta sat down watching the clouds pressing in on the lake, making it turn grey.

Ella was halfway across the parkland when she felt the tinge of regret that she had not allowed her sister to speak. Since Michael's death, when Roberta made every attempt to comfort her, there had only been one time that her sister had tried to speak to her: when she came home from the hospital. Depressed and grieving, she rebutted Roberta, shouting at her, blaming her and throwing ornaments until eventually she locked herself in her room.

Tray upon tray of food was placed outside her room door, but Ella kicked each one across the landing, until the third day, when Dr Haslett was called. She remained doped up to the eyeballs for three more weeks, until one misty morning she got up and dressed. Gathering up the little cardigans, bootees and jumpers she had knitted, she buried them in a shallow grave at the far side of the lake.

Ella wanted to sneak in the back, but Muriel, holding court at the outside tables, waved enthusiastically and shouted at her to come over. Ella, one hand still on her pocket, shook a smile onto her face. The animated conversation at the table stopped as she approached.

'We are dying to know. When is he coming?'

Ella fidgeted with the stitching of the pocket, pulling at the threads. 'Soon, I think.'

Muriel leaned towards her. 'And?'

'That's it. I can't talk about it, Muriel. Surely you understand.'

The other ladies looked at each other in disappointment; one or two went back to eating their cake.

'Muriel, thank you for looking after the café. Could I draw on your generosity for another little while? I need to go upstairs and catch my breath.'

A little put out that there was so little forthcoming on the letter, Muriel nodded, adding she needed to get back to the post office before lunch.

'I just need a few minutes to put on my face,' Ella said as she made for the front door and stairs. When she passed the café, she noticed it was full and she was annoyed that Muriel was not watching her till as well as she would her own in the post office. She would have to hurry and she felt agitated.

Flopping down, she saw Roberta making her way around the back of the house and she decided she would not even think about why her sister wanted to talk to her. Sliding the letter from its envelope, she pressed it down flat on the dressing table with her hands. It was a printout from a computer with a handwritten part at the bottom. She read it again.

Riverside Drive,
Manhattan,
May 14, 2008

Dear Ella,

I hope you don't mind me calling you by your first name, but Ms. O'Callaghan does seem too formal. I must say I am thrilled at your letter to me and so very sorry at the circumstances that saw us separated after birth. I grew up in a very loving home, and for my parents, Jim and Stephanie, this is a very traumatic time. They had no idea your child was illegally taken from you and are appalled at the situation. They were told you had died; often at key moments, such as my birthday, we would remember you, offering a prayer. My mother told me the star that twinkled the brightest in the sky was my mom from Ireland. In a strange way, it helped me as I got older, because I did not harbor any secret hopes of uniting, realizing I was a very lucky boy to be with parents who loved me so.

I know this may be difficult for you to read, but I state it so that you know: while for you there is a terrible void that cannot be filled, for me there are memories of a very happy childhood and parents who now support me in what I propose to you.

I would very much like to meet you and to help you fill in the gaps of my childhood. My father is frail, but my mother would dearly love to make the trip to Ireland with me. Stephanie would very much like to meet you and asks your permission to do so.

I have got to say, for my part I am very nervous and would appreciate Stephanie's support. Let me know what you think.

I am a lawyer here and have done pretty well in life. We are thinking of coming over in June. Would that suit? I am afraid work commitments mean I cannot come any earlier. Anyway, we can write, talk and get to know each other in the intervening time. Are there any cousins I can meet? Aunts and uncles too? I have never been to Ireland, though in recent years I often thought of making the trip. I wish now I had.

My mother says to include my photograph; I fear I may not live up to your expectations. Can you please send me a photograph, if you have one of yourself and of Roscarbury?

In a handwritten note he had put:

Ella, I can't imagine the pain you have been through and I hope now I can bring some sunshine into your life. I look forward to meeting with you and spending time together.

Your loving son, James.

She slipped her finger across the handwritten part. He used a fountain pen; she liked that: it denoted a man of good education and style. The paper, too, was thick and the envelope heavy. The photo was a small head and shoulders shot, taken on graduation. He was smiling and her heart skipped, to think he looked so like his father. He had the same whip of the head and his hair was Michael's dark hair. She was not sure she could see herself in him, but maybe the wide, honest eyes.

A volley of goodbyes downstairs made her jump and she realised she had spent too long. Carefully, she propped the photograph against the mirror. Muriel could wait another few minutes. The occasion of her son writing required that she wear a brooch.

The daisy brooch: white cabochon-stone leaves, a centre of pink-red crystals, and a long curving stem, as if it had just been plucked in the field. Bernie O'Callaghan thought it too common and never wore it. Every time Ella looked at it, she was back in the field, lying in the grass, surrounded by cowslips and daisies, watching the clouds hurry past. It was a symbol of a carefree time; she felt the giddiness of the frothy clouds against the bright-blue sky and the sun shining on her, melting away decades of fatigue. Pinning it to her cardigan, she fancied she looked years younger.

Muriel was busy washing up when Ella came back into the café.

'I am sorry for keeping you so long, Muriel.'

'Well, is it good news?' Muriel yanked at the sink plug.

'My son is a big-shot lawyer and he wants to meet me.'

Ella stopped, her voice too watery with tears to say more. Without even drying her hands, Muriel went to her and hugged her so hard Ella had to wriggle free.

'I am so happy for you, Ella; you have no idea.'

Thirty-Four

Michael deserves to be remembered right to his son. He wanted that. Please go to the bother of reading his letter: Act One, Hamlet, top shelf in the library. R.

Ella walked straight to the row of books in the library and took down *Hamlet*, shaking it until the letter plopped out. How dare her husband write to somebody other than her? What right did Michael Hannigan have to be remembered kindly? She stuffed the letter in her front patch pocket to be read later.

She slipped a note onto Roberta's library chair.

What is in the past can stay there. Michael Hannigan has no rights now: he is dead. I will not have you spoil the one moment of happiness I have left in the world. E.

In the café, she fingered Michael Hannigan's letter. If she got time later on, she might throw her eyes over it, though she would not let on to her sister.

'I have never seen one linger so long over a cup of tea,' Ella muttered.

Ella took the stranger in. Hunched, her elbows on the table, she was looking intently out the window. A paisley scarf slipped down her front, but she hardly noticed.

'She might just be taking time out,' Fergus whispered as he wandered off to clear a few of the far tables.

Muriel Hearty and a small group of women in the centre tables spoke quietly together, before Muriel beckoned to Ella to join them.

'Have you heard from Debbie?'

'I talked to her on the phone last night. She is being well looked after; I can't say more than that. It is just a waiting game now.'

'She should have stayed; we would all have pitched in.'

'She has her aunt and uncle and friends.'

'But we went through something together; we would not have minded looking after her.'

The other women murmured in agreement.

'That's silly talk and well you know it. She is getting the best specialist care in that hospice. Good intentions can never match that.'

Muriel pulled Ella closer. 'Who's your wan at the window?'

'No idea.'

'Well, she won't boost the café profits,' Muriel tootled, and the other women giggled. They all got up at the same time, noisily scraping their chairs along the wooden floors. 'There is bingo in the hall tonight, Ella. You should come along. Bring Fergus too.'

Ella did not answer but got a tray and began to clear the table. She already had one tray full and was working on the second when the woman at the window rose from her seat and went to the till to pay.

'I will be with you in a minute,' Ella said, grumbling to herself that she should choose this moment to pay for her cup of tea. 'Was everything all right for you?' she asked, putting her hand out for the money.

'Why wouldn't it? Sure, you can't go wrong with a cup of tea.'

Ella laughed. 'I guess you are right.'

'Are you Miss O'Callaghan, the owner?'

'Yes, Ella: Ella O'Callaghan.'

'You won't remember me. I am Fran Murtagh.'

'Fran Murtagh?'

'Mary Murtagh's sister. We used to live beside the bridge in Rathsorney, at one time. I am Frances Rees now.'

Ella looked at the tall, well-dressed woman in front of her. She noted she was wearing an expensive raincoat and that her handbag was leather. Ella undid her apron and walked with the woman back to the table by the window. 'We didn't know any of the Murtaghs were still in the country, or have you travelled from afar?'

'I have lived in Malahide, Dublin, all my life. That is where my family moved after Rathsorney.'

'I see.'

'I was hoping you had a forwarding number or address for Deborah Kading.'

'You know the situation?'

'Yes, that is why I am here. I wrote to the convent seeking help; they did not bother to reply. Unfortunately it appears I am now too late; Deborah has already left the country.'

'And Mary?'

'My sister died of a broken heart in a mental institution, because nobody would believe her insistence that her child had been stolen from her. She was told the baby died, but she never believed it. I think it is only a matter of weeks before she is proved right, but . . .'

'It will be too late for Debbie.'

'Exactly.'

'How is Deborah?'

'Very weak; some days are better than others. She is in a lot of pain, doped up to the eyeballs, so I have to talk to her aunt Nancy mostly.'

Frances shifted in her chair, to move closer to Ella. 'I thought I should tell her she was welcome to our family, that her mother had always wanted her. Was she happy with the Kadings?'

'As far as I know, though she lost her mother when she was very young.' Ella looked away, not wishing to say anything further.

Fran Rees let a tear slip down her cheek and she shook her head, like a horse hoping to dislodge a fly. 'Those nuns have a lot to answer for. I wrote to the convent after I heard Deborah on the radio and got no reply. Any time I rang, I was told nobody could help. It was only when I knocked on the convent door and insisted I would go to the press that Assumpta met me.'

'What did she say?'

Fran looked out the window. The sea far away was glistening like a starry night. A bluster of a breeze was agitating the trees in the far wood and the rhododendron was swaying, throwing its old flowers away. A group of girls were messing as they walked up the driveway, pushing each other into the rhododendron bushes.

'She told me Deborah had gone and everything else was in the hands of the inquiry and gardaí and she could not possibly comment.'

'Sounds like marbles-in-the-mouth Mother Assumpta, all right.'

'Deborah was told Mary Murtagh was her mother?'

'Yes, she was.'

'I can fly out. Bring photographs of Mary.'

Ella felt the tears rise up. 'You would do that?'

Fran Rees twiddled with the cup and saucer Fergus had quietly slipped in beside her. 'I owe it to my sister, Miss O'Callaghan. I was a few years older than her. When she spoke of keeping her baby, I never let on that I knew my father would not in a million years let it happen. I let Mary plan, knitting matinee coats in several colours and crocheting little bootees. I suppose I was too caught up in my own life; I was planning to marry Richard then. When she had the baby, she was told it had died; I did not say anything.'

She stopped to gulp a mouthful of tea.

'I was brought up to believe my parents knew best. When they put her in the mental hospital, I never thought she would be there so long. Every time I visited her, which to my shame was only at Christmas and Easter, she begged me to find her child. Even though I had my suspicions my father probably had the child adopted and it was more than likely alive, I never said that to Mary. I wronged her, don't you see? I am now trying to right that wrong.'

Ella reached over and patted Fran's hand. 'You were young. Looking back and regretting is always the easy part.'

'Do you think it would mean something to her now?'

Ella squeezed Fran's hand. 'I know it will mean everything.

Book the flight straight away.' She reached into her pocket, pulled out a notebook and jotted down Debbie's address and phone number. 'Take it, and let me know how you get on.'

The other woman could not muster any words but smiled her appreciation as Ella, hearing the young girls come up the stairs, quickly disappeared behind the counter.

Thirty-Five

Marian Hospice, Ohio, April 2008

'She's my aunt, Mary's sister?'

Nancy nodded, tears brimming up. 'You don't have to see her if you don't want, darling.'

Debbie tapped Nancy on the wrist. 'Don't be silly, of couse I want to meet her. How did she find out where I was?'

'Ella O'Callaghan. She just walked into the café.'

That had been three days ago, when Debbie could still chat. Now every sentence was an effort and she wondered if her mother's sister would make it on time.

She asked Nancy to pat a bit of powder on her face, and pink lipstick, because for some reason even though she was dying she wanted to look good meeting this woman for the first time.

'It's time; I'll see if she's arrived,' Nancy said, making for the door, but stopping halfway. 'Are you sure you're up for this, Debs?'

Debbie smiled. 'Go, Nance, please. Don't worry.'

Frances Rees nervously waited in the reception area and

wondered how everyone could be so cheerful in a place where dying was the business. It had been an easy decision to come here, and when she had rung ahead, Nancy Slowcum cautiously welcomed the plan.

'She is near the end. You do understand that, don't you?'

'I have some photos of her mother. I don't want to intrude, but I thought it might help.'

Nervously holding a package of family photographs, Frances wondered if she had been mad to declare her family interest in this woman: Mary's daughter, her niece, dying in this place where everybody spoke gently.

A plump lady in a tracksuit, her face heavily powdered, walked towards her, two arms extended. 'Mrs Rees, we're almost family, aren't we? It was so good of you to come.'

Frances Rees was pulled in to a bear hug by Nancy.

'Debbie is very eager to see you, but she gets tired easily, so it won't be for very long,' Nancy said, leading her down the corridor to a blue door. 'She has a beautiful view across the gardens, though she says it will never match the loveliness of Roscarbury Hall.'

Nancy opened the door slowly, beckoning Frances to follow. Debbie was propped against several pillows, as if her bed had been specially arranged for this moment.

Her voice was low, but definite, when she spoke. 'I am so grateful you made the journey; come sit with me.'

Nancy hovered at the end of the bed until Bert called her out of the room.

'She fusses over me, always has done.'

'Deborah, I am sorry . . .'

Debbie put up her hand. 'Frances, let's not waste time. Pull up a chair and tell me about Mary.'

Frances sat on the edge of the chair and started to gabble on. 'Call me Fran; everybody in the family calls me that. Mary was five years younger and I can tell you a right strap when she was a young woman, always going off to meet some young lad or other.' Frances hesitated.

Debbie smiled. 'Please, don't hold back.'

'I don't want you to think less of her. She was a kind, generous girl, a bit shy, and a pair of hands on her that could style any type of hair. I worked in Arklow, hairdressing, but it was Mary who had the real talent. It all just came naturally to her. She once dyed her hair pure blonde; needless to say, my father went mad. And then there was the time she straightened her hair; she decided to iron it—she ruined her long tresses that day and had to go for a boy's cut; that was before girls went down that road. She looked so sexy, in the boyish cut and the short skirts.

'My father couldn't contain her. We all admired her spunk, and all the young lads were after her. She only had eyes for one man, though. He was no good, and married.'

'My father?'

'I am afraid so. She would do anything for him. Meet him in Arklow, standing for hours waiting for him by the cold stone bridge, and he would not have the decency to give her an explanation when he arrived. Sometimes he could not stay more than half an hour. She was besotted with him. He was only married a short time too, but there was no telling her he was no good.' Frances stopped as she felt the tears rise inside her. 'One day, she said they were going to go away together, away from Ireland, and he would find some way of marrying her. Even if they didn't, they would be together. She loved him dearly, was prepared to turn her back on her family for him.'

'Who was he?'

'A good-for-nothing who strung her along, that is who.'

'What do you mean?'

Frances took a deep breath. 'She did not tell him about the baby until she was well on and could not hide it any more; the red welts on her hips were huge from the corset she had to wear all the time.'

Debbie closed her eyes and Frances was not sure whether she should continue.

'I am tiring you out. Will I go?'

Debbie put up her hand, as if to stop Fran from leaving. 'Who knows if there will be another time?'

Fran burrowed in to her seat. 'He would have nothing to do with her. She came home that night in bits; he said he had a wife and family and she would have to get rid of it.'

'But she was months pregnant.'

'Exactly, the bastard. He wanted to bring her to a woman in Dublin, have a back-street abortion.'

'He doesn't sound as if he really cared for her.'

'A married man having an affair with a young girl? He was only thinking of himself; that was not going to change.'

'She must have been devastated.'

'She knew she wanted to have you; she kept saying the two of you would move to Dublin once you were born and have a life together. It was not something that ever had any reality to it, not when my parents found out about the pregnancy.'

'Betty Messitt told me she was locked in the house.'

Frances gulped back the tears. 'I had a flat in Arklow, so I was away for most of the week. To my eternal shame, I was so caught up in my own life I paid little attention to Mary at the time. She was given a hard time by my father. We all knew there was no way he would let her keep the child, but she was persistent and stubborn in her plan for your life together.'

'Would your father ever have relented, do you think?'

Frances shook her head vigorously. 'There was never any question she would be allowed to keep the baby; she must have known that deep down it was not the thing to do.' Frances reached into her packet and pulled out a few photos. 'I thought you might like these. Mary was some looker, don't you think?'

Debbie took in the wide smile, the over-the-top hairdo and the slim frame, her hands on her hips like a model.

'She had a style of her own didn't she?'

'And a mind of her own: that was her trouble. You were whipped from her straight away; she said she never got to hold you, never even saw your face.'

Frances stopped as the tears rolled down Debbie's cheeks.

'It might be time for me to go.'

'Please, tell me what happened to her.'

'The family never went back to Rathsorney: my father got work in Dublin and we moved to Coolock. He thought the change to the city would make Mary forget, but it was terrible. She cried and cried and cried; even in her sleep, she screamed her baby had been stolen. She threatened to go to the gardaí. My father said there was no way they would believe a slut like her. He took to locking her in the house all day. When she continued to fight him, he signed her into the mental home.'

'And they accepted her in?'

'She was heavily sedated. I went to see her once a week for a while, but it was incredibly upsetting. She was in with a lot of old women, and she sat babbling to herself that her baby had been stolen. If anyone new walked in, she would run up to them to try and tell her story.'

'You could not do anything to help her?'

'My father was the only one who could have got her out of that place; he was never going to do that.'

Relief washed over Frances when a nurse stuck her head around the door to check if they needed anything. She arranged her scarf and flattened her hair, in an attempt to compose herself.

'How did she die?'

Frances took a deep breath. 'I had taken to visiting once a month; I dropped it down to once every two months. I am ashamed of that now. Daddy rang me and said Mary was dead and to come home for the funeral. She slashed her wrists with an old piece of glass, left over after a few panes of glass were replaced in the day room. Nobody found her, until it was too late.'

Debbie reached and took Frances' hand. 'This was not your fault.'

Frances pulled her hand away. 'Don't you see, if I had listened to her, believed her, I might have been able to help her. I was too goddamn selfish, getting on with my own small life.'

'You are being too hard on yourself.'

'I am not; I should have been there for her. If the roles had been switched, she would have fought Daddy tooth and nail for me.'

'Who was my father?'

Frances shifted uncomfortably on her seat. 'He is dead. He died before Mary; we never told her.'

Debbie pulled herself up further on the pillows. 'Why don't you want to tell me?'

'Haven't I told you enough things to cause pain? Why can't we leave it?'

'It is a vital missing part of the jigsaw, Frances. Do other people in the area know?'

'He would only ever meet her away from Rathsorney, so nobody really knew. She told me, but that was when she was so sure of him.'

'The name, please, Frances.' Debbie's voice was firm, her face determined.

'Michael. Michael Hannigan.'

'Ella's husband?'

'Yes. He was an awful cad after he left Mary to deal with her pregnancy; he took up with another young one. That wife of his was a saint.'

'Does Ella know this?'

'She does not, and she won't hear it from me; I think it would kill her.'

'I'm tired, Frances.'

She reached out her hands and let Frances gently hug her.

'I can come again tomorrow; we can talk about nicer things.'

'It's such a long time to tomorrow, it's hard to plan, but I'd like that.'

'Can I get you anything before I leave?'

'I'll rest, until Nancy comes fussing.'

Debbie closed her eyes. Swirls of colours pulled her away. She heard Frances walk to the door; she mustered the strength to call out to her.

'Frances, did she ever say what she was going to name me; had she picked names?'

Frances beamed with delight. 'I should have told you. She was convinced she was going to have a little girl; she was going to call you Rachel, because that sounded like a posh name, and girls with posh names had grand lives.'

'I like that. Can you do one thing for me?'

Frances moved closer.

'Tell Ella thank you from me.'

'Of course I will.'

Debbie spanned with her hand across the locker. 'The brooch Ella gave me: is it still there?'

Frances picked up the brooch, the stones glinting as she pressed it into Debbie's hand.

Debbie closed her eyes as Frances quietly let herself out of the room, softly closing the door behind her.

She remembered now, the surge of excitement that she had a gold star, the sound of the screen as she pulled it too hard, and the thud of the front door as she threw her weight on it.

Flinging her schoolbag on the ground, she called out to her mother. Debbie felt young again, running to find her mother.

'Mommy? Mommy?'

Skipping to the sitting room, she expected to see her by the window. She stooped to pull up her socks before fixing her hairband; Mommy liked her to look neat. Walking over to the sewing machine, she reached out to the lace-trimmed silk blouse, shimmering blue, bundled to the side and still attached by a thread to the needle. Fingering it gently, she admired the buttons, silver and pearl, in the shape of flowers.

'Mommy? Mommy?'

She danced to the kitchen. A cup of tea was cold on the table; a muffin lay half eaten and mashed on a plate.

'Mommy? Mommy?'

Calling louder, she glanced out to the garden and the washing line, her cheeks flushed pink with excitement, her heart bursting, the Big Chief tablet notebook sweaty in her hand. She opened it to check the shiny gold star the teacher had carefully pinned to her spelling test. Running to the stairs, she stopped to put her head around the dining-room door. The table sparkled and the room smelled of polish. A pink envelope with her father's name printed heavily but neatly was propped against a jug of spring flowers.

'Mommy? Mommy?'

Growing more agitated, she could feel the sting of tears as uncertainty crept over her. She called out again, but her voice was not sure any more. She climbed three steps before stopping to check the coat rack in the hall. The white raincoat and rain hat were there, her mother's handbag on the chair inside the door.

'Mommy? Mommy?'

The steps seemed higher than normal, the house too quiet.

Her heart began to pound; the bones in her knees were hurting.

'Mommy . . . ?'

Her voice faltered; her mouth dried up. Gripping the banisters too tight, so her fingers cramped, she felt the sweat ooze from the roots of her hair. Tears gurgled up.

She saw her silk shoes first, the shoes Mommy had specially covered to match her dress last Christmas. She kept them high up, wrapped in tissue in a box at the top of the wardrobe. The diamante heart on the front of each shoe caught the light, glinting, beams of colour stalking her brain. Mommy was not wearing nylons.

'Mommy?'

A roar thundered through her, making her insides hurt, but no sound came.

Mrs Balcomb next door called out to her poodle. Mr Haussmann over the street spluttered loudly, clearing his throat as he settled himself in to the rattan chair on the veranda.

Mommy was wearing the pink satin dress with the butterfly collar and the seashell buttons. She was still, her slight frame hanging over the second landing.

The notebook slipped from Debbie's hand; she thundered down the stairs and into the garden, gobbling up the fresh air, not knowing what else to do, afraid she would throw up and make a mess. The door of the small potting shed was ajar. She pushed it and burrowed under the table, beside the stool where Rob liked to sit, pressing little slips and seeds into small boxes of earth. Rolling into a ball, she held her knees tight and hummed a tune she did not realise she knew. Humming over and over, she heard the sirens. She hummed and hummed, hugging her knees. Her father called her name, but she did not stop humming.

'Debbie. Debbie.'

She stuttered in her humming as she felt Rob's large hands lift her to him.

Rob called her now softly and beckoned her to follow him; she was ready. Her fingers wrapped around the brooch; she felt the whisper of butterflies, the shift in the air as their wings gently flapped, calling out her name, lifting her away.

Thirty-Six

Three months later

Ella stood by the window, watching the avenue. There were two hours to go, but she could not settle to doing anything else. The ladies of the village passed in and out of the hallway on the way to the Ballroom Café. She flattened her silk dress with her hands, worrying she was overdressed, that the crimson was too gaudy for a woman her age. Maybe she should have picked the navy one with the white lace collar that shop assistant Hetty Flood had recommended. Her hair felt tight, her scalp itchy from the perm in Rathsorney yesterday morning. She fingered the happy brooch at her collar and checked her watch; little time had passed. Oceans of time left until they arrived.

He had a nice voice, proper and polite, she thought, as she spoke to him last night on the phone. He spoke slowly and clearly, and she tried to do the same, though her mind was in a rush to say so much.

'Stephanie and I can't wait to meet you. We thought it best

to sleep off the jet lag and drive down in the morning. How is that for you?'

'Fine, just fine. Come any time.'

'I reckon it will be around lunchtime, one o'clock.'

'Marvellous. I will be waiting.'

When he rang off, she thought she sounded like a right fancy cow. She never used the word marvellous, maybe once in the last ten years. It popped into her head, just like that.

Iris walked down the avenue to put up the closed sign, as the last few women chatted at the outside tables. Muriel had brought a big bunch of flowers this morning. All dressed up, she was, as if she expected to be invited to the lunch.

'It is your day, Ella; enjoy every minute. We have to meet this boy of yours soon.'

'In time, I am sure, Muriel, in time.'

'Will he be staying here in Roscarbury?'

'I have booked him and his mother into Neary's Hotel off the N11.'

'Oh.'

'It will give us all a bit of space.'

'He is bringing his mother?'

'Of course, I want to meet her.'

'I don't know if I could do that. You are something, Ella O'Callaghan.'

They stood in the hallway, Ella fidgeting with her rings until Muriel took the hint, saying she had better get along.

'They will be in from the mountains for the dole this morning and Matthew will go mad if I don't lend a hand.'

She flustered down the avenue, not entirely satisfied with her morning's gossip.

Iris tidied up the tables at the front, leaning the chairs against the tables before she came back into the house.

'That is me finished, Ella. I have pushed two tables together in the café and laid for three. You will want a bit of room. All you have to do is set up the coffee machine. The food is laid out on the counter, a few of the good tea towels on top.'

Ella swallowed hard. 'What would I do without you, Iris?'

'Pay somebody else good money, that's what.'

'It won't be long now. Are you sure you don't want to stay?'

'Me? What would I be saying to them?'

'I suppose.'

'You know there is only one other person you should be asking, but I will say no more.'

Ella touched her happy brooch. 'I don't want anything to spoil the day.'

'I will leave you to it; Molloy's have a lunch special, so I am off.'

Iris closed the front door behind her. They had done a good job on the house: the glass in the windows sparkled and the front gardens looked tended, pots of petunias spilling over the front steps, hedges neatly trimmed, the edges of the avenue outlined sharply with a spade. She saw Ella inside the drawing-room window. Roberta, sitting at the library window, sipped a sherry. Iris noticed she was wearing her grey suit, the one she had bought in Gorey two weeks ago, the collar of a pink blouse contrasting nicely with her delicate features.

★

Roberta knew when Ella got her hair done that the time had come. Iris up the ladder washing down the outside of the windows and Sheehy brought in to cut down the grass on the parkland several weeks too early were another giveaway.

She never asked what day he was due to arrive, but Iris blurted it out two days ago, as if she couldn't but tell her.

'Will he be staying?' Roberta asked, never moving her eyes from the newspaper she was pretending to read.

'I don't think so. Ella is closing up the café so they can have lunch.'

'Was she ever going to tell me?'

'I don't know. Don't let on you heard from me?'

'It is not as if we will be chatting about it,' Roberta said, her voice stiff.

'Will you want to meet him?' Iris was worried she may have caused an upset for Ella.

'Why wouldn't I?'

'No reason, no reason,' Iris said, before filling up another bucket of soapy water for the windows at the back.

'I doubt if he will be worried whether the windows have been washed or not,' Roberta called after her, reaching for a pen to scribble a red note.

I have a right to meet my nephew. Make no mistake of that. Don't think you are the only one who would like to grasp at the straw of happiness. R.

★

They were driving down from Dublin, so they would be hungry. Ella went upstairs to check the café. Iris had put on linen tablecloths, and the good china, only taken out on special occasions, sparkled. Muriel's flowers were placed in a glass vase to the side of the counter. Trays of food covered in linen cloths were placed inside the counter ledge; a trolley laden with whiskey, brandy, sherry and liqueur along with two cans of beer was by the far wall.

Feeling sick, Ella began to pace up and down, dodging between tables, counting the knots on the floorboards. When the phone rang, she ran downstairs, slightly slipping on the last step in her rush.

'Ella, we're going to be delayed. My mom wasn't feeling well this morning, so we're starting off later than intended.'

'I am sorry. Is she all right?'

'Nerves, I would say. It may be two-thirty by the time we arrive.'

'Drive carefully.'

Ella made her way to the kitchen. She felt cross; the dress was sticking too much to her, the brooch picking at her through the thinness of the silk. When she heard Roberta in the hallway, she pushed the kitchen door, hoping she would not come in.

Roberta checked the avenue for a car before making her way down the hall. She noticed Ella's shoulders hunched as she stood looking out the window at the sink.

'Are they not coming?'

Ella watched the old dog sitting whining, tied up by Iris before she left. 'The dog is making a show of us,' she said to nobody in particular and went out to untie it, pushing it away harshly when it jumped up on her dress, wagging its tail.

Roberta was sitting at the kitchen table when Ella came back in. 'Is there something wrong?'

Ella took her in, noticing the new clothes, the hair brushed into a tidy bun and the drop earrings. 'They are late.'

'What time now?'

'Two-thirty. I don't want trouble.'

'You won't get any.'

Ella threw the last of her tea down the sink and rinsed out her cup. She was skirting past the table when Roberta spoke again. 'Have you heard the rumour about Mary Murtagh?'

Ella stopped, the sweat pumping out of her now, squelching through the tight curls of her new perm. 'So?'

Roberta hesitated, running her finger across the table-cloth. 'So the American may be entitled to her claim on Roscarbury.'

Ella thumped her fist on the table. 'She or anybody belonging to her will not have a claim on Roscarbury Hall. That is rightfully my son's and that is the way it will stay.'

'But if Deborah Kading is his daughter?'

'We don't know that. Talk is only talk. Mary Murtagh is long gone. There is no way of proving the gossip. Gossip holds no legal sway.'

'I am glad.'

Ella, spit spilling out the corner of her mouth, sat down. 'Debbie has passed away. I don't know if you've heard.'

'I am sorry.'

'She had such little time.'

'She did.'

They sat, the dog scratching in the corner the only interruption to their thoughts.

Roberta eyed Ella closely before she spoke. 'Michael Hannigan left his fair share of pain.'

'More trouble than he was worth; I only wish I'd known it back then.' Ella reached for a spoon and twisted it around her hands.

Roberta picked at the tablecloth, like it was something she had to do. 'Me too,' she said, picking deeper.

They sat quietly opposite each other, the clock ticking on

the mantelpiece and the chuntering of the hens on the back step the only sounds. Roberta got up and took the bottle of sherry from inside the tall spaghetti jar in her cupboard.

'I told Muriel if she continued to spread gossip about Michael, I would go to a solicitor.'

'You did?'

Roberta spun around. 'Don't I love Roscarbury as much as you?'

Ella shook her head, trying to dislodge the tears she felt bubbling up. 'I know,' she whispered.

The phone ringing in the hall prevented her saying more. As Ella rushed to answer it, Roberta poured a sherry and made her way to the library. She had settled into her chair at the window when Ella put her head around the door.

'They have made better time than they thought. They are coming into the town. Five minutes at most,' Ella said, her voice shaking.

Roberta did not answer immediately, concentrating instead on fixing the old blanket over her knees. 'I will stay out of the way.'

Ella hesitated but did not answer, walking away slowly to take up position by the drawing-room window. She wanted to run to the toilet, but she knew if she did they might come and it would be terrible to have nobody to answer the door.

The sun was streaking across the gardens, dazzling around the old ash tree and making the water on the fountain sparkle. Her mouth was dry; a pain ran up the back of her neck. She felt so sick she thought she might throw up, so she squeezed the back of the old velvet chair to distract herself. When she saw the big black car turn up the avenue, she thought she would pass out. She knew her face was as flared red as the dress and she cursed her stupidity at picking such a young person's colour.

The car moved slowly, the driver wary of the potholes. She should have had Mick Hegarty fill in the bad one, midway between the gate and the entrance, but it had never occurred to her until now.

She leaned, but could not get a glimpse of the driver. The woman in the front looked heavy and appeared to be wearing a hat. Ella patted her hair and cleared her throat; her body was stiff with expectation, her head pounding with pain. So transfixed was she watching the avenue, she did not hear the drawing-room door push open.

Roberta walked up and stood beside her sister. She was not sure if Ella noticed. The car came to a halt at the front steps, but the driver reconsidered the position and reversed slightly, so that the steps were clear. Ella gasped as the car pulled back.

Slowly, Roberta reached out and caught her hand, squeezing it gently. Ella pressed her fingers into her sister's frail skin. Roberta did not say it hurt, nor did she pull away.

They watched in silence, holding hands as James got out of the car, looked around with a broad smile on his face, and gave a low whistle.

'So like his father,' Ella said, her voice faltering.

'Yes,' Roberta answered, squeezing her sister's hand tighter.

'Michael would have liked that,' Ella said, squeezing Roberta's hand back. 'Shall we go and meet him together?' she added quietly.

Roberta did not need to answer, and they walked hand in hand to the front door to greet their guests.

Acknowledgments

My late father, Patrick, was a born storyteller; my mother, Anne, a huge reader. They reared their five children in a house of stories and books. Patrick and Anne O'Loughlin lived in a small place in the west of Ireland, but they opened up the world for us through their love and support. I owe them everything. Thanks is such a small word for the support they gave to me and my dream of writing. Neither would the dream have become a reality but for the unstinting support of my husband, John, and my wonderful children, Roshan and Zia. Not once did they let me give up; I love them all the more for it.

A big thank you to my agent, Jenny Brown, who never wavered in her belief in my writing, and to all at Black and White Publishing, especially director Alison McBride, my editor Karyn Millar and rights manager Janne Moller for their good humour and expert advice.

To all my friends in the world of journalism and law, as well as my local community and those dear to my heart in India; I would never have been able to stay on the road to publication without your warm words of encouragement.